Paperback: 978-0-8253-1028-7
Ebook: 978-0-8253-0907-6

For inquiries about volume orders, please contact:
Beaufort Books
sales@beaufortbooks.com
Published in the United States by Beaufort Books www.beaufortbooks.com

Distributed by Midpoint Trade Books, a division of Independent Publishers Group
www.ipgbook.com

Interior Design by Mimi Bark

For anyone who ever dreamed about
growing up to be a pirate, fighting a pirate,
or falling in love with a pirate.

———————

CAROL ANN COLLINS

the Seafarer's Secret

BEAUFORT
BOOKS

Dear Father,

Remember when you told me how our deeds might not be fully known while we lived? That some would never understand their purpose for being born and only in death would their importance be made clear?

I hope you were right.

— JOURNAL OF AN UNKNOWN WOMAN, EARLY 1700s

E va Knightly watched the old man shuffle his feet, slowly making it to the corner table the way he did every morning at six thirty. After he sat down, a waitress brought him coffee just the way he liked it—black with one packet of sweetener, the yellow kind, not the blue. She was present many times when he told anyone who would listen that one of his granddaughters was a doctor in Tennessee and she said the blue stuff would kill you.

As much as he spread her advice, he wasn't one to believe her. He said if God had seen fit to spare his life this long, it was doubtful the Lord Almighty would decide to call him home over a packet of blue sweetener. But Eva knew his granddaughter had made him promise he wouldn't use the blue stuff anymore, and he always kept his promises. At least that was what he told his friends.

Just like every other day, the waitress placed his coffee on the table in front of him and asked if he wanted anything to eat. "Not right now, sugar," he replied, and thirty minutes passed before he waved the waitress over and gave her his breakfast order. He called her *sugar* because he liked to tease her. She let him because it always made her smile. And it didn't hurt Elbert always left a hefty tip.

By the time his breakfast hit the table, two women, Maxine and Francis, and another man, Herb, all equally aged, joined him. Herb had a copy of the local newspaper, and once they all were sufficiently caffeinated, they began to discuss the news. This was their morning ritual, repeated almost daily, including Elbert's ongoing battle with blue-packaged sweetener.

Eva discovered the quartet's routine shortly after her move to Eden, and as a result, she always got up at an ungodly hour to ensure she sat at a table close enough to eavesdrop on them. Because the best place to get the news in Eden was not from the paper Herb brought into the diner. It wasn't even the muted television perched in the back upper right corner. Oh no, it was from the four people off to her side gossiping over breakfast.

Granted, the sleepy coastal town of Eden, North Carolina was not known to be a hot spot for news junkies or those wishing to engage in political debates. In fact, the majority of those who had even heard of the town had only done so because they had passed through it on the way to one of Eden's more famous Outer Banks sister towns, Kitty Hawk or Nags Head.

The remaining people who knew of Eden could be divided into two groups: residents of Eden and history buffs.

Eva happily considered herself a member of both groups. She bought a house in a small Eden neighborhood about five years ago. However, she soon learned that living in Eden didn't make you a resident to the other people in town. Residents had to earn their stripes if they didn't grow up there, and it was only in recent months that most of the citizens in the close-knit community had accepted her as one of their own.

Eva also fit perfectly in the second group—she was definitely a history buff. Not that anyone was surprised. She was the staff historian at the Outer Banks Historical Society as well as Head of Exhibits and Visitor Experience at the museum the Historical Society owned and operated—the Coastal Carolina Museum. The other side to history, of course, was the present, and Eva discovered a long time ago that the present is typically told best through gossip. In Eden, no one gossiped more than her breakfast foursome.

"Body was found this morning down at the cove," Elbert said, immediately stopping his tablemates' chatter. Of the four, he was the one who always had the most up-to-date details of nearly anything going on in town. He wrote a weekly opinion piece for the local newspaper and somehow managed to obtain all sorts of information by introducing himself as a newspaper reporter. "I don't have any other details."

Maxine snorted. "That's a first."

Elbert glared at her. "They're not using the radio. It was pure luck I heard what I did."

"Wonder who died?" Francis asked. "Must be someone local, don't you think? The last time they went radio silent was when the chief's wife, Catherine Harper, was found over a year ago."

As always, the mention of her late friend made Eva's heart ache. Not only had she lost her best friend, but Eva also blamed herself. According to the autopsy report, Catherine had been walking home from a local bar at one in the morning, fell into a sand hole on the shore, and died of asphyxiation. She found herself unable to get out, the medical examiner indicated, due in part to the high level of alcohol found in her blood.

But Catherine had only been at the bar because she and Eva were celebrating Eva's appointment as chairman of Eden's annual Blackbeard Festival.

Eva told Catherine she'd always been drawn to the man known as Blackbeard and thought he'd been portrayed incorrectly by history. She was certain she'd bored Catherine to tears that night in the bar by detailing the thesis she'd written in graduate school on the pirate, but Catherine had still celebrated right along with her. Of course she had. That was Catherine. Always there for her friends, and Eva and Catherine had been friends since Eva's second week in Eden, when the two of them met while digging in the dirt for the Eden Beautification Committee.

"I can't believe that husband of hers is still walking around. To this day, I don't think anyone's looked at him twice in relation to her death," Maxine said to the other three people at her table, snapping Eva from her thoughts. "Nine times out of ten, it's always the husband when a married woman dies. He probably killed her and then buried her body in the sand to make it look like an accident."

"It could happen," Herb said with a nod. "I heard once about a man who killed his wife and hid her body in a big freezer they had."

Eva bit her tongue, not wanting to let on how closely she listened, but God help her if they kept suggesting William had anything to do with Catherine's death. She would have to speak her mind.

"It couldn't have been the chief," Francis said. "Catherine died the weekend of that big storm, remember? He was doing storm prep the entire night she died. Half the county's lawmen can say they were with him."

Maxine gave a *hmph* that informed everyone of her opinion on Francis's reasoning and added, "If he didn't do it, he paid someone to do it for him. They were separated, remember?"

"I don't know," Francis said. "Not long after her body was found, I was in the Piggy Wiggly produce section and overheard two women who work near the Tattered Flag Art Gallery—"

"The what?" Herb asked.

"The art gallery in Nags Head that has all those paintings of Catherine's. Don't interrupt me," Francis said. "Anyway, one of them was saying how Gabby Clark was certain Catherine had a thing for her man. And for weeks after, she told anyone who would listen that Catherine was after Hamilton. They think Gabby killed her in a fit of passion."

Hamilton and Catherine? Eva's initial reaction was to laugh, but Francis's matter-of-fact tone caught her off guard and made her think. There was no way, was there?

Sure, there'd been whispers when William and Catherine separated six months before her death, and a good number of those whispers spoke of infidelity. Not wanting to lose either of her friends, Eva had done her best to remain neutral. And remaining neutral meant not speculating on any supposed extramarital affairs. Especially since she'd always been attracted to William and continuously carried the burden of that guilt.

I hope this letter finds you well and that you will forgive me for the delay in sending. I had hoped to have better news, unfortunately, I do not. Because of that, and because of what I will be telling you, once you and Millie have read this, you must destroy it.

LETTER FROM BLACKBEARD TO WIFE, MARY, 1718

Chapter Two

William Templeton and Death had crossed paths many times in the past. It was a known fact of life for anyone working in law enforcement, even for a small-town police chief such as himself.

Death was rarely pretty, and often unexpected, and those two things could certainly be said about the newly deceased, Gabby Clark.

William knew Gabby because she cleaned the house his grandmother, Nana Ruth, left him. Gabby was also known for her on again, off again relationship with Hamilton Brown. One day, they'd be all over the other with borderline lewd public displays of affection, and the next, they'd argue so loud, someone would end up calling the police.

"What do we know?" William asked JJ, the young officer who had been the first to arrive after the group of fishermen called to report a body found that had washed ashore.

"It's Gabby Clark, sir," JJ said. "Appears to have drowned."

"Not to say it's impossible," William said with a frown. "But let's not assume anything. Has the medical examiner been called yet?"

"I called as soon as I arrived, Chief." JJ looked at his watch. "Should be here in about twenty minutes."

They stood in a small cove frequented by locals who wanted to fish without being overrun by tourists. The area was not easily seen from the road but was known by those living nearby. Gabby's body, where they stood, was on one end. A group of three young men were at the opposite end, talking with Darrius, one of the department's recent hires.

"Those the men who found her?" William asked with a jerk of his head toward the group.

"Yes, sir."

Mitch, William's most experienced deputy, walked up to his right side.

"No sign of the press yet," Mitch said. "But who knows how long that will last."

"Chief!" Darrius called.

William shielded his eyes from the sun and waited as the young man walked toward him, holding something in his hand.

"One of the guys found this in her pocket when he was looking for her identification." Darrius held out his gloved hand to reveal a gold coin.

"Shit," Mitch said.

"That's something you don't see every day." It was an odd-looking coin and nothing like William had ever seen. Slightly larger than a fifty-cent piece and shining in the sunlight, it vaguely resembled something found in a pirate film. Of course, it looked too new to be as old as the 1715 date boldly proclaimed. More than likely, it was some sort of replica, but he wasn't sure why Mitch appeared so disturbed by its presence.

Mitch pointed at the coin. "Make sure that's filed as evidence and have the group of guys who found her come down to the station to give statements. Chief," he said to William. "You may want to sit this one out."

William raised an eyebrow. "Why would I want to do that?"

Mitch looked to where Darrius was walking back to the fishermen. "There was a gold coin found on Catherine as well."

"What?" William asked, dumbfounded. "Like that one?"

"I don't know. It was gold. But even if it's not, what are the odds of another strange coin being found on someone else?"

It was as if someone punched him in the stomach. "What does that mean? Are you saying their deaths are related, that they were killed?" How could that be when Catherine's death had been ruled accidental?

Mitch shook his head. "I can't speculate about anything at the moment, and you know I can't talk about anything related to Catherine with you." Before William could reply, Mitch continued, "Damn it. This doesn't make any sense. We're going to have to find out what these coins are."

"You didn't have the one on Catherine looked at?" William asked.

"There was no need to at the time."

Something wasn't adding up right. Why hadn't the coin been given to him along with her other personal items? He made a note to ask Mitch later.

"You should go see Eva Knightly at the Historical Society about that coin," William said. "If she can't tell you anything about it, she'll know who can. I'm going to see if I can find Hamilton."

THREE HOURS LATER, when William returned to the police station, the last person he wanted to deal with was Mayor Atkins. But since the man stood by the desk of William's admin, Peggy, waiting for him, he didn't have a choice. William had been unable to locate Hamilton after going by his house, Gabby's house, and the hardware store Hamilton owned and worked at when the mood struck him.

What he wanted to do after failing to find Hamilton was go home, change, and run along the beach for a few miles. Jogging was his favorite thing to do after a hard day, but there was so much to do at the office, he couldn't justify leaving early.

"What can I do for you, Mayor?" William asked.

"Do you think it's a good idea for you to work Gabby's case?" Atkins asked, getting right to the point.

William wasn't shocked by the question. He'd expected it based on what Mitch said earlier. And truthfully, if the possibility existed that Catherine's death could somehow be connected, he shouldn't be working Gabby's case. On the other hand, did it make sense for William, the most experienced officer in Eden, to step aside before a connection could be established? He decided to push the mayor a bit. "Is there a reason you think I shouldn't?"

"You and I both know how unusual it is to have two women die with an unknown coin on them."

"Yes, but they died a year apart and in different ways," William argued. For some reason, he felt as if he needed to investigate Gabby's death. "Not to mention, you don't even know what the coins are or if they're even the same. I don't think we should jump to conclusions and assume they're related. We have no evidence of that being the case."

"We have no evidence that it's not, either."

William sighed. "If it becomes obvious the cases are related, I'll remove myself from Gabby's case and appoint Mitch as acting chief until we figure out what's going on."

Thankfully, the mayor agreed.

LATER THAT AFTERNOON, William still hadn't made it home for his jog on the beach. After the mayor left, he ate a hurried sandwich at his desk and was working on a grant proposal that would enable the department to build a much-needed addition.

He wanted to get it done because he had a feeling Gabby's case was going to take up a lot of his time in the near future.

He lifted his head at the sound of Peggy's softly spoken, "Knock, knock."

"Sorry to interrupt," she said. "Doris wants to see you."

"She's here?" he asked, standing. "Send her back."

"William?" Doris stepped into his office. Her expression crumbled, but she held her hand out, took a few deep breaths, and finally gave him a forced smile. "Sorry."

Doris was of average height with hair highlighted to a shade of blonde not found in the natural world. But they had gone to high school together, she was one of his oldest and dearest friends, and he loved her like a sister.

"No need to apologize. Sit down." William guided her into one of the two chairs in front of his desk and took the one next to her. "What's going on?"

"I heard a group of young men fishing found Gabby's body in the water at the cove?" She looked at him for confirmation.

It hadn't been twenty-four hours yet since Gabby had been found, but that was the way small towns worked. Nothing he could do about it, and it wasn't like he could deny anything. He simply nodded.

Doris took a shuddering breath. "There's no way Gabby could have drowned."

"Why is that?" William wasn't sure why she felt the need to discuss Gabby's death with him today. Nothing formal had been issued yet.

"Gabby was deathly afraid of the ocean. She wouldn't go near it."

That wasn't what he expected her response to be. He tilted his head. "Then why did she live on a barrier island, surrounded by water?"

"That's just the way she is…was," Doris said, as if those few words explained everything. "She had her trailer out in the woods where she didn't have to see the ocean, but she always knew it was there. She told me once it was her way of having power over her fear."

William wasn't sure he understood Gabby's reasoning, but if it'd worked for her, who was he to judge?

Doris sighed. "I know what people say about her, and I saw how toxic her relationship with Hamilton was, but there was more to her than that. She was one of my best employees. Probably the best."

"If she didn't drown, how do you think she died?" William asked.

"I don't know how she could have died. I just didn't want people to assume she drowned and not look into it like they should."

William nodded before asking her another question, realizing he didn't know much about Gabby's relationship with Hamilton. "Just how toxic was her relationship with Hamilton?"

"I didn't mean to imply Hamilton had anything to do with it. Lord knows that young man has enough issues, bless his heart," Doris said.

"We're not assuming anything," he tried to assure her. "The medical examiner is going to do an autopsy so we'll know exactly what happened."

"Thank you." Doris nodded. "She was a good person. For her to die like that is so unfair."

Unfair was synonymous with life in William's opinion, but he kept that to himself.

Mary looked down and sniffled. My mind raced trying to figure out if she was on the edge of a fit of hysterics or if maybe Edward had to leave, or had been arrested. Mary took a deep breath, and when she looked up, her eyes held an unwavering strength I hadn't known her to possess.

"I'm with child."

JOURNAL OF AN UNKNOWN WOMAN, EARLY 1700s

Chapter Three

Eva grew up in New Jersey, and her parents divorced when she was twelve. The summer following their divorce, her mother took her on vacation to Nags Head in the Outer Banks of North Carolina.

That was the summer she learned how to fly a kite and bait a fishhook properly. They rented a condo for two months, and the neighborhood kids took her in like she was one of their own. Altogether, there were six of them, ranging in ages from eleven to fourteen. At almost thirteen, she was the third oldest. The locals called them the Six Pack, and for two months that summer, she was the happiest she had been in a long time. Her days were filled with sun and sand, while nights were spent listening to tales of Blackbeard, ghost ships, and buried treasure.

When August came, she did everything she could think of to persuade her mother to move to Nags Head permanently, but nothing worked. The only way her mother was able to get her in the car to go back home to New Jersey was to promise they'd come back the next summer. As they left, Eva shut her eyes tight, vowing she would see everything the exact same in ten months.

It wasn't meant to be. On New Year's Eve, almost five months later, her mother was driving home from her job at the hospital when a drunk driver ran a stop sign and hit her car, killing her instantly.

Eva and her mother were close, and she was distraught after her death. She went to live with her father, but he had remarried a woman who didn't have children and didn't want any—especially one who looked like a replica of her husband's blue-eyed and blond ex-wife.

Though Eva wouldn't make it back to the North Carolina coast until college, those two months spent at the beach left permanent footprints on her life's path. After her mother's death, she surrounded herself with history books of all kinds. She started with those written about Blackbeard and the Outer Banks, but she kept on, reading about England and why its people left for the New World; she read about the girl who was queen for nine days, and the horrific things people did in the name of religion and for a minor momentary reward.

Stated simply, she started a love affair with history.

NOW, YEARS LATER, after earning a degree in history and spending several summers interning for the office she currently worked in, she knew she was one of the lucky ones. She'd thought once or twice about trying to look up the other five Six Pack members. Surely one or two of them still lived around the area. But they'd rarely used names that summer; names were for adults and were boring. She'd been known simply as "Jersey."

The Monday after Gabby's body had been found, Eva found herself thinking about the Six Pack for the first time in years as she sat at her usual table in the diner. A family of four was at the front counter, paying for their meal, and the youngest son reminded her of one of the boys in the pack, with a headful of tousled black hair and freckles across his nose. Did he still have the freckles as an adult, and if so, would Eva recognize him if she saw him? For that matter, would she recognize any members of the Six Pack today? She wasn't sure.

"The Devil's Coins is a relatively unknown legend about Blackbeard."

Eva's ears perked up at Elbert's statement. In the five years she'd been in Eden, she'd never heard anyone mention the myth. In fact, while researching for her graduate thesis on Blackbeard, she'd had a hard time getting her hands on the story.

Elbert started, "According the legend, in 1718, Blackbeard fell in love with a young woman named Mary. They say Mary was as beautiful as an angel, and one day, while she was foraging for food, her path crossed with Blackbeard's. He was never the same."

"Wait a minute," Maxine said. "Who are *they*, and how do they know what angels look like? Much less if they're attractive? Has this mysterious *they* seen every angel in the world and can verify they're all beautiful?"

"Put a lid on it, Maxine," Herb said. "Let him finish."

Though she didn't turn around to look, Eva could imagine the silent glare Maxine shot her tablemate.

"Anyway," Elbert continued, "Blackbeard and Mary met in secret for months, and due to Mary's love, the great pirate began to change. He wanted to get out of the pirate business. To settle down and raise a family. Some people say the two of them got married. But there was one problem."

"Oh, I know this one!" Francis said. "Mary was pregnant and had Blackbeard's son, but she sent the infant away because she feared for his life. Blackbeard was off being a pirate, and he didn't know until Mary told him right before she died in his arms." She ended with a dramatic sigh.

"She didn't tell him where his son was?" Herb asked.

"No," Francis answered. "I think she died before she could tell him."

"She probably didn't want him to know," Maxine said. "Especially if she feared for his life so much that she sent him away in the first place."

"Wish there was a way to know with certainty if there was a possibility of a descendant somewhere nearby," Elbert mused. "Or if we had a way to test for DNA at the Blackbeard Festival. There's a planning committee on Sunday; maybe I'll bring it up anyway."

"Ugh, the Blackbeard Festival," Maxine said with a moan. "I don't know why our town wants to celebrate someone as tragic as Blackbeard."

Eva forced herself not to turn around and gape at the older lady. Maybe she'd been looking at the entire event through rose-colored glasses, but Eva had thought everyone liked the Festival.

"What makes you think his story is a tragedy?" Francis asked.

"He is dead, isn't he?" It was either a rhetorical question or a stupid one, but neither deserved a reply, Eva thought. Maxine, however, continued, "By all accounts, it wasn't a pleasant death, and if we decide to believe part of the Devil's Coins legend, his true love died in his arms. That's a tragedy if I've ever heard of one. Of course, Mary couldn't have been over eighteen. How could a young girl like that possibly be the love of his life? Maybe it wasn't tragic that she died, after all. Did you think maybe he was glad not to be tied down anymore?"

"No," Francis said with a grin. "No, I'm a happily-ever-after kind of a girl. I like to believe it's out there. Somewhere."

"Then you're a fool."

"I didn't peg you as a cynic, Maxine," Elbert said.

"That's because I'm not. I'm a realist. Don't you watch the news? There are no happily-ever-afters."

"There are plenty of happily-ever-afters. They aren't reported on the news because doom and gloom are better for ratings."

Always having to get in the last word, Maxine replied with, "Now who's the cynic?"

"Hey Elbert," Herb said. He wasn't a big talker, and Eva assumed he was only doing so now to stop a potential argument between the two women. "Isn't that your granddaughter, Amelia, outside? What's she doing with all those signs?"

Eva didn't have to look to know what he saw. Amelia Morgan, one of Elbert's granddaughters and a friend of Eva's, was running for mayor and was spending the morning putting up signs. She'd asked Eva to help, but she'd had to turn her down because Officer Mitch Montague had called her over the weekend and set up a meeting for eight-thirty this morning. A glance at her watch told her she had about five minutes before she needed to leave.

"Yes, it is," Elbert confirmed. "She's running for mayor. Looks like she's putting campaign signs up."

"Is that her boyfriend helping?" Maxine asked.

"No," Elbert said, as Eva placed cash for her breakfast on the table and prepared to leave. "That's a lawyer friend of hers. He's a good man, but Amelia swears there's nothing between them. Says they tried dating in high school and it didn't work."

Eva's car was parked on the opposite side of the street from where the two of them worked unloading signs from the back of Amelia's car. The lawyer must have said something funny because he was smiling while Amelia laughed. Judging by his profile, he was quite handsome. For a second, Eva thought about blowing Mitch off, but instead, she got into her car and drove away.

The Historical Society's office building was relatively quiet when she arrived, a stark contrast to the diner in the middle of breakfast service.

"Good morning," Julia Baxter, Eva's friend and work colleague said, passing her in the hallway, carrying a cup of coffee. "Just made a fresh pot."

"Thanks," Eva said, trying to calculate if she had time to grab a cup before Mitch stopped by. "Want to go out to lunch today or is Justin taking you out?"

"Yes, if we can go around one-thirty, and no, he's not today." Julia rolled her eyes. "His mother is staying at our house, so he's going to go back home for lunch."

"Ms. Knightly?"

Eva turned and found Mitch standing behind her. So much for coffee. "Officer Montague."

"I'm early," he said. "I apologize. It's a habit."

Eva turned toward Julia. "I'll come by your office at one-thirty."

Mitch watched her co-worker leave. "If you need to take care of something first, I can wait," he told Eva.

"It's nothing. Come on in and have a seat. What can I help you with?"

She removed her laptop from her tote bag. Mitch took a seat, and she couldn't help but notice how uncomfortable he looked.

"I have two coins I need identified," he said, getting right to his point. "And I was wondering if you or the Historical Society could help, or if not, if you knew someone who could." In what came across as an afterthought, he added, "I got your name from William Templeton."

"Are the two coins in question personal?"

"No," he answered. "They're actually evidence." He looked at her open office door. "Can we keep this discussion confidential?"

"Yes. Feel free to close the door."

"Thank you," he said, standing and doing that very thing. "One of the coins was found on Gabby Clark's body Friday, and the other was found on Catherine Harper."

His words were a punch to her stomach. Catherine had a coin on her? And Gabby, too?

Mitch sat across from her, silent.

"Catherine died a year ago," Eva said, not knowing what else to say.

"Yes, but finding one body with an odd coin is different from finding two bodies with odd coins." He paused for a second. "With Catherine, the presence of a coin didn't raise any flags. The same couldn't be said when another was found on Gabby."

Catherine had asked her about buried treasure the night she died. Eva had forgotten until that very second. Did her question have to do with the coin that would later be found on her?

Eva shook her head to clear it. The question would have to wait until later to be pondered, after Mitch had left and she could think in private. "In that case," Eva replied, "you'll need someone with more expertise than me or anyone else at the Historical Society can provide."

"I was afraid of that."

"But the good news is I know someone who would be perfect." Eva reached for her phone. "Emerson Jefferys is a coin expert in Durham. We went to graduate school at Duke together. If anyone can identify the coins, it's him. Hold on, and I'll pull his details up."

She wrote his name and number down and gave the paper to Mitch.

"Do you mind if we call him together?" Mitch asked.

"Right now?" she asked, and at his nod said, "Let me dial."

Emerson picked up on the second ring. "Are my eyes deceiving me, or is Eva Knightly calling me?"

Talking with Emerson never failed to make her smile. Even today. "Hey, Emerson."

"You've never called me during work hours before," he said. "I take it this isn't a personal call?"

"Unfortunately not," she confirmed. "I have you on speaker. Officer Mitch Montague of the Eden PD is in the office with me."

"What can I help you with?" Emerson asked in a serious tone, the levity of the last few seconds gone.

Eva looked at Mitch and waved for him to answer.

"Mr. Jefferys," Mitch said. "We've had two deaths, both unexpected and potentially homicides, and both with odd coins found on the victim. Ms. Knightly indicated you would be the best person to identify the coins."

"I haven't heard about strange coins being found," Emerson said. "I assume you've managed to keep this out of the media?"

"So far," Mitch answered. "Or at least that was the case with the first one. I'm not sure we can keep things under wraps with the second. Especially if we bring you in."

Eva was still shocked a coin had been found on Catherine and she'd only heard of it today. She didn't offer that information to Emerson. And did Mitch say *potential homicide?* Catherine's death had been ruled an accident. Had that changed?

"I'll do anything I can to help," Emerson said. "When do you need me?"

"Yesterday," Mitch replied. "But we'll take you whenever you can make the time."

Silence filled the air. Probably Emerson checking his calendar. Eva knew his expertise was in high need.

"How does Wednesday of this week sound?" Emerson finally asked.

"I would greatly appreciate that," Mitch said and then he winced. "Unfortunately, our department is at overflow and I don't have any room for you at the station."

"I can work out of my hotel room," Emerson said. "It's not a problem."

"You're not going to work out of your hotel," Eva said. "I have an office at the Historical Society and a workroom at the Coastal Carolina Museum. I can't use both at the same time, so you can use one. And don't even think about arguing with me; I insist."

They wrapped up the call, and Mitch left shortly thereafter. Eva waited a few minutes and then dropped her head into her hands.

She had to pull herself together and get to work. There was too much to do with the Blackbeard Festival alone to worry about a few unknown coins. But even as she reached for her laptop to check on the outstanding contracts for the Festival, she knew the worry would never leave her alone.

In that moment I realized Mary had become a woman. She looks different now that I actually pay attention. The girl is still there but the mantle of womanhood covers her. Soon the girl she had been would disappear forever.

— JOURNAL OF AN UNKNOWN WOMAN, EARLY 1700s

Chapter Four

I t appeared as if the entire town of Eden knew something, but no one had bothered to let William in on the secret. At first, when the lady at the grocery store had not so subtly mentioned that her granddaughter was spending the summer with her and that she was single, he thought she was only making conversation. He didn't even blink when his neighbor stopped by while he was working in his yard and invited him to dinner at her house the following weekend because her sister would be in town. Not even when she winked and said, "She's single."

No, it wasn't until the diner sent a newbie employee with his lunch order, three days after Gabby's body had been found, and the poor young woman stuttered and stammered the entire time she was in his presence, that he finally asked Peggy, who was coughing in an attempt to hide her laughter, and failing, what was going on.

"I mean it," he said, watching out the window as the woman in question nearly sprinted back to the diner. "That girl's face was so red when she walked in here, I assumed she forgot to put on sunscreen and fell asleep outside for four hours."

Peggy only shook her head. "William, please. You act as if you haven't lived in Eden for your entire life."

Not only had Peggy lived in Eden her entire life as well, she'd been the administrative assistant for every Eden Chief of Police since she graduated from high school nearly forty-five years ago. Through the years, she'd tell anyone who listened there'd been over a dozen people who held the title of chief. All men. All white. The longest one in office held his position for over eleven years. The shortest, only three weeks.

"I don't know what you're talking about," William replied.

Peggy closed her eyes and took a deep breath. When she opened them, she no longer resembled his easygoing, laid-back admin. She looked resolved and a bit sad. "It's been a year."

That was all it took. William sat down heavily in the chair directly behind him. She didn't have to say a year since what. He knew. It had been a year since Catherine had died, leaving him a widower at the age of thirty-one.

He supposed for the townspeople of Eden that was long enough for him to mourn the woman he'd vowed to love, honor, and cherish forever. In their eyes, he guessed, it was time to brush off her death, like it was nothing but an old unpleasant memory, and jump back into the dating pool. Where, perhaps, if he was lucky, he would find another woman to claim as his forever.

He stood, and even though he was no longer hungry, he took his lunch back to his private office. If he didn't, Peggy would no doubt see it as a sign he wasn't eating and would make it her new mission to fill his freezer with casseroles.

He placed the Styrofoam container holding his baked chicken lunch on his desk and tried to concentrate on completing the report the governor needed by the end of the week, but his eyes kept drifting to the one picture of Catherine he kept out. It was taken days after he'd proposed, and she looked happy. He felt certain she had been, at least on that day. In the picture, her smile was natural, so different from the fake and forced ones he remembered from her last few months of life.

Some time later, Peggy knocked on his door, and he told her to come in. A glance at the clock told him he'd been working for over an hour to write the handful of sentences he'd added to the report. He almost thanked her for the interruption, but as soon as he saw her expression, he prepared himself for bad news.

"What?" he asked.

"I was just emailed the medical examiner's preliminary report on Gabby Clark." She handed him some papers. "I printed it for you."

"Thanks," he said, scanning the first page. "What does it say?"

"Accidental death caused by drowning, alcohol a contributing factor."

"Damn it." He slammed the papers on his desk. The autopsy was wrong. He knew it was. He felt it.

"Isn't it better that it was an accident?" Peggy asked. "The alternative is to suggest we have a murderer running around free."

He took a deep breath. "Gabby spent the last three years working with Doris cleaning houses." He knew this for a fact because after his grandmother died, he hired Doris to clean and keep up her house. She'd been doing so every other week since.

Peggy just looked at him. Had she been twenty years younger, she'd have replied with *duh*.

"Before anyone I hire enters that house," he continued, "I run a background check on them. Which means, I ran one on Gabby. She's clean. Yes, she dropped out of school, but she's never been arrested, has no violations, no tickets. Nothing. Yes, she and Hamilton had some loud and dramatic fights, and often Hamilton would be intoxicated, but Gabby never was."

"That doesn't mean she wasn't drunk that night."

"I know, but it would be so out of character." He knew from Gabby's background that her father was a cocaine addict and her mother had died of lung cancer when she was a child. He'd overheard her tell Doris one day that she never drank, experimented with drugs, or even tried a cigarette. Gabby was afraid she'd inherited an addictive personality and one time of anything could be all it took for her to get hooked.

Peggy pointed to the report, still on his desk where he'd dropped it moments ago. "The autopsy showed alcohol in her system. You can't ignore that. She drank it."

His mind told him Peggy was right. The only other way Gabby could have had the amount of alcohol found in her body was if someone forced her to drink it. Which was too absurd to even contemplate.

He stacked the papers of the report together and placed them on top of his to-do pile. Peggy was probably right. Nine times out of ten she was. But his gut told him she wasn't in this case.

"I'll wait until we get the final report," he said.

Peggy simply nodded. She was never one to push a point. "I wish I knew if this latest report would end the tongue wagging or make it worse."

He cocked an eyebrow at her. "You talk a lot about gossip, but I never see you participate in any yourself."

"No comment."

"What?"

"That's my secret weapon against gossip. When I first started working here, the hardest part was keeping quiet. I am, after all, a Southern woman, and loved nothing more than a tempting piece of gossip. However, I learned quickly that if I wanted to keep my job, the gossiping had to stop. That's when *no comment* became the two most important words I spoke. They're powerful and have never once failed to shut down the busybodies looking for a juicy morsel or a fancy city reporter wanting the 'inside story' or 'exclusive details.'"

William didn't respond when someone else entered the station. He smiled as the man came into view.

The Reverend Robert Neighbors of Eden Methodist Church wiped his forehead with a handkerchief he kept in his pocket. He was slightly overweight, balding, and had a tendency to sweat more than the average person.

"Robert," William said. "How's it going?"

"Can't complain." Robert stuffed the handkerchief back in his pocket.

"Wouldn't do any good if you did," William added.

"There's the 'glass half empty' man I know." Robert nodded to Peggy. "Ms. Peggy, how are you today?"

"Just fine, Reverend." She walked back to her desk as William led Robert to his office.

"What brings you by?" William asked when both men were settled.

Robert had been a good friend of Catherine's years before he became one of William's closest confidants in Eden. Catherine had met him while she was in college. Robert was a few years older, but that didn't stop the two of them from becoming friends. When the Methodist Church moved the reverend from Charleston to Eden, Catherine ensured he met her husband. William found him to be down to earth and easy to speak with, though he did tend to view everything as black and white. Gray was a color that didn't exist in Robert's world.

Over the years, he'd come to consider Robert a good friend. They shared a love for baseball and played together on a men's church league. William could hold his own, unlike Robert, who dropped the ball more often than not. If asked, anyone would agree it was just as well Robert always struck out because it was doubtful he'd be able to run all the way to first base.

But Robert simply loved the game, and though he'd long ago given up his dream of winning the World Series, his joy of being part of a team made up for the fact he couldn't play at all.

"I wanted to see how you were doing. I thought Gabby's death might bring back some memories, especially with the renewed talk about Catherine and the coins."

How was he doing? William wasn't sure how to reply. Should he complain about the difficulties in trying not to let the whispers and shameless stares get to him? Or how somedays his life felt so derailed, he feared he'd never get it back on track?

"William?" Robert asked, and William realized he hadn't answered the question.

It would be easy to brush Robert off with a quick *I'm fine,* but he decided to be honest. "Just as I think I'm finally moving on, something comes along, and it hits me that I haven't moved as far as I thought."

Robert nodded, encouraging William to continue.

"You know, I read once that those who had loved the most found it easier to find love again after the death of a spouse. If that turns out to be true, I might as well count on being alone forever. I still loved Catherine when she died, but I'm not sure I liked her all that much." He looked down at his hands on the table and swallowed. "Thinking that makes me feel guilty because I'm still alive and she's not. And because I know I wasn't able to love her the way she deserved." He couldn't voice the other reason for his guilt—that at times he felt relief that the bitterness and anger and arguments marking the last year of her life died with her. Or that since Catherine's death, he'd found himself thinking about Eva Knightly more often than he cared to admit.

Robert took his time replying. "I'm sure as a clergyman there's probably some spiritual advice I should wisely bestow upon you, but at the moment, it escapes me. So, for the moment, if you don't mind, I'll just sit by your side and be your friend."

MARRIAGE WAS HARD for any new couple. That was what William had always heard and that was why it came as such a shock that his was so easy. Marriage with Catherine was effortless. He worked and she painted. Evenings were spent outside, walking along the beach. At night when he would turn to her in bed, she went into his arms willingly.

It wasn't until after their third anniversary that things started to unravel. At first, it was the occasional headache, and he wasn't able to tell if she really had one or not. All he knew was it felt as if she was pulling away from him. He tried to cut back on his hours, but as the police chief, it was hard to do. He justified it by telling himself he had plenty of time to make it up to Catherine. Once things got settled, he'd be able to take her on a real vacation.

He remembered the day he'd snuck out of the office early. She'd sold a painting the day before at a gallery on Nag's Head, and he wanted to take her out to celebrate. He stopped by a florist first to pick up a bouquet of yellow roses, knowing she would love them.

Catherine's favorite spot to paint was on their back deck. It was early afternoon, and since there was a good chance she'd be out there working, he didn't go inside but walked along the side of the house to surprise her on the deck and was shocked when he didn't see her there. He looked everywhere, but she wasn't home. As it turned out, she didn't get home until well after ten-thirty that night.

That was the first time he suspected his wife was cheating on him.

I couldn't help but think if Edward knew Mary was carrying his child, he'd never leave. At first thought it seemed obvious I should say something. It would be both quick and final. But it is not my place to interfere in their matter. And though I might be mistaken, something tells me Edward doesn't have any other choice but to leave.

Chapter Five

A s a child, William's Nana had taught him to be kind to everyone, to help those in need, and to be a giver instead of a taker. Even more, she lived the words she spoke. Those lessons she'd planted early had taken root and shaped him into the man he was today. Nana was one of the reasons why he became a police officer in Eden shortly after graduating from college, and why he'd worked so hard to become Chief of Police. He was able to live and work in the place he grew up and performed a public service he hoped benefited everyone in the community. For the most part, William enjoyed his job.

But like any career, there were plenty of days he hated his work as well. Anytime a crime involved children, a piece of his soul died. When he knew someone was guilty but lacked the evidence to prove it, he felt like a failure. Thankfully, such extreme cases were few and far between in his small town of Eden, but when they came, they had a tendency to suck the life out of his bones.

The Gabby Clark case wasn't extreme, but he couldn't shake the feeling that there was more to her death than mere drowning. When he took into account she was found fully clothed and paired with what Doris said about Gabby's fear of water, something didn't add up. Most of the whispers he'd heard pointed toward an intoxicated Gabby somehow drowning. But if she'd been as fearful of the water as Doris made her sound, wouldn't she feel the same way about it even after a few drinks?

Late Monday morning, William drove to Brown's Hardware, the store Hamilton had inherited from his parents after they had died unexpectedly when Hamilton was nineteen. Hamilton had always been something of a wild child, prone to see just how far he could push the boundaries before getting into trouble. When he had to take over the store after his parents' death, everyone had hoped he'd settle down a bit, but unfortunately, that was not the case. Instead, at twenty-five, Hamilton came and went as he pleased, leaving the day-to-day operations of the store to his employees.

In William's mind, Brown's Hardware was a shining example of the persistence of the Outer Banks and its people, or at least had been before Hamilton took over. Hamilton Brown's family had owned and operated Eden's only hardware store since the 1950s. In the following years, it became known as a staple to the small town. Once, in the late 1980s, its existence was threatened by the appearance of several of the large national brands. Though one by one they each tried to take over Brown's Hardware, none of them were successful. Eventually, one of the well-known chains decided to open a location in Nag's Head. It did okay, but most Outer Banks natives only shopped Brown's and let the tourists enjoy the cookie-cutter, more recognizable store.

At the moment, there was no one else in the store. Ten years ago, that would have been odd, but according to what William had gathered from listening to people around town, it was now commonplace. No one, it seemed, wanted to shop at Brown's when Hamilton was working. In the last few years his demeanor had changed. No one was sure why, but of course everyone had a theory. William assumed the only reason people still shopped at the store was due to their loyalty to his parents. Why else would someone subject themselves to Hamilton's curtness and rude attitude?

Hamilton had always been on the thin side, but today he looked gaunt. With bags under his eyes and unkempt dark hair, it was clear he wasn't sleeping. William also noted he didn't look surprised to see who'd entered the store.

Though he'd never looked forward to questioning those left behind after a sudden death, William dreaded it even more after experiencing that questioning firsthand from the other side. It made him feel like crap and he hated making anyone else feel that way.

Pushing those thoughts aside, he tried to clear his mind. He was here to collect information, that was all.

"Chief," Hamilton said with a nod.

William returned the nod. "Looks like it's a bit slow today; mind if I ask you a few questions?"

Hamilton showed no concern, he simply shrugged. "Sure, come on back."

He led William to a room behind the counter. With a large glass window looking out toward the store, they'd know if anyone entered. The room itself appeared to be equal parts storage, general office, and break room.

They sat down at a wooden table William guessed Hamilton's mom and dad had put into place and had never been moved since.

"As you might have guessed, I'm following up on Gabby's death."

Hamilton dropped his head. "I still can't believe she's gone."

"I understand how difficult this is," William said, wanting to put Hamilton at ease and to let him know he was sympathetic. "I only have a few questions, and then I'll get out of your hair." Hamilton lifted his head, but remained silent. "When was the last time you saw or spoke to her?" William asked.

"The last time I spoke to her was Thursday afternoon," Hamilton said. "I was at a conference in Raleigh from Tuesday until Friday morning."

The ME had estimated Gabby died around nine at night on Thursday. "About what time was that call?"

"Around five, I think."

"And she sounded fine?" William asked. "Not upset or worried?"

"She sounded like she always did. I told her I was still in Raleigh and I'd see her the next day."

"I need the information and contact details for the conference. Do you have it handy?"

"You don't believe me?" Hamilton pushed back from the table and stood up. "Do you think I had something to do with her death?"

William refused to be rattled. "Sit down."

Hamilton didn't move, but after a few seconds went by and William didn't move either, he sat.

"Thank you," William said. "I'm not accusing you of anything. I'm asking for this information because you were in a close relationship with Gabby. I'd ask the same from anyone in a similar position. Understand?"

"Yeah. I guess." Hamilton didn't appear convinced. "I don't have the convention stuff here; it's at my house."

"That's fine. You can drop it off at the police station in the next day or two."

Hamilton nodded. "Can I tell you something, Chief?"

"Of course."

"I don't think Gabby drowned."

It was not what William thought he would say. "Why is that?"

"She almost drowned when she was little. She'd been playing in the ocean with her mom, and the undertow was stronger than her mom thought. Washed Gabby out of her arms." Hamilton retold the story completely stone-faced. "She wasn't breathing when they pulled her out."

Doris had mentioned Gabby's fear of the ocean as well, though after hearing Hamilton out, William, had a better idea of why. Knowing just how dangerous the sea could be, Hamilton's words painted a vivid picture in William's mind, leaving him speechless.

Hamilton turned his head to look at him. "I can't believe she went near the ocean of her own free will. Not when I couldn't even talk her into eating on the beach."

"Do you know of anyone who might have had reason to want her gone?"

"No, I mean don't get me wrong, she rubbed a lot of people the wrong way." Hamilton shook his head. "But enough to want her dead? No, I can't think of anyone."

"I have one more question for you," William said. "Did you notice anything different in Gabby's behavior a week or so before she died?"

Hamilton leveled his gaze at him. "Are you asking if I saw any hints she might decide to get drunk and try to jump waves?"

"No." If Hamilton was unaware of the gold coin found in Gabby's pocket, William wouldn't be the one to tell him. Though since the coins were such a hot topic at the moment that seemed unlikely. "Did she seem interested or involved in anything new?"

Hamilton shook his head but then stopped. "Actually, she did, but I'd forgotten about it until just now. A few times she asked to use my laptop, and I saw where she'd been searching Blackbeard. She even mentioned us going by that museum, the history one?"

"The one the Historical Society runs?" At Hamilton's nod, William continued, "I know of it, but I don't think I've been inside since it opened."

"I ain't ever been inside, either. I mean it's just a bunch of old junk. Probably be like school, boring as all. But Gabby wanted to go. I told her maybe in the fall, when it's less crowded." Hamilton gazed the window, but it didn't seem as if he saw anything. "Now I can never take her."

THE HISTORICAL SOCIETY wasn't far from the hardware store. William decided to stop by to speak with Eva before heading back to the station.

He didn't know the volunteer working the front desk, but once he gave his name and told her who he wanted to see, he was directed to Eva's office. Her door was open, and she was on the phone. William stood in the hall, wanting to give her privacy, but once she spotted him, she waved for him to step inside.

"William just dropped by," Eva told whoever was on the phone. "Look over those dates and times, and let me know if any of them work with your schedule."

They said their goodbyes and once she'd put her phone down, Eva turned her attention to him. "Amelia said to tell you *hello*."

"Can't believe she's running for mayor," William said. "But I hope she wins."

"You do realize she'd kind of be like your boss if she does?"

He flashed her a grin. "I know. I think she'd shake this town up. Probably do it some good."

"She might shake you up," Eva countered. "Have you thought about that?"

He had actually, and he still wanted her to win. Amelia was smart and wouldn't let him get away with anything just because they were friends. He also knew she'd be open to listening to his ideas and giving them the thought necessary before deciding on a path. He couldn't always say the same for the current mayor. "Who knows," he told Eva, waggling his eyebrows. "A good shake up might do me some good as well."

Eva laughed. "Both she and Elbert have recently joined my Blackbeard Festival Committee, and I couldn't be more thrilled.

She called to see if we could get together soon and talk about Blackbeard." She raised an eyebrow. "Mitch was here earlier. Said you gave him my name."

"I did," he said, leaning forward. "Did Catherine say anything to you about the coin they found on her?"

"No," Eva answered, and she looked away from him. "She didn't. The first mention of the coin I heard was this morning when Mitch brought it up, along with the one found on Gabby."

"Are you going to identify them?" William asked.

"Me?" she asked as if he'd been crazy to think such a thing. "No, I recommended a guy I went to grad school with who's an expert in the field, Emerson Jefferys. Even if I tried to identify them and thought I had an answer, I'd want confirmation from someone like him."

"The fishermen who found Gabby said they thought it looked like a coin from buried treasure," William said.

She laughed. "And they know exactly what treasure looks like because they've seen so much of it?"

"Right?" he asked, with a smile.

"Do you think Hamilton had anything to do with her death?" Eva asked, growing serious. "I know you can't discuss it in detail or anything, but gut reaction?"

"Is there a reason you ask?" he countered instead of answering.

"I overheard some people talking about how Catherine had a thing for Hamilton." She didn't look him in the eye as she spoke. Rather, she focused her attention on a spot over his shoulder. "I didn't believe it, but I couldn't shake the feeling I'd forgotten something. I finally remembered what it was."

William waited. He'd heard similar gossip but didn't think it likely.

"We were in the diner having lunch, maybe two years ago. I can't remember exactly," Eva said. "Hamilton walked in. As soon as Catherine spotted him, she said she didn't like him and didn't trust him."

"Catherine said that?" William asked. Catherine rarely expressed dislike for anyone and had the type of personality that naturally drew people to her. She rarely met a stranger. Which was why her comment to Eva came as such a surprise.

"Yes, and I had the same reaction. It was out of character for her," Eva said. "According to Catherine, she was at your Nana's one day when Gabby was cleaning. Catherine said she typically didn't go there when she knew Gabby would be there because she didn't want to get in the way." William nodded, and she continued, "But she needed some documents for taxes or something. When she arrived, Hamilton was there."

"Hamilton was at Nana's with Gabby?" William asked. "Doris doesn't allow that. It's a liability."

"That's what Catherine said. She said they were standing out- side and Gabby saw her arrive first and told Hamilton he needed to leave because he didn't have permission to be there. He grabbed her by the arm, jerked her toward him and told her he didn't need permission to do anything. Then he let Gabby go, walked over to his truck, and drove away. Catherine said he blew her a kiss as he passed."

"Damn," William said, running his hand over his face, his eye- brows knitted together. "She never told me." Which raised the question, what else had she kept to herself?

Love is a strange thing.

— JOURNAL OF AN UNKNOWN WOMAN, EARLY 1700s

"I have a bone to pick with you," Amelia said when Eva answered her phone late Wednesday afternoon.

"Really?" Eva asked with a smile, hearing the levity in her friend's voice.

"Yes. When you told me a colleague of yours who is a coin expert would be consulting for the Eden Police Department, I pictured a skinny geeky guy with zero fashion sense and even less social skills."

Eva laughed because Emerson was a tall, good-looking, Black man, and he had excellent fashion sense and social skills. Amelia was short, perhaps five foot two with heels, but had always had a thing for tall men. She also had short brown hair and the personality of a firecracker. Engineering never seemed to match up with the lively woman.

"It's not funny," Amelia said in mock chastisement. "You should have warned me he was smoking hot."

"And tall," Eva added with a chuckle. "When did you see him?" Eva knew he had arrived earlier in the day but wasn't sure what time. He'd called her yesterday, and they planned to get together for dinner tonight.

"Around lunchtime I was heading into the library because the young adult novel I told you about that I've had on hold forever finally came in, and Mr. *You Must Be Lost Because You Are Too Hot For This Town* was approaching from Sweet Sandy's Ice Cream next door. I only had a second to decide what to do, so I did the first thing that came to my mind. I dropped my purse right in front of him, and he had to jump out of the way of fifteen lipstick tubes. He stopped to help pick them up, and I introduced myself."

Eva laughed because it was so easy to see the scene happen the exact way Amelia described. "Emerson and I are having dinner tonight at the diner. Why don't you join us?"

"Really?" Amelia seemed excited before replying with a dejected, "No. I don't want to be the third wheel."

"It's dinner at the diner, you won't be a third anything because Emerson and I are only friends. Look at it this way," Eva said, knowing her friend wouldn't turn her down. "You said you wanted a Blackbeard refresher since you joined the planning committee for the Festival, right?"

"Right," Amelia agreed, though a bit hesitant.

"The only thing better than talking to one historian is talking to two. Seven o'clock. Be there. If nothing else, look at it as practice for when you're elected mayor and have to interact with hot guys all the time," Eva said.

"I've seen ninety percent of the people the mayor interacts with, and I wouldn't classify any of them as hot."

"Seven o'clock," Eva repeated and hung up so as not to give her a way to refuse. Right as she did, there was a knock on her office door.

She wasn't expecting anyone and assumed it was someone who'd heard she knew the newly arrived coin expert and wanted to gossip. If that turned out to be the case, they'd be sorely disappointed. She had way too much to do to sit around and chat.

"Come in," Eva said, sitting up straighter and putting her phone down on the desk.

"Sorry to bother you, Ms. Knightly," said one of the volunteers at the center, a new one probably, since Eva didn't recognize her. "Reverend Robert Neighbors is here to see you."

Eva groaned internally, wishing it had been a co-worker wanting to gossip. Anything would be better than having to talk with Reverend Robert Neighbors. Overseeing the volunteers, Julia typically gave the high school kids instructions on how to handle requests from Reverend Neighbors. Before Eva could open her mouth to speak, the young woman held out her hands.

"Mrs. Baxter told me if he came by, I should tell him you're busy and give him your card," the volunteer, who couldn't be more than sixteen or seventeen, said. "But he's a man of God, and it's wrong to lie."

Eva stood up and gave the volunteer a tight smile. "Thank you." She read the name tag she hadn't been able to see while sitting down. "Lindsey."

Reverend Robert Neighbors had been appointed to Eden Methodist Church years ago, and according to what she heard, most of those in the congregation liked him. Eva rarely went to church, but when she did, it was usually to the Episcopalian or sometimes the Presbyterian.

She'd been to service at Eden Methodist Church once. Not long after he moved to town, Eva had a confrontation with him that would forever leave a bad taste in her mouth. At the time, Julia Baxter had been Julia Locklear. Her husband, Adam, had been a worthless excuse for a man who was forever belittling her. Eva couldn't count the number of times her colleague showed up at work in tears over something he'd said or done.

Eva tried to get her to call someone, or to talk him into getting help, but Julia always blew her off, saying everything was okay and she could handle it. Then one morning Julia called in sick.

The two of them had spent the day before in a training class, and Julia had been fine. Eva dropped by her house unexpectedly at lunch and found Julia alone with a black eye.

Fortunately, it didn't take much to get her friend to leave and start the separation process. Not long after her divorce was final, Julia met Justin Baxter. They knew they were moving fast, but Julia and Justin didn't care. Besides, Julia was happier than she'd ever been, and that was all that mattered to Eva.

Shortly after Julia filed separation papers from Adam, Eva attended her first and only service at Eden Methodist Church where she met the reverend. He was all smiles until he heard her name. Upon learning who she was, he told her she had no business interfering with the Locklear marriage and that it was wrong for Julia to leave Adam, especially for another man. Eva had only been able to hold her tongue out of respect for his standing, but since that day, she avoided Reverend Neighbors whenever she could. Any time she saw him, he always attempted to strike up a conversation about history. Eva had no idea why he'd tried to be friendly with her since their first meeting, but then again, she never gave him the chance to tell her, either.

As she approached, she saw him standing in the lobby of the Historical Society, his back toward her, waiting.

"Reverend Neighbors," Eva called, almost laughing at how shocked the man looked at the fact that she'd actually appeared. "What can the Historical Society help you with?"

He shoved a hand in his pocket, fumbling. *Jesus.* Eva averted her eyes, concentrating on the wall over his head.

"I was wondering what you could tell me about these?" he finally asked.

She looked down and froze. In his outstretched hand were two gold coins.

Dearest, you must take heed and be diligent. Trust no one. This is doubly true for anyone working for or living with the governor.

— LETTER FROM BLACKBEARD TO WIFE, MARY, 1718

Chapter Seven

E va walked as fast as she could without drawing attention to herself, back to her office. She slipped her hand into the front pocket of her pants and touched the two coins, almost as if she had to convince herself they were real. Her heart raced thinking about what they could be and what it would mean.

Stop it, she told herself. *Don't speculate.*

Once inside her office, she closed the door behind her, took a shaky breath, and placed the two coins on her desk. If they turned out to be what she suspected, it could be huge. She took a deep breath to calm down, reminding herself she was dealing with one really big *if.* With trembling fingers, she slipped on a pair of gloves before picking up one coin and then the other, inspecting them both while mentally comparing to verified similar items. But her knowledge came only from books. She'd never held any of the extraordinary coins.

When she finished her assessment, she placed both coins back on top of her desk and stared at them. If she matched the markings on the coins and their estimated weight with what her reference books detailed, they appeared to be coins from the early eighteenth century. The only detail that concerned her, or at least the main one, was their appearance. They looked too good to be from 1715. Too shiny. The markings and year were too well defined. They had to be expertly crafted replicas.

Regrettably, as she'd recently told William, she lacked the expertise to confirm what the coins were. The potential of what they could be meant she had to do everything in her power to verify each detail, and be absolutely certain before declaring anything. It was a good thing Emerson happened to be in town and she already had plans for dinner with him tonight.

She froze.

Emerson was in town to look at two coins found on two different women, and Reverend Neighbors just happened to give her two more. It all appeared too coincidental and smelled like shenanigans. Or worse.

She'd asked Reverend Neighbors how the coins came to be in his possession, and, according to him, someone placed the two coins in the collection plate at church on Sunday. He'd noticed them while getting everything together for the weekly bank deposit. He added that even though he enjoyed history and considered himself well-read on the subject, he realized the coins were out of his league. For once, Reverend Neighbors didn't seem to be sticking his nose in areas he shouldn't.

She stared at the coins on her desk seemingly too perfect to be real. Odds are, they would turn out to be just as fake as his story probably was. That being said, she shouldn't plan on mentioning them to Emerson. But she couldn't silence the little voice in her head whispering, "What if?"

What if they were real?

If the smallest chance existed that they were real, she had to look into it. It could also be possible that these two coins were nothing like the ones found on either Catherine or Gabby. *Buried treasure* were the two most common words used around town to describe the coins found on both women. However, there were numerous people living in Eden who had never traveled more than sixty miles away. For all she knew, they might see a Mexican peso and consider it treasure.

She sent a text to let Emerson know she had a few coins she wanted him look over.

His reply was quick.

I'll look over them if you'll teach me your lock-picking secrets.

She laughed.

LOL. I can't believe you remember that day.

They'd had offices across the hall from each other in graduate school. One day Eva walked by his open office door and heard him mumbling because someone had given the history department an old chest, but it was locked and he couldn't get it open. She'd pulled her pick set out of her purse, walked into his office, and said, "Let me try." It was open in five minutes.

Her phone buzzed with another text.

My go-to lock picker recently moved out of state. Thought it was time to learn for myself.

She grinned as she replied.

You're on.

Her smile widened as she remembered how she'd learned. That long-ago summer, when she'd first became enamored with the Outer Banks, gave her more than an undying love for history. On one particular day, Eva had wanted to make it back to the house earlier than normal because her mother had promised pizza for dinner. But when she dug in her pockets, she realized she'd left that morning without the key her mother gave her.

She didn't know what her mother did all day while she played outside, but Eva had assumed she spent most of her time in the house they'd rented. Eva's unanswered knocks on the door proved she wasn't inside that day.

WITH A HUFF, *she turned to sit down on the porch to wait, but standing behind her was a boy she'd never met. He looked about her age, but there was a sadness in his eyes she'd never seen on a kid before.*

Still, he was just standing there.

"You have a problem?" she asked, making her back as straight as possible. It was no use, the boy had about four inches on her.

"No," he said. "But it looks like you do."

"I just left my key inside." She shrugged like it was no big deal. "But it's okay. My mom will be here soon."

"I can help you if you want."

"Help me what?"

He took a step toward her. "Let me show you."

She watched as he pulled what looked like metal sticks out of his pocket, thinking the entire time that he was crazy if he thought he'd get a door open with sticks. Which was why when he opened the door for her seconds later, she grabbed his arm and said, "Teach me."

At first, she thought he'd ignore her, but instead of telling her to get lost, he asked, "What's your name?"

"They've been calling me Jersey this summer."

His forehead wrinkled. "Why?"

"Probably because I'm from New Jersey." She cocked her head to the side. "What's your name?"

"Maybe I don't have one."

"Don't be stupid. Everyone has a name."

He appeared to think that over. "Call me Billy."

"Okay, Billy, teach me how to open doors with metal sticks."

THAT WAS THE DAY Eva learned what would later turn out to be a useful skill to have when opening locked cabinets and trunks people would bring to the Historical Society. They were positive whatever was inside held some sort of historical significance. Sure, ninety-nine percent of the time they were wrong, but with Eva's little set of tools, at least it didn't take forever to find out.

For the first time in my life, I seriously considered becoming a pirate.

— JOURNAL OF AN UNKNOWN WOMAN, EARLY 1700s

Chapter Eight

Amelia arrived at the diner a few minutes after Eva, sliding into the black leather booth with a smile. "Are you sure it's okay for me to join you?"

Eva rolled her eyes. "Ask me one more time, and I'm changing my answer to no."

Amelia obviously took her threat seriously because she changed the subject. "Pops comes here a lot for breakfast."

"He does. I usually stop in before work." Eva wasn't about to tell Amelia the real reason she spent nearly every morning here was to eavesdrop on her grandfather and his friends. "I find it's a nice way to begin my day."

Eva saw Emerson as soon as he entered the diner. It had been years since she last saw him, but she'd have recognized him anywhere. Standing nearly six foot three, he could easily look over the top of the group standing in front of the cashier. His eyes traveled over the crowded place, trying to find her.

"Emerson!" Eva stood and waved. Once he caught sight of her, his face broke into a huge smile and he walked toward their booth. She slid out and gave him a hug. "Good to see you. How was your day?"

"Enlightening," was all he replied with. He looked at Amelia, still smiling, as he and Eva took their seats. "We met earlier. Amelia, right?"

Amelia beamed as Eva made introductions. "Emerson, this is my friend, Amelia. Amelia, this is Emerson. We went to grad school together, and he's positively brilliant."

Amelia and Emerson shook hands.

"She exaggerates," Emerson said. "I'm only moderately brilliant."

"Don't underplay yourself," Eva chided. "People around the world want you to consult with them. Weren't you in Indonesia not too long ago?"

"Yes," he said. "Looking at what was hoped to be the resting spot for a Portuguese ship rumored to have over two billion dollars' worth of treasure on it when it went down in the middle of a storm in the early 1500s."

"It wasn't?" Amelia asked.

"Unfortunately, no," Emerson said. "It turned out to be a ship, but it wasn't Portuguese, and the coins found onboard weren't overly rare or valuable."

"This might be a stupid question," Amelia said, "but what are you doing in Eden, North Carolina, if your job typically takes you to places like Indonesia?"

"I'll answer for him," Eva said. "Because whatever answer he gives you will be much too modest."

"Eva." Emerson shook his head.

"Hush, you," Eva told him and then turned to Amelia. "He only charges the corporations and such who hope to make a mint off rare coins. Anything like what we have, a humanitarian issue, he does pro bono."

Emerson looked a bit embarrassed, but Eva wanted Amelia to know Emerson was more than a pretty face. As someone who was currently running for mayor, Amelia would appreciate and respect the side of Emerson that valued the same.

"You know I look at old coins all day," Emerson said after the server had taken their orders "What do you do, Amelia?"

His question gave Eva pause. He wasn't much for small talk, so something about Amelia interested him. For a few minutes, she leaned back and watched her two friends get to know each other. Either they didn't notice she'd stepped out of the conversation, or they had and didn't care, because neither of them looked her way. She looked around. It was so interesting to people-watch. Her focus didn't return to the table until she heard her name.

"Eva said you were interested in Blackbeard," Emerson said and shot her an amused smile, as if knowing she hadn't been paying attention. "What kind of information are you looking for?"

"Enough to be able to provide something useful to the Blackbeard Festival. I recently joined the planning committee Eva runs. To get involved with the community on a new and different level."

"As part of your run for mayor?" he asked.

Eva almost choked on her iced tea and noticed Amelia wore an expression of shock as well.

"How did you know I was running for mayor?" Amelia asked.

"There are signs with your name and picture on them all over town that say so," Emerson replied. "I'd have to be blind in both eyes to have not noticed. Why does that surprise you?"

Amelia shrugged. "I never thought anyone would really look at them."

"I have to admit, I tend to ignore such things, but yours drew me in. How's your campaign going?"

Across the table, Amelia's blue eyes sparkled, and her cheeks flushed. "Pretty well, but between the three of us and this table, I think it's going to be rough to break into the *good ole boys'* club."

"I don't doubt for a second you can handle it," Emerson said, his voice full of sincerity.

Amelia's flush deepened. "Thanks."

"Let me know how I can help," Eva said. Amelia would end up doing it, just as she knew the vivacious woman would be great in public service. They had met soon after Eva moved to Eden when Eva wanted to do some major landscaping. Because her new house was considered coastal property, the county required one of their engineers to approve the plans. The two women had been friends ever since.

Amelia waved her hand. "Okay. Okay. But for now, back to why we're here. Let's talk Blackbeard."

Emerson nodded toward Eva. "She's the expert on him. I can chime in as needed."

When Amelia turned her way, Eva recalled her saying before how she didn't want to be the third wheel, and she nearly laughed. Who was third wheel now?

"What's the most interesting thing to you about Blackbeard?" Amelia asked.

Eva grinned. "By all accounts, he was a marketing genius."

"Seriously?" Amelia said once the shocked look on her face disappeared. "That's not what I was expecting to hear."

"Exactly." Eva chuckled. "Which is why I led with it. Now, what comes to mind when you hear his name? Just a word or two."

"Ruthless. Dangerous. Violent."

"Yes," Eva said. "Almost three hundred years later, we still picture and imagine him the way people did in 1718. Now, can you name a pirate peer of Blackbeard's?"

"You mean another pirate from that time in history?"

"Yes, and they can come from anywhere. Worldwide. Name another pirate."

"I told you I could barely remember Blackbeard and you want me name one of his cronies?" Amelia closed her eyes, thinking, and smiled when she opened them. "Captain Jack—"

Emerson laughed.

"A real pirate. Not a movie character." Eva cut her off before she could finish and rolled her eyes for good measure.

"Damn." Amelia snapped her fingers.

"For the record," Emerson said, "I liked your answer."

Amelia thanked him and then sat unmoving for a long minute, gaze focused on the top of the table, before finally looking up and admitting, "I can't. Blackbeard and fictional characters are all I know."

"Exactly," Eva said, satisfied because Amelia had given the answer she was looking for. "He was so good at marketing, not only is he still selling it three hundred years later, he's managed to shut out his competition. It stands to reason he did some really despicable things to earn such a tarnished but well-known name, right?"

"You would think so," Amelia said, though her voice was hesitant as if she knew there was more behind the question.

"You would, but there are no records of him ever killing anyone until his last fight. The one he was killed in."

"That is surprising." Amelia's forehead wrinkled. "Given the level of violence we associate with pirates, as well as how we view him today, you would think he did *something*. At least to get people talking about him."

"Right? How else would he have become the most feared pirate, ever?"

"I have a feeling it has to do with marketing somehow, but I'm not sure how. I mean, how can you market yourself as a badass pirate unless you *are* a badass pirate?"

"Proper pirate branding." Eva waited a second to see if Amelia had a reply, but she remained quiet. "If you want people to think of you as the world's most fearsome pirate when they see you or hear reports of you, you have to appear to be the world's most fearsome pirate."

"And you do it all by branding yourself?"

Eva couldn't help but notice Amelia sounded as if she didn't believe that could possibly be the correct answer. "Yes, but properly. Here's how he pulled it off—when he came into possession of his ship, *Queen Anne's Revenge*, he added forty cannons to the sixteen it already had."

"He had a badass ship. Makes sense."

"Not only a badass ship," Eva corrected. "But the *baddest* badass ship. It's the first thing his prey or enemies saw, and that sight alone made many of them surrender without a fight."

"The best way to never lose a fight is to never be in a fight. I see his logic there. That way you don't lose any men or resources." Amelia nodded. "I have to say, I'm impressed with how well-thought-out he seems to have been. I never would have viewed it as intentional."

"That's part of why I love history so much," Eva said. "To dig into a person—you think you have figured out completely, only to find they're the exact opposite."

"Or to look into an item or place you think is nothing special," Emerson added. "And then realizing it's the most extraordinary thing you've ever beheld."

"Sounds a lot more interesting than what I do all day," Amelia said, and they all laughed.

The server came by with their entrees, and they sat for a few minutes in silence, eating.

"Tell me more," Amelia said in between bites of meatloaf.

Eva had a bite of fried pork chop in her mouth and waved for Emerson to take over.

"Have you read about how he dressed before a potential battle?" he asked. A good question in Eva's opinion.

Amelia shook her head. "If I did, I can't remember."

"He would decorate his beard with lit fuses to give the impression it was on fire, and he'd cover himself with weapons. Guns, knives, you name it, he'd strap it on himself somewhere. They said he looked like the devil himself." Emerson shook his head. "Can't say I blame them; if I saw someone walking around with a fiery beard, I'd more than likely think the same thing."

"I imagine he was a sight to see." Amelia gave an exaggerated shiver. "No, thank you."

"You want to know something crazy?" Eva asked.

"There's something crazier than what you two have already told me?"

Eva swallowed a snort. "I know it seems preposterous, but yes, there's more."

Amelia's smile grew bigger. "Hit me with it."

"The pirate known as Blackbeard was only active as a pirate for two years." That fact had always amazed Eva whenever she read about the man or was asked to speak at one of the numerous elementary or middle schools in the area. Two years as a pirate and he'd done enough to be remembered over three hundred years later? Crazy. Especially when you considered that much of his name was solely reputation.

Amelia, however, seemed to think differently. "That actually makes sense to me."

Eva lifted an eyebrow. "How's that?"

"I'm assuming he lived the life of a pirate until his death, correct?"

"Yes."

"It makes sense because it stands to reason that piracy has a fairly high fatality rate." When Eva didn't say anything else, Amelia asked, "What else can you tell me?"

"There's a bit more that isn't well known," Eva said. "One, the public record seems to point to a marriage between Blackbeard and a young girl by the name of Mary. And two, it appears as if he attempted to go legit sometime in 1718. Which is also the year he died."

"Really?" Amelia asked. "I know I've never heard that, no way would I forget *that*. What happened?"

Eva had scoured every text she could find, but they all contradicted each other. "It's unclear," she finally said. "I'm not sure I've read two accounts that agree. Some scholars say he went back to pirating because life on land bored him. Others insist he was blackmailed. But they all have one common thread—the sitting governor of North Carolina at the time, Governor Eden."

"The man our town is named after," Amelia added, like she didn't know.

Eva had unintentionally formed an opinion about Governor Eden after her research, but decided to keep it to herself for the moment. She only gave Amelia the facts. "Yes. It's accepted by most historians that after Blackbeard surrendered to him and promised to stop pirating, Governor Eden pardoned him, much to the anger of the surrounding colonies. Everything seems to point to Governor Eden being the man who performed the wedding ceremony between the pirate and Mary. And it's suspected by some he had something to do with Blackbeard's return to the sea. There's even evidence the governor received a cut of whatever Blackbeard and his crew collected."

"The governor had dirty hands," Amelia said, reaching the same conclusion Eva had.

"Yes, the question, however, is how dirty?" It was a question Eva couldn't answer, and silence filled the table.

Emerson cleared his throat. "I read once, and I can't recall if this is real or something made up. Maybe Eva can tell us for sure. But the night before the fight Blackbeard would die in, one of his men asked him where his treasure was buried. Blackbeard replied that no one but himself and the devil knew where it was."

His words reminded Eva of the Devil's Coins legend. Perhaps there was some truth layered somewhere in the old tale, after all.

"I've read similar accounts from a number of sources. I'd wager it to be real."

Amelia spoke first after a server cleared their dishes. "We should do something with the pirate branding thing for the Festival."

"Make your own pirate?" Eva asked.

"Something...maybe have a contest or something? Create a pirate logo? Let me brainstorm, and I'll bring some ideas to the next group meeting. Sunday night, right?"

Eva nodded, liking the logo idea. "Sounds like a plan."

Emerson looked at his watched and winced. "Ladies, I hate to eat and run, but I promised Officer Montague I'd meet him at the station tonight to talk about getting the coins first thing in the morning and to go over a few case details. He had to take off unexpectedly this afternoon, so I wasn't able to catch up with him before dinner."

"No worries," Eva said. "You're coming by the Society tomorrow morning?"

"Bright and early." Turning to Amelia, he reached in his back pocket and pulled out a card. "I had a really nice time talking with you." He took a pen from the table and wrote on the card before handing to Amelia. "Here's my personal number, if you'd like to talk some more."

Knowing Amelia, Eva thought she'd probably call him later tonight. And knowing Emerson, he'd probably be thrilled.

Emerson stood to leave and took the handwritten bill the server dropped on the table a few minutes prior. "And dinner's on me tonight. I'll take care of this on my way out."

"Emerson," Eva called out to his back. "I'm the one who asked you to dinner."

He didn't turn around but lifted his hand in the air as he walked. "I can't hear you."

Eva and Amelia giggled as they watched him stop at the cashier, give them one last wave, and then step outside to walk to the station across the street.

"You're welcome," Eva said with a grin.

Amelia gave a happy sigh. "He seems like such a nice guy, and there aren't very many of those around these days."

"You've got that right," Eva said thinking about her last long-term relationship.

It ended when the man she'd been seeing for nine months, Greg, a plastic surgeon, decided to move and join a practice in Miami, Florida. He'd asked Eva to come with him and she refused, not wanting to give up a place and a job she loved. When Greg said he didn't understand why she couldn't do her "history thing," as he called it, from Miami, she became furious. She pointed out that obviously he had no clue what she did. His reply saying her work didn't matter because history was dead, ended that relationship.

Eva pushed thoughts of her ex away. Amelia was looking at her strangely.

"What?" Eva wiped the corners of her mouth. Did she have food on her face?

Amelia took a swallow of her iced tea before answering. "Have you ever met Stefan Benson? The real estate attorney? He lives and works in Nag's Head."

Eva searched her head, but the name didn't sound familiar. "Not that I can remember. Why?"

"Then you haven't met him," Amelia said, waggling her eyebrows. "Trust me, you wouldn't forget him."

Eva groaned. "Tell me you aren't trying to set me up."

"I see it more as me retuning a favor. I was thinking of my single guy friends, and it hit me the two of you would be perfect together." Amelia leaned forward. "He's helping me with my campaign. Honestly, he's the nicest guy."

Eva wanted to shake her head and say she had too much going on at the moment to even think about a man. But she had a sudden flashback to the diner not too long ago when a man Elbert mentioned was a lawyer helped Amelia put up signs, and how he'd made her laugh. Likewise, she remembered wanting to stay and join the two of them. Surely, it was the same man.

Amelia didn't wait for her to reply. "Listen. We went out a few times in high school but just never clicked, you know? Now we're just friends. Anyway, I remember his dad had all these old…" Amelia's eyes grew large. "That's it. That's the angle you'll use."

Elbert had also mentioned Amelia had dated him in high school. It had to be the same man. "I don't know why I need an angle, but I'm pretty sure I won't like it," she said, but wasn't sure she meant it.

Just as well since Amelia continued as if she hadn't spoken. "Maps. Old ones. Hanging all over the place."

"Okay," Eva said, finally giving in to her curiosity. "Now you have my attention."

"Stefan has all these old maps hanging all over his office. He renovated his office not too long ago, but it wasn't until I went by there last week to discuss the campaign that I saw the finished project. He didn't have the maps up before. I don't know what date they're from or if you'd even be interested in them. Either way, since you're a historian, it wouldn't be unheard of for you to call and ask if he'll let you look over them."

"I don't know. I'm not in the market for a hookup," Eva said. Even if she wanted to, she shouldn't. Not with everything going on with the Blackbeard Festival, Catherine, Gabby, and those coins Reverend Neighbors insisted she take. Yet some part of her was intrigued by the gentleman lawyer Amelia described.

"Technically, it's not a hookup." Amelia dug in her purse and pulled out a sheet of paper. After writing something down, she held it out. "Technically, all I'm doing is giving you the phone number of a guy who might have some cool maps to look at."

"I guess when you put it that way…" Eva took the paper and put it in her pocket.

They were both silent, lost in their own thoughts for a long moment.

Eva jumped when Amelia slapped her hand on the table. "Enough of that," Amelia said. "Tell me everything you know about Emerson."

Mary was going to be late for her own wedding, and I wasn't going to waste the breath to tell her again. I'd already warned her three times, and each time she merely blew her nose with her handkerchief, and said it'd serve Edward right for her to be late.

— JOURNAL OF AN UNKNOWN WOMAN, EARLY 1700s

Chapter Nine

William had grown up in Eden listening to stories of ghost ships, wandering lost souls, and the assorted demon or two. As an adult, it wasn't that he didn't believe in such things, he just hadn't made his mind up quite yet.

An odd thing, he supposed, for a man of his age, but one justified, he believed.

He'd never seen anything remotely resembling a ghost ship or a lost soul. The only demon he'd ever witnessed was Peggy's three-year old grandson who had single-handedly brought an end to the local Baptist church's summer Vacation Bible School last July, but he supposed he couldn't count that.

Though he'd never had any sort of interaction with the supernatural, several people he knew had. Supposedly. They seemed convinced of the experience, and he respected them enough that he didn't feel comfortable assuming they were wrong.

Buried treasure, on the other hand, was different. He'd always assumed that pirates buried their treasure. After all, there weren't any banks to keep their bounty safe and even if there had been, it was doubtful pirates would be welcomed customers. What else was one to do other than bury it?

In William's mind, the experts seemed to contradict themselves. One would expect treasure to be found all up and down the Outer Banks Coast. In fact, it was well known many pirates, specifically Blackbeard, had been very active in the area. Yet the experts hadn't found any buried treasure. If it ever was, though, it'd make sense any treasure found in the area would have to be Blackbeard's.

He wouldn't go so far as to claim the coin found on Gabby was treasure. Honestly, he didn't know what real treasure looked like. When he heard the word, all he pictured in his mind were images from his childhood. A big wooden chest with a pile of gold coins filling the inside, along with an occasional ruby and emerald, and a crown of some sort on top of it all. He'd let Eva's friend, the coin expert, Emerson Jefferys decide what the coins were.

Though he tried telling himself it was all in his head, he couldn't shake the feeling that he knew what Emerson would find. An odd, old coin found on the body of one woman was strange, but believable. For the same odd, old coin to be found on the body of two women was something else entirely.

If Emerson determined the coins were the same, not only would William have to pull back from Gabby's case, he'd have to step down as chief, as well. There was no way he'd be allowed to hold the position if Catherine's death was reopened as a potential homicide. He needed to prepare Mitch. There was no one else he trusted to handle the job responsibilities in his place. Damn, but the whole situation was going to be awkward.

That didn't mean William was going to stop what he was doing. Hell no, he'd keep investigating Gabby's death even if he said he'd officially stepped back from the case.

On Wednesday, his focus was learning what he could about Gabby's last few days. He'd called Doris the night before to see if she could meet with him. In addition to giving him Gabby's schedule for the week, he hoped Doris would be able to shine some light on what, if anything, could tie the young woman to the coin. Doris ran her business from her house on the other side of town from both his office and home. He decided to head her way before going by the office, making sure to call Peggy and let her know his plan.

"William," Doris said, answering his knock on her door. "Come into my office. I went ahead and pulled everything from the week you were asking about."

He followed her into the dining room she'd converted into an office. "I get more use out of it this way," she'd told him years ago when she first made the change. She had a small desk in one corner with two filing cabinets and a work table filling most of the remaining space. Next to the desk, a large brown dog slept on top of a huge dog bed. At their entrance, it opened one eye, wagged its tail, and went back to sleep, but only after William rubbed its graying head.

Doris smiled as they both sat down at the table. "Rascal's going to outlive all of us," she joked.

"How old is he now? Eighty?" He remembered playing with Rascal as a puppy.

"Close. Eighteen." She shook her head. "Vet said he should have died two years ago. Shows you what they know. Not a thing."

William chuckled. Doris had never liked anyone in the medical field, not doctors, nurses, vets, or dentists. He thought it ironic her daughter currently attended medical school in Durham and planned to be a vascular surgeon.

"I know not everyone in Eden agrees with me, but I'm glad you're not assuming this is a simple case of drowning while waiting on the final report. I still can't find it within myself to believe she drowned." She handed him a sheet of paper, and he felt her watching as he looked it over. "I listed out the day she worked and where she cleaned. I also put on there how frequently she cleaned each place. I wasn't exactly sure what you were looking for."

Monday, Tuesday, Wednesday, and Thursday were typed on the left side of the paper with the name, address, and cleaning schedule of clients beside the appropriate day. Gabby had cleaned his grandmother's homestead on Tuesday, and did so every other week. Of course, he'd expected to see that. The Maritime Property Law office was on the list as being cleaned every Thursday. He noted she cleaned Eden Methodist Church on Monday and Wednesday, and was supposed to return on Friday. The medical examiner estimated her time of death to be late Thursday, which was why Doris hadn't included Friday.

"Out of curiosity," he said, keeping his eyes on the paper. "Where was she scheduled to work on Friday, other than the church?"

"Only the church. That took most of her day because she had to make sure it was ready for Sunday. I remember Reverend Neighbors calling me in a huff, all upset when she didn't show up at eight that Friday morning."

William made a note on the paper to make sure he stopped by the church to speak to Robert. "Did Gabby clean all these places alone or was there another employee with her?"

"She cleaned alone because she was one of the few I could always count on to clean properly without me breathing over them the entire time. That was why she had most of my best clients, along with my pickiest ones."

"I've heard Hamilton Brown sometimes showed up while she was working." William had debated over whether to bring it up to her. It was Catherine, after all, who had witnessed it, but it was Gabby's death he was investigating. While he could see it might be a gray area for some, in his mind, talking to Doris about an employee's work habits wasn't the same as getting involved with his late wife's case.

The way Doris pressed her lips together told him she wasn't hearing this for the first time. "Yes," she said. "A few of her clients brought that up before. I actually had a conversation with Gabby about a month ago after the last complaint. She was informed that if he showed up again, I'd have to let her go." She wiped away a tear. "I didn't want to get between her and Hamilton or to make things difficult, but it's a liability."

"Did you ask her why he kept showing up?" he asked.

"According to her, he was horribly jealous and convinced Gabby was cheating on him. He accused her of having men over to whatever house she was cleaning and sleeping with them."

William remembered the scene Catherine told Eva she witnessed. It seemed to fit what Gabby had relayed to Doris.

"Are you aware of Ms. Clark ever inviting anyone to a property she was cleaning or doing anything other than her job while on the clock?" he asked.

"No." Doris shook her head. "It's like I said, she was one of my best." She leaned forward. "I know how *animated* she was around town, like someone lit a fuse, but had no idea how long the fuse was. I'm telling you, she was different at work. Night and day."

"Why do you think she was like that?"

Doris opened her mouth, but then closed it and shook her head.

William chuckled. "You're one of the most opinionated women I know, and I love you for it, so I know you have thoughts on why she seemed to have two different personalities."

He didn't think she'd change her mind about telling him, but she finally took a deep breath.

"I think Hamilton brought out the worst in her."

HALF AN HOUR LATER, he was still thinking about what Doris had said when he pulled up to the police station and parked, but instead of going inside, he walked to the diner across the street. Being that odd time of day between the breakfast and lunch crowd, there were only a few patrons inside. He went up to the counter to order a sweet tea to go when he noticed Elbert Morgan sitting alone at a nearby table, reading the newspaper, and walked over to sit with him instead.

"Hey, Chief," Elbert said, looking up from his paper when William made it to the table's side.

"Mind if I join you?" William asked.

"Not at all. Have a seat." Elbert folded his paper and put it down.

A server appeared at his elbow, and William ordered a slice of pecan pie to go with his tea.

"Anything new with you?" William asked Elbert when both had been delivered to their table.

He didn't really have to ask. Elbert enjoyed talking so much, he more than likely would have launched into one thing or another. It was actually a bit odd the man had been silent for so long. Maybe William shouldn't have sat down after all.

"I have the Festival meeting coming up on Sunday," Elbert replied. "What do you know about Blackbeard? We're supposed to have new ideas to suggest to the group for things to do."

"I don't know much," he admitted. "He was a pirate around here and every so often someone gets the great idea to dig up my property in the hopes of finding his treasure."

Elbert chuckled. "I remember Ruthie going on about folks doing the same thing."

Ruthie. Nana, who he still missed daily. She'd passed away a few months after he married Catherine. He thought she'd held on at the end because she wanted to make sure he wouldn't be alone.

Little did she know.

"She probably handled it better than I do," William said.

"That's only because your grandmother had a way with words

and people. She'd invite you over for a glass of iced tea, and right as you were getting nice and comfortable, BAM! That's when she'd tell you how she really felt."

"Yeah." William laughed, remembering. "She could do that. I can't believe it's almost time for the Festival again. Feels like we just had it." He knew it was good for business, but to him it only involved hordes of people over and above the normal for high season and having to bring in outside help to ensure everyone's safety.

"That it does," Elbert answered. "I heard more people are expected this year because of the coins."

William couldn't stop his wince. Catherine's death was going to be seen as good for local business. There was so much wrong with that.

"Sorry, Chief," Elbert said, even though William hadn't spoken. "My mouth got ahead of my brain there for a second. I'd say it's because I'm getting old, but the truth is, it's always been like that."

"No need to apologize," William said, seeing, not for the first time, why Elbert's nickname was Mouth of the South. "It is what it is. Just remember, neither coin has been identified yet. They could be anything from anywhere." He'd learned when you spoke to Elbert it was best to be as vague as possible, or else you'd later hear yourself referencing something everyone would take as the gospel truth.

"Right, but you've brought in an expert to do just that."

Neither Emerson nor his reason for being in town were a secret, so William nodded.

"I heard he arrived in town." Elbert leaned closer to him. "Can you tell me if he's started looking at them yet, and if he has, what he's found?"

No one William had ever spoken to knew exactly where or who Elbert got his information from. Nor would Elbert tell. If asked where he'd heard something, more times than not, his reply would be, "Here or there." All William knew for sure was that it wasn't from him. And that wasn't going to change today.

"I haven't been in the office since yesterday," William answered. "And if I had been or if I'd heard something, which is unlikely since I'm not involved in Catherine's case, you know I couldn't tell you."

Elbert leaned back in his chair with a grin. "You can't fault a man for trying."

LATER THAT AFTERNOON, a few minutes before two, William stood beside his cruiser in the parking lot of Maritime Property Law, waiting for the employees to return from lunch.

A car pulled into the spot next to him, drawing him away from his thoughts. A middle-aged Black woman with long braids stepped out, shooting a questioning look his way. She opened the back door of her car and pulled out a stack of books.

William stepped away from his car. "Can I help you?" he asked. "Those look heavy."

She shook her head. "No, I'm balanced now, if you took some I'd probably fall over. But if you could grab my keys?" A jiggling sound came from below the books.

"Absolutely," he said, taking the keys when she lifted the books up. "Are you sure you've got those books? I feel like a horse's ass only carrying keys."

"I'm good. I promise," she said as they approached the front door of the office. "It's the key with the green top."

William unlocked the door and held it open for her. Once inside, she placed the books on the front desk and turned back to him. "Naomi Spencer." She held out her hand.

He shook it. "William Templeton, Eden Police Department. I'm actually here to discuss Gabby Clark."

"You'll need to talk with Stefan Benson. She talked with him the most. He joked he was going to steal her away from Doris because she was the only person who ever cleaned to his satisfaction. He'll be back from lunch in a few minutes." Naomi went behind the desk, moving the pile of books off to the side. "Feel free to wait."

"Thank you. I'll do that." He nodded toward the stack of thick hardback books. "Looks like you have some light reading to do."

"I'm going to school part time to be a paralegal. Mr. Benson lets me borrow what I need."

He'd gone to high school with Stefan, but they'd never been part of the same social circle, even as adults. Stefan's family came from old money, and William always thought it pretentious that his name was spelled with an *f*, but he supposed that blame fell on the man's parents.

When the door opened a few minutes later and a tall, trim man walked in, William recognized him instantly. Stefan wished Naomi a good afternoon, and then turned to William.

"William Templeton." William outstretched his hand. "Stefan Benson? We went to high school together."

Stefan shook his hand. "I remember you. Track athlete, right?"

"That's me," William confirmed. "You were in student government."

"Yes. Those were the days, weren't they?" Stefan shook his head. "I'm sure you didn't stop by to reminisce over old memories. What can I help you with?"

"I wanted to speak with you about Gabby Clark," William said.

"Of course. I still can't believe she's gone." Stefan turned to speak to his admin. "Naomi, hold my calls. Come on back to my office."

William stepped into the room at the back of a short hall, and they both took a seat on the visitor's chairs placed in front of his desk. The rich leather and wood in Stefan's office was nothing like William's cramped space at the department. But while he could appreciate the subtle elegance, including a series of colorfully illustrated maps framed and placed along one wall, he felt certain real estate law would bore him to death.

"What do you want to know about Gabby?" Stefan asked.

William studied Stefan, taking in his body language. He looked calm and relaxed but looks could be deceiving. "This was the last place she cleaned before her death sometime Thursday night."

"Was it?" Stefan's forehead wrinkled. "I wasn't aware of her cleaning schedule."

"Did her behavior seem off in any way that Thursday?"

"Is that when she drowned?"

William reminded himself he needed to be careful around Stefan. The man might be a real estate attorney, but he was still an attorney. "That's the assumption everyone's made, but the medical examiner hasn't issued their final findings yet. I'm trying to get a feel of her last few days."

Stefan nodded. "I don't remember anything standing out. I remember it was raining, and she made a joke about dripping all over everything."

"Do you remember what time she left here that day?"

"Unfortunately, I wasn't here. I left around three for a meeting at Nations Bank in Manteo. She was still here when I left."

If it had been someone who wasn't an attorney, William would ask for the name of the person Stefan had met with and then he'd call to verify that a meeting had, indeed, taken place. But Stefan was, and William would expect him to withhold the information based on the principle.

"I can get the names and numbers of the people I met with if that would help," Stefan added.

William was so shocked he volunteered and didn't try to play the ego game with him, he almost told Stefan not to worry about it. "That would be great," he said.

"Hang on a minute and I'll print it out for you," Stefan said, standing and walking to his desk. In less than three minutes, he handed William a printout of the appointment from a calendar app with the names and numbers of the people he was meeting, as well as the place and time.

"Do you have any other questions?" Stefan asked.

"No, that's it for now," William said. "Do you mind if I speak to Naomi for a minute?"

"Of course not."

Naomi was sitting at the desk talking to someone on the phone about rescheduling a meeting for Stefan, while typing fanatically away on her laptop. At her elbow what appeared to be a textbook was opened to a page with several lines highlighted in yellow. A middle-aged couple walked in, the woman carrying a folder stuffed with paper. Naomi waved to them and mouthed that she'd only be a minute longer.

William swallowed a sigh and stood off to the side to wait until Naomi had a free moment. She looked his way with a quizzical expression.

"I can wait," he assured her.

"It might be more than a few minutes," she said, with her hand over the phone's mouthpiece.

"Take your time, I'm not in a rush."

William watched as she efficiently rescheduled the client on the phone, showed the couple into Stefan's office, and finished the email she'd been writing.

"Now," she said, with a teasing grin. "What can I help *you* with?"

"Do you have time for a few questions?" he asked, expecting any second for a stampede of clients to break the door down.

"As long as you're fast."

"Got it." William glanced at his watch to note the time. "I'm following up on Gabby Clark, talking to people who had contact with her in the days before her death. What can you tell me about that Thursday?"

"It was raining pretty bad when she showed up," Naomi said, and William noted Stefan had said the same. "I remember because as soon she stepped inside, she saw Stefan and the two of them joked about it. She refused to park in our lot because she said it was for clients. According to her, she enjoyed the fresh air and the walk energized her, except when it was raining. That's the type of person she was, most of the time."

"Most of the time?" William asked. "What makes you say that?"

Naomi glanced at Stefan's closed door. "Sometimes her boyfriend would stop by, but only if Mr. Benson wasn't here. She'd always get rid of him quickly, but she'd be in a bad mood for the rest of her time here."

"How often would he come by?"

"She was only here on Thursdays." Naomi pressed her lips together, thinking. "Maybe once or twice a month? It really depended on Mr. Benson's schedule."

"When was the last time he came around while she was here?"

"It's been a while." Naomi waved her hand. "Two or three months?"

"Do you remember what time she left or if she had any plans after work that last Thursday?"

"She usually left around three or three thirty. Wait." Naomi's forehead wrinkled. "But not that day. She was running behind due to the rain and not being able to get into Stefan's office until he left for an off-site meeting. Gabby didn't leave until nearly four-thirty and she said she wouldn't have time to stop and talk with Reverend Neighbors because he left the church at four on Thursdays. She said they were friends. I have to admit based on the way I saw her and her boyfriend act out in public, I was surprised at that. Maybe she was more like her work self around him. But still, it's hard to imagine someone as strait-laced as Reverend Neighbors being friends with Gabby."

Her tone of voice made it sound as if the relationship was

somehow scandalous, and William felt it necessary to defend Robert. "I'm sure the Reverend is friends with a great number of people."

But even as he spoke the words, William couldn't help but wonder why Robert hadn't told him about his friend, Gabby.

It was, without a doubt, the smallest wedding I had ever been to. Not counting the couple themself, who could have been getting married on Edward's ship for all they seemed to notice, there were only four people present. The governor, who officiated. One of Edward's men. Me. And the governor's wife, Penelope, who looked as if she'd rather be anywhere else for the majority of the service.

— **JOURNAL OF AN UNKNOWN WOMAN, EARLY 1700s**

Chapter Ten

"**A**re you trying to say that Catherine and Gabby were killed because of a curse Blackbeard put on his treasure?" Maxine asked on Thursday morning after Elbert brought up the Devil's Coins again. "Because if you are, that's assuming a lot."

Eva wasn't surprised at the foursome's topic of choice for the day. Once word got out about the coins found on both women, there was little else anyone in the town wanted to discuss.

"What is it with people calling about those coins?" Julia had asked her at work the day before. "Not only are they part of active investigations, but that guy you know only arrived today, so he hasn't even determined what they are yet. For all we know, they might not be anything at all."

Since Julia oversaw the Carolina Coastal Museum's volunteers, she begrudgingly had to move some to phone duty due to the number of calls they'd had as a result of word spreading about the discovery of the two unknown coins.

"True," Eva had replied, trying to come up with something positive to say on the matter. "But think of how much we could do for the museum if even a fraction of the phone calls turn into visitors and Festival attendees."

Julia hadn't been able to argue with that.

"I saw the medical examiner drive by when they found her body Friday morning," Francis said, bringing Eva's thoughts back to the present. "Obviously, somebody thinks it's more than a curse." Francis lived in an old white house near Eden's one highway. As far as Eva could tell, most of her time was spent watching the comings and goings of the town from her front porch.

"It was an unexpected death," Elbert said. "The medical examiner always gets involved in those cases."

"Aren't most deaths unexpected?" Herb asked, but no one answered.

"It was probably Hamilton. Haven't I told you most murders are done by people who know the victim? That's why they brought in the medical examiner."

"You stop it right there, Maxine," Elbert said in an authoritative voice Eva hadn't heard him use before. "I just finished saying the ME is always brought in for unexpected deaths. That doesn't mean murder and you know it. You shouldn't go around throwing out things like that, someone will overhear and think it's the truth. Look what happened to William, over a year later people are still saying he might have had something to do with his wife's death."

"You're a fine one to talk," Maxine said, not sounding remotely abashed. "Besides, she was his *estranged* wife which means the two of them had problems."

"Doris has been telling anyone who'll listen that Gabby was scared of water and would have never gone anywhere near it." Francis rushed to change the subject before pausing and seeming to think. "And she didn't have a bathing suit on when she died. She was fully clothed."

"Probably drunk," Maxine added under her breath.

"I'm just glad William Templeton is able to run this

investigation," Elbert said. "I've always thought he had a good head on his shoulders. Knew it before he got that scholarship to NC State."

"I don't think he went there," Herb said. "I think I remember hearing he went to Chapel Hill."

"Lord have mercy, Herb," Maxine said. "He didn't go there. Everyone knows Chapel Hill isn't nothing but a bunch of drunks."

Francis snorted. "At least it wasn't Duke."

"Please," Maxine chastised her. "He isn't a Yankee. Of course, it wasn't Duke."

"I thought he went to some la-tee-da private school that wasn't Duke," Francis said.

"No," Maxine said. "You're thinking of his wife. Catherine went to some girls-only college in Charleston. I have to say, I never cared for the woman. I always saw her as snooty and odd because she didn't take her husband's name."

"That's what happens when these young folk go off for schooling instead of staying here and going to the community college like everyone else," Herb said. "They run off to Raleigh or Charleston and get these wild ideas. Back in my day, when a woman got married, she took her husband's name. Didn't matter what it was. There used to be a dental hygienist in Nag's Head named Sally McCarthy who married Ronald Sallie. She didn't keep her last name or hyphenate it; she went by Sally Sallie."

"I'm fairly certain the reason Catherine didn't change her name was because she was known in the art world as Catherine Harper," Elbert said, once more bringing the group a much-needed voice of reason.

Herb huffed. "I still don't like it."

"Then it's a good thing she married the chief and not you," Elbert said, ending the discussion.

SHORTLY AFTER SHE left the diner, Emerson met Eva at her office, and they walked across the shared parking lot to the Coastal Carolina Museum's back employee entrance. Inside, she had a private work room. Frankly, she was rather proud of the well-appointed room she'd designed for herself. Two long tables took up much of the space, but there was a small desk in the corner, and a large cabinet along one wall that allowed her to keep almost anything she'd need in the room without making it look or feel cluttered.

"This is nice," Emerson said, looking over it all. "Much nicer than working out of my hotel room."

"It's yours for as long as you need it," she said. "Or a month. Whichever comes first."

He chuckled and began taking items out of the backpack he had with him and organizing them on one table. Eva had stopped by the bank to pick up the coins after leaving the diner earlier. She handed him the storage box with the coins and took a step back to let him work.

"Are these the two coins you'll teach me how to picks locks for if I look at?" He wouldn't give an opinion before studying them in detail, but from the look in his eyes, he seemed eager to get busy.

"Yes. Mind if I hang out with you?" she asked. "I have a few emails to send out about the Blackbeard Festival, so I won't be in your way."

"Of course I don't mind, and even if I did, it's your workroom." He caught her eye and smiled. "And this way, you can fill me in on Amelia."

She laughed and placed her laptop on the desk. "Funny, that's the same thing she said about you last night."

Neither of them spoke while they worked, and though Eva was able to send out the emails she needed to, she was actually aware of Emerson as he measured, weighed, and inspected all four coins. Whatever data he collected, he entered into his laptop.

It was early afternoon when he finally pushed away from the table and stood up. He stretched his arms over his head and groaned. "Ugh. I'm much too old to sit in one place for that long." Eva bit her thumbnail and waited.

His expression was unreadable when he spoke. "You recall the wreckage of the Spanish ship found off the coast of Florida? It was about five years ago."

Eva nodded. It had been a huge find for the historical community. She'd devoured every paper and article she'd been able to get her hands on pertaining to the wreckage.

"I was called to help with the identification of the coins found," Emerson said. "And there were numerous coins found."

Eva remembered. She thought there was something else, though, but couldn't recall exactly what.

"What was able to be taken from the wreckage site were mostly common coins of the early eighteenth century. Granted, there were enough of them to be a small fortune, but it wasn't those common coins that the ship was known for. According to Spain, there was an undisclosed number of rare gold coins on board as well. They claimed as much in 1715 when the ship first went down, and they were still claiming it three years ago when it was reported there were no coins of that nature found in the remains of the ship."

That was what she'd forgotten. Spain had gone so far as to say they didn't believe the report stating the gold coins were missing.

"At the time, there was a lot of speculation. Had one of the ship's crew or passengers taken the gold and abandoned ship? Was it buried below the wreckage in a spot we weren't able to reach?" Emerson's eyes flashed in excitement. "Or was it possible the coins weren't on board when it wrecked?"

"Not on board?" Eva asked. She didn't see how that was possible. From what she could tell, it was well known and accepted that the gold had been on its way back to Spain.

"Not on board," Emerson repeated. "Because someone else had them."

"What?" Eva asked. "Who else would have them?"

Emerson put his finger against his lips as if to hush her. "Stay with me for a minute. What happens to metal when it's in the ocean for a long time?"

"It can become discolored or corroded," she answered.

"Yes," he said. "And I've been around a lot of coins that have been in the ocean as well as those that haven't been." He pointed to the coins, still on her workbench. "These have never spent much time in water, much less salt water. They've been on land."

"Okay," Eva said slowly because she felt as if she was missing something very simple.

"I told you all of that because there was one gold coin found in the wreckage we never disclosed to the press."

Eva's mouth fell open.

"The management running the site felt it would be more believable to say we hadn't found any of the gold coins as opposed to saying we only found one." Emerson shrugged. "I didn't agree, but I was overruled. After thinking about it later, I realized what might have happened to the rest of them."

"What?" she asked.

"My guess is the coins weren't on board when the Spanish ship met its end. Maybe because a pirate had attacked the ship before then and stole them. Maybe most of them." He nodded toward the workbench.

"Blackbeard was thought to be around that part of Florida in 1717," Eva said. "What are the odds that two years later, he found the coins there?"

"It's certainly possible," Emerson replied. "Where did the two coins you have come from? You didn't tell me."

"The pastor at the local Methodist church says someone put them in the collection plate."

"That's the craziest thing I've heard of." Emerson's forehead wrinkled. "I need to call the police department. Is it okay if a few of them come by here? I'd rather not transport the coins unnecessarily."

Eva nodded, unable to shake the feeling that the crazy had only just started.

"Love has brought you joy and it is a blessing to observe."

— JOURNAL OF AN UNKNOWN WOMAN, EARLY 1700s

When Mitch stopped by his office after lunch on Thursday to tell William that Emerson needed to see them both, preferably today, William had a suspicion he knew what the coin expert had found. He and Mitch drove to the museum together. Mitch didn't say a word, leaving William to wonder if Emerson had given him a hint of his findings.

He'd heard Emerson was working out of the Coastal Carolina Museum, but until entering through the back door, William had been unaware he was doing so out of Eva's workroom. William had never been to the museum and didn't think today changed that since all he saw was the employee-only section.

Though he wasn't surprised by the cleanliness and organization of the room, he was surprised to see Eva waiting with Emerson for their arrival.

"Mr. Jefferys," Mitch said, taking charge and shaking Emerson's hand. "I assume you have news for us?"

"Yes, and please, as I mentioned yesterday, call me Emerson."

"Ms. Knightly?" Mitch asked. "Are you staying for this?" His tone indicated he thought it best if she did not.

"I asked Eva to stay," Emerson said. "Not only because we may need her expertise, but she is in possession of two of the four coins I examined today."

"What do you mean two of the four?" Mitch asked and shot Eva a look that seemed to imply she'd done something wrong.

Eva, however, appeared unconcerned. "Reverend Neighbors of Eden Methodist brought them to me recently. He said someone put them in the collection plate on Sunday."

That was news to William, who couldn't help but wonder why Robert hadn't mentioned the coins to him.

"He said he didn't know what they were and thought I could help," she added, with a glance toward William.

William was aware Eva didn't care for Robert, but she knew the man was a friend of his. It made sense Robert would involve her if he didn't know what the coins were.

"If I may?" Emerson asked, and everyone nodded. He pointed to the table behind them. "The condensed version of my findings is that all four coins were part of a collection of gold coins from Spain. Originally, they were on a Spanish ship. The ship wrecked off the coast of Florida in 1715, all souls lost. The wreckage was discovered about five years ago, and three years ago I was part of the team that analyzed the remains. It's my opinion that all four of these coins are from the doomed Spanish ship. They're all the same," he said, softly. "Incredible, the world thought they were lost forever, and yet there are four right here."

William tried to let that knowledge sink into his head but couldn't for all the questions spinning around inside it. "How does something like this happen?"

"I don't know," Emerson confessed. "Fortunately for me, my job is only to identify the coins. I'll leave the rest up to you."

"I think you should start with Reverend Neighbors," Eva said. "I thought his story was ridiculous when he first told me, and this only makes me think so even more."

"You don't believe him?" William asked.

"I'm not sure. It doesn't make sense," Eva said. "He had to know if they were real, they'd be worth a lot of money. And if someone put them in the collection plate, they obviously wanted the church to have that money."

From the side of his eyes, he saw Emerson nod in agreement, but couldn't read Mitch's expression.

"Reverend Neighbors said they were the Devil's Coins and he wanted nothing to do with them." Eva didn't look at him as she spoke. "Even if he didn't want the coins, the least he could do was sell them and use the money to fund charitable projects. So yes, I think there's something off in his story."

"But why?" Emerson asked. "Why would he lie?"

"He wouldn't," William said in a no-nonsense voice and with an expression to match. "I've known him for years. He's not a liar."

Eva wanted to argue back, he could tell, but she didn't. There was a time and place to let William know what she thought about Reverend Neighbors, but here, today, in front of Emerson, wasn't it. "For the moment, we'll have to agree to disagree."

William sent her a silent thanks. "Can one of you tell me how coins that should be buried in the ocean made their way to Eden?"

Eva glanced at Emerson and at his nod, she replied. "Our best guess is that they were stolen from the Spanish ship, and whoever took them continued to the Outer Banks area and buried them here."

"Blackbeard?" William asked.

"More than likely," Eva said. "He wasn't the only pirate along the coast during that time, but he was the most active. It all fits."

"Most experts agree Blackbeard's treasure doesn't exist," William said.

Eva gave him a small smile as if she'd read his thoughts. "I'm well aware of that."

"And you're going to sit there and tell me they're wrong?"

"I prefer the term misguided, but yes, they are," Eva replied.

William looked at Emerson. "You, too?"

"Every day and twice on Sunday," Emerson replied with a grin.

"Thank you, Emerson," Mitch said, taking control of the meeting. "I look forward to reading your report, but you're right. You've done your job, and now it's time for us to do ours. You ready, Chief?"

No, he wanted to say. He'd prefer to stay with Eva. He liked how she refused to back down when she believed something and the way her blue eyes sparkled when she talked about history. She had the ability to make him smile even while disagreeing with him.

He kept all that to himself, though, and followed Mitch out of the room and back to the cruiser they'd shared on the quick drive over. Mitch, again, remained silent as they made their way back to the station, and William appreciated him not bringing up what they both knew.

He wasn't surprised when the mayor knocked on the door to his office less than an hour later.

"Word travels fast." William stood and waved to the set of visitor's chairs. "Have a seat."

When they were both seated, the mayor cleared his throat. "After hearing what Mr. Jefferys and Ms. Knightly said about the coins, I think it best you remove yourself from the investigation into Gabby Clark's death and step down as police chief until this mess with the coins is straightened out."

Just because that was his plan, didn't mean William liked it. He dropped his head into his hands and exhaled deeply, scrubbing his hair with his fingers.

"I remember you being very clear when we discussed the possible connection between Catherine and Gabby's cases. Now that it's been confirmed that the two coins are part of a collection that's been missing for over three hundred years *and* that two other matching coins were given to Ms. Knightly by your friend, Reverend Neighbors, I think you're too personally involved."

"I'm not trying to argue with you, am I?" William asked, lifting his head. "I know what needs to be done. That doesn't mean I have to like it."

The mayor sighed deeply. "Look, William, I know the last year has been difficult—"

"No, you don't know." William stood. "You haven't had to face the death of a spouse, speculation and suspicion about your role in that death, and then told you have to let someone else do your job while waiting to hear exactly how your wife died. It's been more than a year, and I still don't know for certain if her death was an accident, and I still can't walk down the street without people looking at me like I'm a dangerous animal who should be locked up. So no, you don't know anything, and I'd prefer you not say you do."

Without waiting for a response, he turned and walked out.

To say her parents didn't take the news of Mary's nuptials well would be like saying the beach had sand. They tried to complain to the governor but since he had preformed the ceremony, their complaint didn't go very far. For two days after hearing about the secret wedding, her mother wailed around the house distraught and certain her offspring's choice of mate would ostracize her from society.

Fortunately, most of her friends told her it was romantic and charming, though I am certain that in private, they gave silent thanks it wasn't their child who eloped with an infamous pirate.

— JOURNAL OF AN UNKNOWN WOMAN, EARLY 1700s

Chapter Twelve

Ten small towns off the North Carolina coast, from the northernmost, Corolla, to the southernmost, Ocracoke, form the over one hundred mile stretch of islands known as the Outer Banks. With year-round populations varying between under five hundred to a little over six thousand, these towns collectively grow from fifty-thousand residents in the off season to more than two hundred thousand in the summer.

Tourism was a fact of life for those living in the Outer Banks. While traffic sometimes swelled to nightmarish proportions during the summer, it was hard to complain about an industry that employed one-third of the permanent residents. Not to mention the over one billion dollars visitors spent annually.

Eva reminded herself of that fact on Sunday evening as she drove to The Tattered Flag, the art gallery in Nag's Head where the Festival planning meeting was to be held. She'd always thought it strange for the word *tattered* to be part of an art gallery's name, but then again, a lot of people thought she was strange to live on a barrier island.

What was not strange was how difficult it was to find a place to park, especially when it looked as if all two hundred thousand tourists decided to visit the upscale outdoor shopping center the art gallery was located in, all on the same day. Even though she expected to have a hard time finding a place to park anywhere during the month of June, Eva couldn't help but mutter, "If everyone comes to the Outer Banks to get away from it all, why does everyone wind up here?"

It didn't help that she was running late, and she was never late. Damn that phone call. It'd lasted over an hour and she hadn't had time to process anything about it. She finally found a spot in a far corner of the parking lot, though it appeared to be miles away from where she wanted to be.

"I'll consider this to be my work out for today," she mumbled to herself as she hiked across the steaming parking lot and tried not to think about how sweaty she was getting along the way. Forget about scrambling eggs on the sidewalk. She'd feel lucky if the soles of her shoes hadn't melted away by the time she reached her destination.

The air conditioning washed over her as soon as she stepped inside, momentarily freezing her to the bone as the cold air met her sun-heated skin. She stepped further inside and smiled at the group members already sitting at a small table toward the back of the gallery.

"Come on in, Eva," the gallery's owner, Paul, said, waving her toward them. "We're all here."

She walked over and took a seat next to Amelia. Looking around, Paul had been correct, everyone was waiting for her. The group included Elbert, a twenty-something newlywed couple from the area who held hands the entire time, Paul's partner, Mac from Boston who didn't care for the beach but loved history and Paul, and Taylor, a high school junior who reminded Eva of herself at that age.

"Thank you for coming, everyone," Eva started. "First of all, I apologize for running late. I was on the phone with the chairman of the board, and our call went longer than anticipated."

She took a deep breath, not knowing how to best phrase what she had to say. "There have been comments made to the board suggesting the Town of Eden cancel the Blackbeard Festival this year as a result of the two recent deaths."

A low-level murmur started within the group, and Eva waited for them to quiet down before continuing. She couldn't blame them because the news had been a shock to her as well.

Before the phone call she'd been excited about the Festival projections. Though she was never one to assume a victory before it happened, everything had seemed to point to this year's Blackbeard Festival having one of highest attendance levels ever. A few weeks ago, she'd made some discreet calls to a handful of local hotel managers and discovered rooms were booking fast for the Festival weekend.

According to what she'd been told on the phone, that was no longer the case.

"In addition," she said. "The board has confirmed with local hotel owners and managers that there has been an increase in cancellations for the weekend of the Festival. The board isn't ready to shut the Festival down yet, because that would lead to the potential closing of the Coastal Carolina Museum, but it's a possibility unless it can be proven that Eden is a safe place to visit."

The chorus of voices asking what they could do to help cheered her up, but she knew, in reality, the only thing that would convince the board to allow the Festival to continue would be for the medical examiner to rule both Catherine and Gabby's deaths as accidents or for the person responsible to be found and locked away.

She gave the group a smile. "I propose we move forward as if this is going to be the biggest and best Blackbeard Festival, ever."

Because, so help her God, if she had to solve those cases herself, she would.

Energized, the meeting continued with everyone listing the new ideas they'd brainstormed. Eva wrote them all down so they could go through and discuss in more detail later. As she expected, several had merit, like a dramatization of a ship battle, which unfortunately, would probably have to be vetoed due to budget restraints. And several did not, such as the idea of pirate bingo, which they'd tried two years ago with dismal results. Regardless, they were all jotted down.

Everyone's favorite idea was Amelia's pirate logo contest, especially when she suggested they ask local personalities to judge. She brought up a weatherman everyone loved for his sense of humor, a bestselling author who'd recently bought a vacation home, and a reality TV star who moved to the area after a stint in rehab. Amelia even took on the task of asking everyone, saying she knew them all from work. Eva couldn't help but wonder if charisma was a Morgan family characteristic or if Elbert and his granddaughter were the only two with a knack for knowing everyone.

Eva gave the group an update on the various vendors, and Elbert took on an action item to follow up with William Templeton about security. *Surely, he'd be reinstated as chief of police by then,* she heard whispered around the table, but chose to ignore.

The last item on the agenda was an update on the silent auction Paul and Mac had volunteered to sponsor. It would be the first silent auction the Festival had ever had, and while Eva wasn't convinced it'd be a hit with the attendees, the two men had agreed to do all the work themselves. She wasn't about to turn down an offer like that.

As the meeting drew to a close, Eva wasn't surprised when the chatter turned to Blackbeard's treasure. Especially with it widely circulated that a coin expert was in town and that he was a friend of Eva's. Eva answered as many questions as she could, but she and Emerson gave their word to the police not to say anything about the coins just yet, and she intended to keep that promise.

"What's to say his men didn't go back to dig it up after Blackbeard died?" Elbert asked at one point, and she sighed in relief that neither her nor Emerson and the coins had been discussed for long. "If I'd been on his crew, I'd have looked for it."

It was a good question, though Eva expected no less from the lively older man. "Most of the men who fought alongside him that day were killed in battle. And a good number who were ashore and passing time in a local tavern were arrested and executed. Any remaining survivors would have probably left town as quickly and quietly as possible." She paused to think. "Even if they did return to the area, they might know of one or two locations but not all of them."

"How did Blackbeard die again?" Taylor asked.

The high school student wasn't one to ask many questions, so Eva was happy to share her knowledge with the group. "The lieutenant governor of Virginia, Spotswood..." Eva rolled her eyes at the collective giggles around the table. "Yes, that was his real name. He didn't like what he saw as Governor Eden being too lenient with Blackbeard. Spotswood somehow received word on Blackbeard's location—from who, no one knows—and moved two ships into position. One day in late November, Blackbeard is on his ship, and most of his men are not because he gave them leave to go ashore, very strange behavior for Blackbeard."

"No one knows why he did that?" Amelia asked.

"Not that I've ever been able to find." Eva shuffled through a pile of papers and put a map of the North Carolina coast on the table. "Spotswood's ships move into position, blocking him in. Blackbeard fires at them. I think he knew who they were, as well as what Spotswood thought of him. Blackbeard's shots caused considerable damage to the boats."

"All those cannons he added," Amelia mumbled.

"He thought he'd killed the majority of them," Mac said, taking over. "So he boarded their ship, only to find that Spotswood and most of his men were hiding below deck, waiting for him."

Elbert let out a low whistle. "Damn."

"Right?" Mac agreed. "I can't believe he didn't anticipate that."

"He was definitely off his game," Elbert nodded. "And I can see why Blackbeard's men weren't too keen to go digging for his treasure after that."

"Exactly," Eva said. "But you would think the least they could do was write down where it was so someone, someday, could find it. Or maybe they did write it down, but the paper they wrote it on went down with the rest of the *Queen Anne's Revenge.*"

"Have you ever gone treasure hunting?" Paul asked.

Eva replied honestly, "Of course I have. I'm guessing Mac has, too."

Paul didn't press further, and Mac simply chuckled and replied he certainly had.

People started leaving after that. A few stayed near the table and chatted, while others meandered here and there, looking over the paintings on display. It'd been years since Eva last visited the gallery, and she wanted to take a few moments to wander around. First, though, she caught up with Amelia.

"Can you and I get together next week to go over those records you mentioned?"

After Eva answered several questions about Emerson at the diner, Amelia mentioned data she was gathering to produce family trees on local historical figures. This meant she might have a way to identify potential descendants of Blackbeard, and Eva was beside herself with excitement. Unfortunately, Amelia confessed she hadn't been able to get the information she needed on the pirate, not only because there was little information to be found, but most of her free time was spent on her run for office. Nonetheless, she added, she did have some interesting profiles.

"Absolutely," Amelia said. "I'll look at my calendar and give you a call." At Eva's nod, she continued, "Speaking of calls, have you made one to Stefan yet?"

Eva winced but replied honestly. "No, but only because work has been so crazy lately, especially since Emerson's been here. I plan to call him soon."

"You won't regret it," Amelia said, and Eva hoped she was right.

The child within Mary continued to grow. I watched as her countenance took on a glow due to the new life inside her, even as one week became two without word from Edward.

— JOURNAL OF AN UNKNOWN WOMAN, EARLY 1700s

Much to the dismay of his new bride, most of the property Nana left William was marshland, and therefore uninhabitable, but William didn't care. To him, it meant when they did build on the land able to support a house, he wouldn't have to worry about nosey neighbors. In the early days of their marriage, he could picture their future home so clearly, with floor-to-ceiling windows overlooking the water, a huge deck and patio for barbecues and entertaining friends, and everywhere he heard the laughter of children.

Unfortunately, his wife didn't share his vision. Catherine Harper didn't want to live "off in the swamp" but rather in town where she could walk to where she wanted to go and had people to talk with. Plus, she'd said that with his job it only made sense for him to be in town so he wouldn't have to travel far when calls came in. He begrudgingly admitted she was right.

They agreed to live in the "marsh house," as Catherine nicknamed it, while waiting for their house in town to be built. He knew how she felt about the place, but he was young and their marriage new, and he was certain she'd change her mind after they spent time together in the house he loved so much. Then they could sell the house in town. It didn't happen.

William had to admit Catherine tried to make the most of the experience. Never one to keep her feelings to herself, she surprised him by not complaining once, even though he knew Nana's place was far from her ideal. He told her how much he appreciated her willingness to spend that small amount of time with him in the place that meant so much to him growing up.

He was under no illusion, however, that her silence meant she'd changed her mind about her preferred location for their residence. Once construction on the house in town was completed, William set aside his dream home plans, but he insisted on keeping Nana's place up. Catherine agreed to help, and when William couldn't visit the house because of work, she would visit on his behalf. He appreciated that she knew how much the house and land meant to him. But the dream house with the big windows overlooking the water and the backyard for parties was gone. As was the sound of children's laughter.

After Catherine's death, he thought about selling the house they had shared in town and living in the marsh place, the way he had been since the separation. But with all the questions surrounding Catherine's death in the very beginning, he didn't have time to move. Plus, he believed it was too soon and would look unseemly.

Since allowing Mitch to become the acting chief, William found himself working more of the everyday calls with a handful of his recent hires. He didn't mind working in the trenches with his team. Surprisingly, he discovered he enjoyed getting to know them and the people of the community better. The experience would make him a better chief when he was reinstated, and he would be, he vowed. Mitch had called the lab to get a status of Gabby's labs and final report, but so far, he hadn't heard back.

Late Sunday night, after working over the weekend, William jumped in his truck and headed toward the only place that ever felt like home. He was off for the next two days and though he'd had a positive weekend, he felt a bit run down and hoped the time away from town would recharge him. As it turned out, it didn't even take that long. He ran into very little traffic, and the twenty-minute drive helped to calm his mind. By the time he pulled up to the small two-bedroom cottage, a familiar peace surrounded him. Being in the quiet place always cleared his head and allowed him to think.

Over the past year, he'd realized how little he knew of Catherine's day-to-day life. Obviously, she was an artist, and while he knew she didn't sit around sketching and painting all day, every day, it shamed him to admit he had no idea what she did when she wasn't painting. Nor, he admitted to himself, would he have been able to answer truthfully about any change in Catherine's habits the last week of her life. Perhaps that would be acceptable since they had been separated for the last six months of her life, but the fact was, he'd *never* given thought to how she spent her time when she wasn't painting.

The last year of her life, he'd suspected Catherine had been having an affair which had led to their separation. She never told him who it was with, and he'd never attempted to find out. If Catherine had strayed, it was all on her.

But what had once been guilt over not knowing how his estranged wife spent her days had morphed into something that felt more sinister. It bothered him Catherine had a rare gold coin on her when she died because that only added to the numerous questions surrounding her death. Had she been aware of how rare the coin was? Why hadn't she mentioned it to anyone? He could see why he wouldn't be the first person she'd tell, but why hadn't she talked to Eva?

An unrelenting need to know what Catherine did during the day ate at him until the answer came so clearly, he felt stupid for not seeing it sooner. Catherine had a planner she kept everything in, and he was almost certain he knew where it was.

After her death, he hadn't thrown any of her things away. Instead, he'd packed everything in boxes, brought them to Nana's, and tucked them out of sight in the attic. His reasoning being that when he felt ready to go through the boxes, he'd do better mentally at Nana's than he would at his house in Eden. But once he brought the first box down from the attic and stared at it for who knows how long, he realized his location didn't matter. It was going to hurt wherever he was.

It was nearly midnight when he found what he was looking for.

He'd brought the third box down from the attic, opened it in the living room, and found the worn black leather binder Catherine had called "her life." In a world where everyone and everything seemed to be going digital, the one thing Catherine absolutely refused to give up was her planner.

He could see why. It was color coded and more organized than anything else in their house. The downside was Catherine wrote using initials and her own made-up code he'd quit trying to break early into their marriage. He flipped through a few pages and chuckled at the combination of letters he had no way of ever translating that she'd used for about half of her entries.

One of the first things he noticed was her frequent notation of PC, often more than once a week. It appeared she'd finally taken his advice and scheduled herself computer time to transfer all her paper accounting to digital. He'd been on her forever to do that.

Not knowing what he was looking for, he flipped through more pages. She'd had a few meetings scheduled for the week after her death. He wondered if they ever got canceled because he'd never done so.

The pain of her death wasn't as sharp as it had been. Lately, it had become more of a gnawing ache. Still painful but more bearable. Tonight, however, looking through her planner and seeing she had a life he more than likely knew nothing about, one he saw written in her own handwriting, the sharp pain returned. Not only because he'd lost her a year ago, but because he knew he'd lost her long before then.

Today it became obvious Edward wouldn't be home for the birth of his child and I fear I can no longer keep Mary's condition a secret. Not and keep the vow I gave to him to keep her safe.

— JOURNAL OF AN UNKNOWN WOMAN, EARLY 1700s

Chapter Fourteen

"**A**cting Chief Montague thinks Catherine and Gabby's deaths are related," Francis announced to her three breakfast companions early Tuesday morning. "I saw the evidence myself."

Eva had to force herself to remain still. She knew the police thought there might be a connection, but nothing official had been released concerning any such potential. How would Francis have gotten any information? Elbert, Eva believed, could have come across that tidbit, but not Francis.

"From your front porch?" Elbert asked, clearly not believing her either.

"Yes."

"I don't think you can make a determination like that from watching cars drive by your place."

"Don't act so put out, Elbert," Maxine chided. "You're not the only person in this town allowed to know things. And stop scowling at me, do you want your face to freeze like that? Go on and tell us what you saw, Francis."

"Montague and Templeton went to meet with that coin expert last week, and shortly after they got back to the station, Templeton flew out of the parking lot like a bat out of hell," Francis said, excitement building in her voice. "And before you try to tell me I can't see the police station from my porch, Elbert, I can. I told my Eddie I needed binoculars for bird-watching, and they arrived two weeks ago."

Francis's son, Eddie, lived in Chicago and saw his mother maybe once a year. He probably actually believed his mother wanted binoculars for bird-watching.

"Oh." Maxine gave a nod of approval. "That's a good idea. I want a pair."

"Do they have ones with night vision?" Herb asked.

"Lord, help us all," Elbert mumbled under his breath, echoing Eva's thoughts.

"I heard that," Francis chided. "Anyway, as soon as he was able to, after work on Sunday, he drove out of town again. I assumed to that house Ruth left him."

"I don't see how this relates to Montague thinking the deaths of Catherine and Gabby are related," Elbert said.

"If you'd be quiet for five minutes, I'd tell you." Francis gave a dramatic sigh and continued. "Gabby always cleaned Ruth's place every other week, and the week she died, she'd recently cleaned there. They say she died sometime Thursday night, and we know she had a gold coin on her. If you remember, William owns all that marshland where they say Blackbeard may have buried his treasure. Both women died with a coin, and both had a connection to William and, as a result, to the marsh and whatever treasure it holds."

No one spoke for a long moment.

Elbert broke the silence first. "I think you should stick with watching birds."

EVA WAS STILL thinking about Francis's words a few hours later. Was she implying that since William was a connection between the two deaths that he had something to do with them? Surely not. There had to be a good number of locals with ties to both women. No, more than likely she was trying to link William's land to both women. Of course, that didn't make sense either.

She looked up when one of the servers, Gina, came by to ask her if she wanted another refill.

"I better not," Eva said. "I've already had three, and if I have another, you'll be watching me climb the walls."

Gina nodded. "Let me know if you change your mind."

Eva assured her she would and looked to the door. She had called Stefan after the Festival meeting, and he suggested coffee in Eden's diner today, Tuesday, as he had business in town. Since they agreed to meet at nine-thirty, Eva hadn't left after breakfast like normal. Instead, she'd brought her laptop with her.

She couldn't help but think that since Greg had left, she'd only been out on two dates, each with a different guy. Neither of whom had been worth a second date. Who knew? Maybe the third guy would be the charm. It didn't hurt he'd been vetted by Amelia.

Though she had never met him, she recognized him as the man who had been helping Amelia put out signs for her campaign the morning Mitch stopped by her office. Amelia hadn't lied. There was no way Eva could have met Stefan before, because there was no way she would have forgotten the man. He stood out as soon as he walked in, and to say he was easy on the eyes was an understatement. Eva recognized his suit as belonging to an Italian designer's collection, thanks to her ex's yearning for a similar one, although Greg would never have been able to wear one as easily as the man before her. The high-end apparel would overpower most men, instead of complimenting them the way it did Stefan.

But it was more than the suit, or even his blond good looks, that captured one's attention. Stefan had the most unusual shade of blue eyes she'd ever seen. Light blue. So light, she wasn't sure they were even considered blue. Like Amelia had said, he seemed to have an easy smile and the lines around his month hinted at a man who enjoyed laughter.

He wasn't William, though. She forced herself to smile at the man walking toward her.

No one would be William, she scolded herself, and the sooner she realized that, the better.

"You must be Eva," he said, shaking her hand. "Stefan Benson. So good to meet you."

"Amelia's told me all about you," Eva said with a grin.

"I'm not sure if that's a good thing or a bad thing," he joked. "We've known each other since elementary school."

They sat down, and he waved a server over to take their order.

"Amelia said you work for the Outer Banks Historical Society," he said. "I'm surprised we haven't run into each other before."

"Really? Why does that surprise you?"

"I've always considered myself a bit of a history nerd, and my mother was on the board of directors for the Coastal Carolina Museum."

"That is surprising. I thought I knew everyone on the board." Eva would at least have thought she'd heard of Stefan if his mother sat on the board. If from nothing else than at the annual Christmas party.

"She served on the board until she passed, seven years ago," he clarified, as his coffee and her water were delivered to the table.

"That explains it," Eva said. "I moved here five years ago."

Stefan raised a quizzical eyebrow. "Moved here? You aren't from this area?"

"No."

"Hmm." He sat back in his seat, appraising her. "I truly had you pegged as a local."

She smiled at the compliment. "I'm from up north."

"A Yankee?" he asked in mock outrage. "And they let you work at *our* Historical Society?"

Eva couldn't help but laugh. Their conversation turned to the maps he had in his office, and he told Eva to call his admin in the morning to set up a time to come by when she was free to see them. He apologized profusely for not having his schedule with him but confessed his admin no longer allowed him to have edit capabilities over it because he always screwed up the calendar system.

"You got roped into heading up the Blackbeard Festival?" he asked. "Isn't that just one big treasure hunt?"

They had been discussing their hobbies, and Eva joked she didn't have time for anything other than work and the Blackbeard Festival.

"I wasn't so much roped, but rather handed it and told to get busy." She shook her head. "I was actually having fun with it. I love Blackbeard."

"*Was* having fun?" he asked. "Why past tense? I have to admit, the adventurer in me thinks an old-fashioned treasure hunt sounds like fun. And I've always thought Blackbeard was an interesting character."

"The board might cancel the Festival this year because of the deaths of Catherine Harper and Gabby Clark; and even if *they* don't, visitors are already cancelling their lodging. Without the funds from the Festival, the Coastal Carolina Museum will more than likely have to close. We've already had to cut our open hours dramatically during the off season. Even now we're stilling having to close on Mondays."

"That's awful."

"Yes." She didn't want to turn their first meeting into a downer, so she added, "But until they pull the plug on me, I'm going to keep planning like it's going to happen. And I have a lot more in mind for activities than a treasure hunt."

"That's the spirit." Stefan lifted his coffee mug to her and changed the subject.

She hadn't planned on enjoying her talk with Stefan, but he was smart and funny, and a bit flirtatious—nothing over the top. Most surprising of all, he acted very down-to-earth for a man as well-off as he appeared.

Glancing at his watch, he frowned and said he had to leave the diner in about ten minutes. "I have a meeting concerning some legal issues about an old restaurant property, Sam's."

"Sam's Sandwiches?" she asked. "I'd forgotten about that place! Is it still open?"

Stefan looked at her oddly. "No, it's been closed for fifteen years, but the grandchildren have a new place over in Nags Head."

"I came to the Outer Banks with my mom when I was a kid, and as soon as you said Sam's, I remembered sitting at a booth in Sam's laughing hysterically at something my mom had said." Eva blinked away the unexpected tears the sudden recollection triggered. "It was the hardest I ever laughed. I wish I remembered what it was that made me laugh so hard." She shook her head. "My mom died shortly after that vacation. It was a long time before I laughed again."

"That must have been hard, losing your mother as a child," Stefan said.

"Yes." She wiped under her eyes. "Sorry for almost becoming a sobbing mess."

"Don't apologize," he said. "Memories are funny, aren't they? What you remember and what you don't. How does your brain decide? And how it is something long forgotten can be triggered by the most random things?"

She was getting ready to answer when the bell above the diner door rang announcing someone's entrance. William. His eyes caught hers, and he made his way toward their table but stopped abruptly when he caught sight of who sat with her. A look of surprise flashed in his eyes but disappeared so quickly she thought it was all in her imagination. Jealousy? It couldn't be.

He continued walking. "Eva," he said with a nod when he reached them.

"William," she said and motioned to Stefan. "I'm not sure if you know—"

"We went to school together when we were kids and saw each other for the first time in years a few days ago," William said, nodding in acknowledgment. "Good to see you again, Stefan."

"Likewise."

"I don't mean to interrupt, but since you're here," William said and shifted to face her. "I need to speak with you about something. Would it be possible for me to stop by your office around nine tomorrow morning?"

"I have a meeting then," she said.

William glanced at Stefan before adding, "Your place six o'clock tomorrow? I'll bring dinner."

He certainly appeared jealous, Eva thought while confirming tomorrow at six would be fine.

William bid them both goodbye and went to the take-out counter to pick up an order.

"Are you two friends or dating or something?" Stefan asked with a smile after the bell announced William's departure.

"Why?" Eva teased. "Jealous?"

Stefan's eyes danced. "Maybe."

She shook her head. "William and I are just friends. His wife was Catherine Harper."

Stefan's eyes grew big. "I hadn't realized. The different last names threw me."

"They throw off quite a few people."

Stefan glanced at his watch again, and Eva knew their time was up.

"I hate to end this on a sad note," he said. "But I have to leave now or else I'll be late."

"Of course. I understand."

"I enjoyed talking with you," he said, standing. "I hope we can do it again soon."

As she agreed and watched him walk away, she was surprised at how much she was looking forward to seeing him again. She smiled, picturing Amelia's *I told you so* face.

If it hadn't been for the midwife, both Mary and her son would have died. They most certainly wouldn't be as they were after, with Mary resting in bed looking exhausted and enamored at the same time.

Mary said the child looks like his father, but I thought that was doing Edward a disservice. His son looked more like a wrinkly red grape that had been out in the sun too long.

— JOURNAL OF AN UNKNOWN WOMAN, EARLY 1700s

ike numerous other small towns in the southern United States, Eden had a large number of churches. Most of them were Protestant, though there were a few places of worship for Catholics and Episcopalians, and there always seemed to be a disproportionate number and types of Baptist churches to be found. As far as William knew, there was only one type of Methodist church. Nana had thought it foolish there were so many denominations in the Christian faith. William just shook his head; even as a child he'd learned how rare it was for a group of people to agree on anything.

As a teenager, he'd attended a non-denominational church with Nana. William liked it better than the more traditional churches, if for no other reason than they had drums and guitars instead of the dreadful pipe organ. The sound of a pipe organ always made him feel as if he was at a funeral.

Early Tuesday afternoon, William pulled into the parking lot of Eden's only Methodist church. Once he stepped inside, he was met by the church's administrator, Evelyn Davis, whom he'd went to high school with.

Evelyn had graduated the year before William did. She was somewhat of a rebel in high school, so he always thought it was humorous she now worked at a church. The multicolored hair and crazy outfits she'd favored when they were teens had been replaced with a neat, shoulder-length, light-brown bob, a drab gray suit, and a bit too much of whatever perfume she used.

"William," she said, eyes wide, and using his first name as most of those he'd grown up with did. "What a surprise to see you. Is everything okay? Someone in trouble?"

He tried to relax his frame, knowing he often came across as irritated or pissed off. That had not always been the case. There had been a time when happy days outnumbered the ones where he just made it through. At least he thought there had been.

Today he actually *was* irritated, specifically at the fact that he was about to question his friend, albeit on the sly. No matter that Eva thought differently, William couldn't believe Robert would lie about the coins, but he knew he had to go through the motions.

If William went with the assumption Gabby's death wasn't an accident, it made sense someone might want to get rid of coins that could possibly be seen as suspicious. Dropping them anonymously in a church collection plate was a fairly elegant, though unusual, way to get the job done.

Along those lines, if it turned out Gabby had been murdered, did that make it more probable Catherine had been as well? That would mean he'd failed as both a husband and police chief.

He forced a smile, hoping to put Evelyn at ease. "Everything's fine," he assured her. "Today's actually my day off. Is Reverend Neighbors here?"

The tension left Evelyn's shoulders, and she let out a big breath of relief. "He's in his office. Why don't you go on back?"

"Thank you, Evelyn," he said, and made his way toward the staff offices. Robert sat behind his desk, typing, his eyes on the computer screen in front of him. At William's knock, he lifted his head.

"William." He stood and walked from behind his desk to give William a one-armed hug. "I wasn't expecting you today. I was just thinking how we need to schedule some time to go out to the batting cages. My cousin in the mountains has a new bat, and he swears it increased his batting average. I thought I might look into getting one for our games this summer."

William swallowed his laugh. It was going to take more than a new bat to increase Robert's batting average, but there was no way to ignore the man's undying passion for the game.

"I could use an hour or two of swinging practice myself." It hit William that this would be the first summer he'd be playing where Catherine wouldn't be on the sidelines, cheering them both on, and his chest ached. William hadn't played the year before because the season started so soon after Catherine's death. He wasn't sure if Robert had played last year. "Everything's so busy at the moment."

Robert must have heard the change in his tone when he mentioned being busy. He led William over to the two chairs in front of his desk, taking his seat after William. "Want to talk about what's going on?"

"What's not going on is the better question," William said, forcing himself to ignore the pain the new reminder of Catherine's death brought. "Especially when you factor in Gabby Clark's death."

"Such a tragic death." Robert shook his head. "She worked here three times a week, cleaning. Delightful young woman, most of the time. But I suppose we're all like that, aren't we? We all have our moments."

"Some of us more so than others," William said, and Robert laughed.

It was the perfect opening for William to follow up on the question he had after talking with Stefan's admin, Naomi. "Since Gabby was here the Wednesday before she died, I was hoping you could tell me if she acted odd or did anything outside of her normal habits?"

"What do you mean?" Robert looked confused.

"For the most part, humans are creatures of habit. Did she do anything out of habit on Wednesday?"

"I don't think I can help you. I didn't know her well enough to be aware of her habits."

William kept his voice as even and calm as possible. "It was my understanding that the two of you were pretty close?"

All at once, Robert's face flushed, but William couldn't tell if it was due to embarrassment or rage. "I'm not sure I understand what you're saying."

William shrugged. "Just that Gabby referred to you as a friend."

"She was here three days a week," Robert scoffed. "Of course I was friendly to her. I'd like to think I'm pleasant toward all my staff. But that doesn't mean there's anything inappropriate going on."

"Hold on a minute." William held up his hands, surprised at how defensive Robert had gotten over one statement. "No one said anything about being inappropriate. I was making conversation."

Robert closed his eyes and took a deep breath. When he looked at William again, he appeared calmer. "I'm sorry if I took your words the wrong way. It's an automatic reflex, I guess. You hear all those stories on the news about clergy, and the horrible things some of them do." He took another deep breath. "But you know me. How hard I work to ensure there's never a hint of anything questionable about my behavior. It makes me a bit defensive."

A bit? William wanted to ask. "I guess I probably shouldn't ask about the coins you gave to Eva Knightly." He'd worded it that way because he knew Robert wouldn't be able to stop himself from wanting to know more.

"What about them?" Robert asked, exactly as William intended.

"Where did you get them?"

"I thought she would have told you." Robert's expression remained unchanged. "They were placed in the offering plate, the Sunday after Gabby's death."

"You don't know who put them there? Have any suspicions?"

Robert gave a small smile. "You and Catherine attended here for a good number of years. You know we don't snoop around offerings people don't want to be recognized for. Nor do we question anonymous gifts."

William knew of a least a dozen times Catherine had dropped cash into the passed plate without any sort of information as to who it was from. He suspected Robert knew she had done so as well. But maybe that wasn't the same case with the coins.

"Why don't you want the coins back?" William asked. "They might be worth a lot." He knew for a fact they were. When he made it home after learning what they were from Emerson, he'd looked up the estimated value online. For Robert to refuse a gift that large made no sense.

"I don't think God wants anything to do with the Devil's Coins."

"Perhaps God wants you to redeem the coins. To use them for good." William couldn't understand Robert's reasoning for giving them away. "If someone dropped them in the offering, surely they wanted you to do something with them. Change some lives. Give to missionaries. Heck, do you know how many families live in poverty in our county alone?" The more William thought about it, the more he couldn't see where Robert was coming from.

"I don't think so. Not those coins."

"Why not?" William pressed. "They're only metal. Surely metal can't hurt anyone."

"Because they're cursed." Robert's voice grew louder, but he wasn't yelling. Yet. "Cursed and so will be any man, woman, or child who dares to lay claim on them."

William had only seen Robert this worked over a few times before. Always, it'd been over an issue Robert was passionate about. William found it hard to believe old coins fit into that category, no matter who they might have belonged to once.

William chuckled, trying to lighten the fear in Robert's voice. "Come on. You don't really believe that, do you?" But it was clear he did.

"Of course I do, and if you were smart, you would believe it too and have nothing to do with those coins."

The midwife told me before she left, while Mary and her new-born son slept, that I would be the one called upon to protect little Alexander Edward. I didn't know what she meant, but the one thing I did know was I would fight to the death anyone who threatened one hair on the head of that precious baby.

— **JOURNAL OF AN UNKNOWN WOMAN, EARLY 1700s**

Chapter Sixteen

"You must be a mind reader," Eva teased William later that day when he arrived at her house with his naturally warmhearted smile and holding bags of Chinese takeout. She led him into her kitchen. "I've been craving egg rolls all day."

"Just a lucky guess." He placed the bags on the countertop and looked around the open concept layout of her first floor. "It's been a while since I've been here. Have you painted?"

He hadn't been over since Catherine's death, but she didn't want to bring that up. "Yes, but only the downstairs. The old color was too dark." She took the paper cartons out of the bag to put them on the table. "Please tell me you got chicken with garlic sauce. Oh, you did. I hope you got something else for you. I could polish this off all by myself."

"I like the lighter color. And, yes, there's broccoli chicken in another one."

"Broccoli?" She wrinkled her nose. "Yuck."

"That's why I got it."

She reached into her refrigerator and pulled out two bottles of locally brewed beer and raised an eyebrow at William.

"Hell yes."

They sat down at the table, and Eva could almost pretend there was nothing between them. But that's all it would be, pretending. Unacknowledged and unspoken, it hummed in the quiet spaces of their conversations, unwilling to leave even as they ignored it.

Eva shook her head at him. "I can't believe you're using a fork."

"As opposed to what?" he asked. "Little wooden sticks?"

"Chopsticks. They're called chopsticks."

"I know what they are, and believe it or not, I do know how to use them." He speared a piece of broccoli with his fork. "I just use a fork better."

She rolled her eyes. "Whatever."

He reached over to where she sat and took her chopsticks.

"Hey," she said, trying unsuccessfully to get them back. "I was using those."

"I'll give them right back." Holding them as if it was something he did at every meal, he effortlessly took a good-sized bite from a nearby container of fried rice, and held it to her lips. "Do you believe me now?"

She nodded and opened her mouth, assuming he was going to feed her. Her heart raced. That was not ignoring the electricity between them or pretending it didn't exist. But at the last second, the right side of his mouth quirked up, and he moved the chopsticks to his own mouth and ate the rice.

"Ass," she said, snatching her chopsticks out of his hands and returning to her own food. He didn't respond, probably because he knew there was no way he could deny what she'd said.

"So," Eva said, after they'd finished eating and cleaned everything up. "What's on your mind?"

William placed on the table a leather-bound book he'd brought in with the takeout.

"The other day I was at Nana's, and I found Catherine's planner." He opened to one page. "I noticed that after we separated, she spent a lot of time at the Coastal Carolina Museum. I was surprised. I hadn't realized she was that into history."

"She was painting the mural for the children's section."

Part of Eva wasn't shocked William didn't know about the mural. She'd seen firsthand that things weren't sunshine and roses for the couple after the separation. Part of dodging landmines and being friends with both of them meant not talking about certain subjects with one or the other. Catherine painting at the museum wasn't something she'd have discussed with William.

Even with her attraction to William, Eva had always hoped he'd get back together with Catherine.

Before the last year of Catherine's life, she and William loved to talk about their joint history and how they got together. Though they graduated in the same class, Catherine always gave William a hard time because during their high school years, William ran track, which made him a jock. According to school hierarchy, jocks were expected to date either cheerleaders or sporty girls, someone from the volleyball team, perhaps. Nerds and art students were viewed as untouchable for jocks. Catherine had the dubious honor of being both. According to her, William ignored her during their four years of high school and was a wuss for following stupid rules made by brainless teenagers.

This was the point when William would typically chime in and agree that, yes, he'd been a wuss but that he never stopped thinking about her after graduation. Even with them attending different colleges, he insisted, he at a public university in Raleigh and she at a private one in Charleston.

Catherine would roll her eyes whenever he said that, because they didn't see each other again until their tenth high school reunion. By then, William was back in Eden, working on the police force with his eyes on the position of police chief. Catherine lived in Nags Head, waiting tables and painting every free minute she had. They both attended the reunion alone, and when their paths crossed that night, that was all it took.

Six months later, they were dating exclusively. Eighteen months later, they were engaged. Twelve years after graduating from high school and two years after the reunion, they were married.

"She what?" William asked, bringing Eva back to the present and a mural he hadn't known about.

"Catherine painted a mural for the children's section of the Coastal Carolina Museum. When I get into the office tomorrow, I'll look at the schedule and see when I can show it to you privately."

William nodded, a hint of sadness lurking behind his eyes. "That sounds good."

"For what it's worth, she seemed to enjoy painting it." Eva remembered Catherine saying it was refreshing to work on something other than a landscape. "In fact, she enjoyed it so much she wouldn't let us pay her for it."

William gave a small chuckle. "That sounds like her."

"Right? I didn't listen, of course, and gave her a check for the agreed upon fee, anyway. Catherine took it, didn't say a word, and three days later an anonymous donation was made to the Historical Society for the exact amount."

His chuckle was bigger this time. "And that sounds *exactly* like her."

Eva couldn't help but smile as she remembered opening the donation envelope and realizing what Catherine had done. "It's a beautiful mural. We hear all the time how captivating it is, especially the way she was able to incorporate as many different elements as she did."

The mural had been finished not long before her death. It was a whimsical piece, an intriguing combination of historical events overlaid with present-day landmarks, and various cartoonish

historical figures were present as well. Eva remembered thinking Catherine looked happier painting the mural than she had
in a long time. Yet there were times when Catherine thought no
one was watching, and she'd let her jovial mask fall away for a
second. In those times, Eva saw that Catherine wasn't as happy
as she wanted those around her to think, but she could never get
her friend to confide in what was going on, beyond the obvious.

"I wasn't aware she was painting during the separation,"
William said, not quite meeting her eyes. "She had some of her
supplies at Nana's. I called and asked if she wanted me to bring
them to her, but she said no. Said she couldn't find her muse."
He shook his head, as if clearing it of unwanted thoughts, and
looked around.

"You know what?" Eva asked standing, remembering suddenly. "I have pictures of Catherine and the mural. Hold on a
minute."

She turned and took a few steps past William, who had stood
when she did, to her bookshelf. Most of the space was filled with
reference books, but she did have a small space on a lower shelf
where she kept photo albums. Taking a slim black volume out,
she verified it was the one she was looking for, and handed it to
William.

He took it with hesitant fingers and opened to the first page.
Watching him, it was as if the past came back and punched him
in the gut. He dropped into the chair, the breath leaving his body
in a big whoosh.

The small photo book mostly contained pictures of Catherine.
Some by herself, some with the mural, and some with the Historical Society and museum employees. There were a few showing
only the mural. Tears prickled her eyes as she remembered that
day. How pleased Catherine had been with the way the mural
had turned out. She'd been so happy and insisted on taking Eva
out to lunch to celebrate.

God, she missed her.

"She was very talented," he said. "Normally, she painted land-scapes. It looks like she really enjoyed doing something different."

"I like to think so."

"Was the mural in the paper?" William asked with a frown.

"No," Eva replied. "We did take a few pictures for a press release. But once Catherine finished it, we'd decided to wait until closer to last year's Blackbeard Festival. We thought that would be the best time because we'd be able to reach more people. Now, we aren't sure if or when we should run a press release. I want to make sure it doesn't look like we're trying to capitalize on her death or the fact that the mural was the last known piece she worked on. We're still discussing how to do it and not be seen as unseemly, especially with it being over a year since the mural was completed."

But if it would save the Coastal Carolina Museum and there-fore jobs, she just might have to be unseemly.

Watching William reverently look through the images of Cath-erine and the mural, the ache in her heart caused by the loss of her dear friend intensified. But it was more than that. It hurt seeing how much William still felt for Catherine.

"You know what?" she asked, wiping a tear away and prom-ising she would ignore the attraction she felt for him. "I have something else I think she'd want you to have."

She went to the desk tucked into one corner of her living room and pulled out a framed drawing. It was a rough sketch of a lighthouse, and though there were several to be found along the Outer Banks, she couldn't identify which one Catherine was depicting. She handed the frame to William, who took it with tentative hands.

"Catherine?" he asked.

Eva nodded and saw his fingers tremble. "Yes. It's from when she was painting the children's mural. It's a sketch she was working on while trying to decide which lighthouse she would use. When I first saw it, she was getting ready to ball it up and throw it away. I told her she was crazy to throw something that beautiful away, and she gave it to me."

William remained silent, studying the sketch.

Eva continued, "I put it away after she died because it was hard to look at it and think about how much life she still had left to live. I came across it a few weeks ago and decided her work was too beautiful not to be seen." She swallowed around the lump in her throat. "So I had it framed but could never bring myself to hang it up. Now I know it was because the sketch is meant to be yours."

I wish I were able to tell you I would be home soon, but I will not lie to you. Please know I am doing whatever I can to get back to you as quickly as possible.

— LETTER FROM BLACKBEARD TO HIS WIFE, MARY, 1718

Chapter Seventeen

H is wife had spent months painting a mural for the local museum, and he hadn't known. Granted, they were separated, but William had the feeling that even if they hadn't been, he still wouldn't have known. If that didn't sum up the state of his marriage, nothing would. He wondered off-handedly if she'd have mentioned the mural to him before the article ran in the paper. The very fact he had to ask himself the question made his heart ache. God, they really had made a mess of their marriage.

William couldn't stop staring at the pictures. Catherine looked beautiful, but of course, she always looked beautiful. It wasn't until the last year of her life he realized she used her looks as a shield to protect herself. Maybe if she hadn't died, he'd eventually gotten behind that shield. He was fairly certain she'd never even dropped it for him. Of course, maybe he hadn't dropped his either.

He turned a page to find a large photo of the mural and took a few minutes to look it over. He swore he could almost see her heart and soul better in the whimsical mural than he could in the landscapes she was known for. Unfortunately, it was so large that in order to capture it in its entirety, the details were lost. But even without seeing the details, her talent was visible. It hurt to think of where her talent might have taken her if it weren't for that walk along the beach.

Hell, these days, simply hearing her name hurt.

And then Eva gave him the lighthouse sketch, and he thought he'd lose it. "Thank you," he managed to get out. Lifting his eyes to meet hers for the first time since looking at the mural, he saw how hard the discussion had been on her. She had been happy earlier in the evening. Joyous even. Now she looked sad.

He knew he should leave and head back home, but instead he lingered. Not wanting to leave. To somehow bring her happiness back. His gaze swept over Eva's desk and fell on a photo he remembered taking almost five years ago of Catherine and Eva. The two women knelt on the ground of the small communal garden they'd helped the Eden Beautification Committee plant. It was where Catherine had met Eva for the first time. Catherine had joined as a way to make herself take a break from painting and Eva had joined to meet people.

He remembered Catherine talking about the new historian at the Historical Society. She'd told him Eva reminded her a bit of his Nana. At his raised eyebrow, she'd added they both had a feisty personality tempered with kindness and a natural curiosity about the way the world was. He'd told her that was well and good, but she might want to keep that thought to herself because while he'd never claimed to be an expert on women, he doubted there were many who wanted to be compared to someone's grandmother. Catherine had laughed.

She had a beautiful laugh.

His first interaction with Eva had occurred not long after, just following a thunderstorm. It was during the summer, and a group of beachgoers discovered the skeleton of a ship uncovered by the storm's wind. Not an entirely uncommon event for the Outer Banks. Strange and wonderful things were always being found buried in the sand, especially after heavy winds. This particular ship, though somewhat persevered, wasn't safe, and he needed to keep people away from it until it could be removed by the state.

But apparently, Eva Knightly didn't think the "Keep Off" sign he'd put up applied to her. A few days after the ship had resurfaced, and the town of Eden was still waiting for the state to come by, he found her climbing on it. Of course, he didn't know who she was at the time.

"Are you looking for something or someone?" he'd asked her.

"Neither, *Officer*?" she'd asked, obviously wanting to get his name.

"Templeton," he answered.

Her eyes widened at his name, and he assumed that meant she'd at least heard of him.

"And you are?" He'd lifted an eyebrow.

"Trying to see if I can identify this ship."

"Yes, I can see that." He'd felt a bit awkward having a conversation with someone climbing the skeleton of ship. "I was hoping to get your name."

"Eva Knightly. Recently hired historian at the Historical Society. I think I met your wife the other day."

He gave her an amused smile. "Hello, Eva Knightly. Welcome to Eden, and yes, she mentioned you."

"Thank you." She had the appearance of someone who spent most of her life indoors and not out in the sun. Not only was her face pale, but her blonde hair was a light shade. He hoped she'd put sunblock on before heading outside.

He'd put his hands on his hips. "Is there something I can help you find?"

"No, I just need to gather a bit more information and maybe take a few pictures here."

"Unfortunately, I'm going to have to ask you come back down. As you can see, there's a sign telling people to keep off."

A look of outrage and disbelief had covered her face. "But I'm with the Historical Society!"

"I don't care if you're with Santa and the Easter Bunny. The sign says, 'Keep Off.'"

"But surely you don't mean me."

"I'm afraid I do, so I need you come down before I have to arrest you. Trust me, arresting you won't be fun for either one of us. You, because you'll be in jail, and me because I'll have to complete a pile of paperwork and more than likely piss off my wife."

She hadn't argued after that but climbed down. He'd thanked her, and they went their separate ways. When he told Catherine about it that night, she laughed and immediately called and asked Eva over for dinner. Noteworthy only because his wife barely knew how to boil water, much less cook, which meant it would be William preparing a meal for Eden's newest resident. Not that he minded; he enjoyed cooking, and from those first few meetings, a friendship was born.

Looking at the picture now, he was glad that Catherine had someone like Eva as a friend. He knew the separation had been difficult for Eva, and she'd done everything she could to not pick a side but to remain friends with him and Catherine both. He was grateful for her friendship.

Though the more he thought about it, neither grateful or friendship sounded intense enough.

"You really don't mind if I keep these?" He held up the photo album.

"No," Eva said, unshed tears glistening in her eyes. "You should have them. I think Catherine would have wanted you to have them."

"Thanks," he said. "I told you I removed myself from Gabby's case?"

"Yes," Eva said, eyeing him warily. "I think it was the right decision, for what it's worth."

"I know, but I can't do it." He looked down at his hands before looking up and continuing. "I went to Eden Methodist on my day off and talked to Robert about Gabby. Asked him questions."

"Are you kidding me?" she asked in an angry whisper. "Are you trying to get fired?"

"No," he replied. "I just can't sit around. Besides, Robert's my friend. It wouldn't strike anyone as strange for me to talk with him." He shrugged. "As long as I'm discreet about what I'm doing, and don't do anything stupid, I'll be okay."

Eva didn't reply right away but took a few seconds to think. He waited for her to tell him how foolish he was acting, and instead she shocked him.

"I really can't say anything, I guess," she said. "After hearing what the board was thinking about doing, I decided if I had to do the investigation myself, I'd do it."

He wouldn't have tried to stop his grin if he could. "Is that your way of offering to help me?"

She rolled her eyes. "Like I'd let you do this on your own. I'll have you know I can be very handy riding shotgun."

If I thought Mary had changed upon marrying Edward and becoming mistress of her own home, it was nothing when placed beside the changes now that she is a mother. I would have never thought the same girl who used to complain about getting up out of bed of a morning would rush to her newborn's side at every sigh, peep, or snore he made during the night.

— JOURNAL OF AN UNKNOWN WOMAN, EARLY 1700s

Chapter Eighteen

"**H**eard from Emerson?" Eva asked Amelia that Friday night over pizza. She didn't miss the way her friend's cheeks flushed at the question.

They'd called for delivery from Amelia's waterfront condo. The location would drive Eva batty. She didn't think she'd be able to deal with being surrounded by an ever-changing parade of tourists. Amelia, sounding exactly like her grandfather, shrugged and said she loved meeting so many new people all the time.

"Yes," Amelia said. "There's an estate sale he's going to in Beaufort tomorrow. He called yesterday and asked if I'd like to meet him there."

"He's a great guy, and an estate sale sounds like fun." Eva watched as Amelia refilled her plate with another slice of the veggie pizza she preferred. "It's an abomination to have that many vegetables on pizza."

Amelia rolled her eyes. "Just because you grew up eating New York pizza doesn't mean you're an expert on the subject."

"Yeah, it does."

"Whatever," Amelia said. "Tell me, oh wise one, if Emerson is such a great catch, why haven't you scooped him up?"

Eva wrinkled her nose at the thought. "Me and Emerson? No way. That'd be like dating my brother."

Amelia laughed. "You don't have a brother."

"True, but if I did, it'd be Emerson."

Amelia took a bit of her pizza and seemed to be thinking as she chewed. The smile she flashed at Eva spelled nothing but trouble.

"I heard your meeting with Stefan went well," Amelia said, eyes dancing.

Just as she'd thought, nothing but trouble. But the only person she could have heard that from was Stefan himself, which made Eva smile. Obviously, Stefan had been talking about her. Shouldn't she feel butterflies or something? "He's a nice guy," was all she said back, and he was. But that didn't mean he was the one for her.

"Fine," Amelia teased. "Don't tell me anything. I'll find out one way or another."

"There's really not that much to tell," Eva said. "We met and chatted. Had some coffee. He told me to call his admin and set up a time to come by his office. I'm seeing him on Tuesday."

"I knew the two of you would hit off," Amelia said with a self-satisfied smirk.

Eva gave her a questioning look. "Because of the maps?"

"Not just those, but yes, they're one reason. I also think your personalities complement each other. You both have this witty sarcasm that somehow draws people to you, but you're more grounded. He's more devil-may-care and exuberant. You both have that same drive to help."

Eva tilted her head in acknowledgement, remembering Stefan and Amelia laughing as they set out signs. Nope. Still nothing there.

"He's never changed," Amelia said. "He was the same way in high school, funny and charismatic. Always willing to lend a hand."

"I love how you and William know half the town from high school."

"Small town living." Amelia's brow furrowed. "Though I'm not sure Stefan and William ever spoke to each other in high school."

"I don't think they did based on what they told me." Eva shivered remembering the look of jealousy that had flashed so briefly when William saw her sitting with Stefan.

"Makes sense," Amelia nodded. "With William being a jock, and Stefan being class president, athletes and student government types rarely interacted."

Eva couldn't help but laugh at the ridiculousness of it all. "And what group were you in?"

Amelia's eyes danced with mischief. "No one could ever decide, so I considered myself a member of them all."

Her response was so perfectly Amelia, Eva laughed harder. Amelia joined in, and for several seconds, that was all they did.

Amelia grew pensive looking when they'd calmed down. It was such a startling contrast, Eva asked her what was wrong.

"I wonder if William will ever get married again?" Amelia asked, looking over Eva's shoulder.

"Are you serious?" Eva replied, nearly choking on the bite she'd just taken. "Catherine's only been gone for a year. Tell me you aren't trying to set him up."

"No, of course not."

But Eva knew her far too well. "Not yet, anyway."

They both laughed.

"You're probably right."

"I know I am," Eva said. "Aren't you the one who introduced Justin and Julia?"

"Yes, but even I thought they moved way too fast."

"I think it'll be a long time before William's ready to go out with anyone," Eva said.

"Why do you think that?"

"I think he feels guilty because things weren't great between him and Catherine, but he always thought he'd be able to fix it somehow. No one expected her to die, and now he's left with memories that probably aren't always the warm and fuzzy ones. And there's no fixing anything now. Plus, you know how he is, he won't be able to move on until he forgives himself, and I think it'll take a long time for him to do that."

"I always hated that they split up," Amelia said. "They seemed to be made for each other and were so happy when they got married."

Eva hesitated before asking her next question, not wanting to appear as if she was gossiping. "Do you know who Catherine was...seeing when her and William split?"

"No, I don't think anyone does." Amelia's voice indicated she believed what she said one hundred and ten percent. "But I do think something was going on with her for quite some time before she died."

Eva recalled thinking the very thing several times while Catherine worked on the mural in the museum. "Catherine and I had a standing coffee date every Tuesday after work," she told Amelia. "I remember one day, probably a few weeks before everything came to a head, and they separated, William sent her a text letting her know he was working late, and for her to grab something to eat before heading home because he wouldn't be there in time to cook dinner."

Amelia nodded. It had never been a secret that Catherine might have been the world's worst cook.

"I had the strangest thought that she looked sad and shouldn't be by herself and asked if she wanted to grab something with me," Eva continued. "But she didn't answer me. Instead, she said she shouldn't have married William because he was too good for her. Then she started talking about high school and the big crush she'd had on him then." She swallowed around the guilt that never seemed to leave.

"I remember that." Amelia wiped a tear away. "She totally did."

Eva nodded. "What shocked me was when she said if she had it to do over again, she'd force him to leave this godforsaken place but that now it was too late."

They were both silent for a moment.

"I hope he's able to be happy one day," Amelia said with a forlorn look on her face. "He's truly a good guy."

Eva agreed. "I remember the time he organized the first Back-to-School Drive to collect supplies for at-risk children to ensure they had the necessary items for class. Catherine told me William saw to it personally that there was a backpack for each child who needed one. Not long after, I was eating at the diner one morning when William came in for a cup of coffee to go. As he waited, a little boy came up beside him and tugged on his hand. William bent down to the child's level to see what he needed. The little boy thanked him for his backpack and told him he wanted to be a police chief when he grew up."

A long silence stretched between them. Finally, Eva shook her head. "I mentioned to William the other day how you'd be his boss if you're elected mayor."

"Right?" Amelia's eyes lit up. "How much fun would that be?"

"Too much," Eva agreed. "But seriously, how's the campaign going? I feel awful I haven't been able to help."

"Don't feel bad. You are more than busy at the moment," Amelia said. "Believe me, I'll have plenty for you to help with when the Blackbeard Festival is over."

"At least you didn't say canceled," Eva muttered.

"I'm not allowing myself to even consider that an option," Amelia said, lifting her chin. "Here. Take a look at this family tree. I think you'll be surprised."

Curious about the genealogy project Amelia mentioned at the last planning meeting for the Festival, and eager to get her mind on something else, Eva watched as she pulled a stack of papers from her messenger bag and placed one of them in front of her.

Eva noted the name at the top had been blacked out. "Is this a person I know?"

"Maybe," Amelia said. "They probably wouldn't care, but I don't feel as if I have a right to flash around someone's genealogy. We'll call this person Mr. X."

"As in X marks the spot?" Eva teased. "Does that mean Mr. X is a treasure?"

Amelia laughed. "I can't believe I didn't think about that."

Eva chuckled and glanced down at the paper. Still smiling as she skimmed, her breath caught at a name she recognized. "Wait a minute." She picked up the paper to make sure she read it right, and then followed the lineage. "Is this for real?"

"Of course," Amelia said, her eyes dancing in merriment.

"Mr. X is a direct descendant of Governor Eden?"

"Yes, but to be honest, he told me he was years ago," Amelia leaned over and whispered. "That's one of the reasons I picked him as my first to research. The second was, I wanted to see if he was lying."

"Sneaky."

Amelia didn't reply either way.

"What time are you meeting Emerson tomorrow?" Eva asked.

"Nine in the morning." Amelia's smile lit her entire face. "Do you have plans for the weekend?"

"Festival planning," she admitted, which sounded even more lame when she said it than it had in her head.

Because we had not informed anyone of Mary's pregnancy, we had no way to explain the sudden appearance of a baby. It kept me awake all through the night, sick with worry.

— **JOURNAL OF AN UNKNOWN WOMAN, EARLY 1700s**

Chapter Nineteen

On Monday morning, William and Eva met in her office to discuss security for the Blackbeard Festival. He'd asked for the meeting because he was concerned about the possibility of its cancellation.

"If I go with your initial request for security, I'll need to work with every police department and sheriff's office in five counties," he told her. "And I might have to bring in a private firm or two as well. But I don't want to line everyone up if it's going to be canceled."

Eva sighed. "And if you wait until too close to the date, no one will be available."

"Right."

"I understand why you need a more accurate projection," she said. "But I'm afraid if I push the board for an answer on the Festival's status, they'll decide the easiest thing to do is to go ahead and cancel it altogether."

William agreed. That was his fear as well.

"How close are we to getting the medical examiner's final findings on Gabby?" she asked.

"I wish I knew." William ran his fingers through his hair. "Mitch has called twice for updates but hasn't received anything solid. I keep thinking we'll hear something any day now, but I've been thinking that same thing for weeks. I've always known the lab is slow and has a backlog, but it's never struck me as how slow it could be or how much was on the backlog." He swallowed any further comments, knowing complaining about the lab wouldn't get the results to arrive any quicker.

"Can you wait a little longer before doing anything with security?" she asked.

"I suppose it won't hurt, but I'd be lying if I said I truly believe we'll know more any time soon."

She tapped her pen against her desk. "Why don't you come over to my place tomorrow night? We can put our heads together to see if we can find a new angle on the cases, and after we can eat dinner and watch the game."

Before Catherine died, the three of them, or four, when Grant had still been in the picture, would often get together to watch baseball. The closest national team was in DC, but they didn't care. Besides, Eva pulled for New York and was a lot of fun to annoy when they were down.

Yet another example, he knew, of how life kept going. Watching a game with Eva and not Catherine would feel just as odd as it would be to play a game with Robert without her being there. Sometimes grief felt how he assumed it would be to walk through a minefield, wondering if the next hour or minute would arrive carrying with it a memory destined to bring him to his knees.

"Sounds good," he said. "But let me bring dinner again. I might even cook something this time. It's been too long since I've had the opportunity to cook for more than just me."

Eva gave him a small smile. "I was talking with Amelia the other day about how Catherine couldn't boil water."

"The only thing she could do was reheat a casserole." William laughed as a forgotten memory came to mind. "I wasn't able to get through all the frozen casseroles people brought over when she died. Not that I'm complaining, I love that our community takes care of their own. I think every woman in Eden brought me a casserole. Every woman except one. You."

"Me?"

"You stopped by a week after her funeral, and the first thing I noticed was you didn't have a casserole dish. We sat on the swing outside."

"Yes," Eva said. "You said even though everyone knew we were friends, you didn't feel comfortable inviting a single woman into your house so soon after Catherine's death."

He nodded. "Do you remember what you told me?"

"No."

He wasn't surprised with her answer; she'd been close friends with Catherine and had still been grieving. "You spoke about your mother's death and how it felt as if everyone except you had moved on three days after the funeral, so you purposely came late to let me know how you understood there was no timeline for grief." His smile got bigger. "Then you reached in your purse and pulled out gift cards, one for Bliss Burger and one for American Pie Pizza. In case I got sick of casseroles, you said."

Eva wrinkled her eyebrows. "I actually had planned to cook you something, but when I made it to the grocery store, they were all out of cream of mushroom, and I said to myself, 'that man's probably sick of casseroles.'"

"American Pie makes a great pizza," William smiled. "And a very welcome change after seven straight days of casseroles."

Today, two months after Alexander Edward's birth, Mary received the letter she'd been waiting for, Edward would be returning home within the week.

— JOURNAL OF AN UNKNOWN WOMAN, EARLY 1700s

On Tuesday, Eva contemplated not doing breakfast, and sleeping in. She was tired because she'd stayed up late into the night trying to decide the best way to continue planning the Festival, and when she finally made it to bed, she found herself wide awake. But she'd missed breakfast for the last few days and wanted to eavesdrop on the foursome more than she wanted sleep, so she made herself get up and out of the house.

"I was at the police station yesterday," Elbert shared with his three companions, and his words jolted her awake more than the two cups of coffee she'd just downed.

"What were you arrested for?" Francis asked. "Talking too fast?"

"Or for sticking your nose into a no trespassing zone?" Maxine asked.

Both women cackled as if they'd told the best joke ever.

All Herb did was ask, "Who got arrested?"

"No one," Elbert said. "No one got arrested. I was there to talk to Peggy about the Vacation Bible School that First Baptist Church is doing next month."

"Are they starting that back up?" Maxine asked. "Lord, help us all. Were you telling her she wasn't invited if she brought any grandkids? I'm not sure the church has recovered from the last batch yet."

"The Lord said, 'Let the children come to me,' Maxine," Elbert said.

"Fine, then let them go to Him via Eden Methodist Church. They're having one, too."

"Anyway," Elbert said, trying to regain control of the conversation. "While we were speaking, a phone call came in for Officer Mitch, from Raleigh."

"The final report on Gabby?" Francis asked. "I thought that was due back days ago. They're late."

"And they'll be even later because some lab work has to be repeated, and the lab is having instrumentation issues."

"How much later?" Maxine asked.

"I don't know," Elbert said. "Mitch got pretty heated at that point, and Peggy closed his door."

Eva bet the acting chief wasn't the only one who got heated upon hearing the news. Until the final report was released, William wouldn't be able to reclaim his position. But what bothered her even more was what Elbert said before then. He'd said labs had to be repeated, but not why, only that the lab had instrumentation issues. Was it because of equipment failure, and they didn't believe a negative result? Or did something unexpected show up in the first result and they'd been unable to confirm?

She bit her thumbnail. It never occurred to her there was a possibility Catherine's death had been something other than a tragic accident. Her brain couldn't make sense of it. Who would have killed Catherine?

Along with that thought came the uneasy realization that if both women had been killed, the Festival probably did need to be canceled.

She wasn't ready to accept that yet.

They needed both cases closed, and it needed to happen now. She was so glad William would be over later tonight. They had a lot of work to do.

She glanced at the time. It was still too early for William to be at work, but she looked over her shoulder to check the parking lot at the police station anyway. As expected, she didn't see his truck, only the cruiser he generally left in the lot overnight.

"I was thinking," Maxine said.

"Not again," Herb muttered.

Maxine sent him an icy stare. "Let's suppose those lab tests do come back showing something on Gabby. That probably means there's a connection to Catherine's death. And you know, just because Catherine was found in the sand, doesn't mean she died there. Maybe she was killed and then buried in the sand."

"I guess it could happen that way, but I don't think it did. Haven't you read the warnings about sand holes?" At Maxine's shrug, Elbert continued, "Why are you so certain it wasn't an accident?"

"Because it makes more sense to me that it wasn't an accident and, like I've said before, most of the time it's someone close who turns out to be the culprit," Maxine replied.

"Chief Templeton didn't kill his wife," Elbert said.

Maxine didn't say anything, and even though Eva wanted to crane her neck to see if she'd made any kind of expression, she held herself still.

"I can't believe what you're suggesting," Elbert said, anger evident in his tone.

"I didn't suggest anything. I didn't say a word." Maxine sounded just as angry as Elbert. "But since you brought it up, Catherine fell into a hole and died? You can't tell me anyone believes that's what happened. It might be the stupidest way to die I've ever heard of."

The sudden silence caught Eva off guard, and she looked around to find the nearby tables had all stopped talking, entranced by the foursome's much-too-loud conversation. Eva risked a quick look at Maxine. The older lady had meticulously painted red nails and her powder gray bouffant had likely been professionally poofed recently. What struck Eva the most, however, was the absence of any remorse or shame.

Maxine calmly stood, took a twenty-dollar bill out of her purse, and placed it on the table. "Speechless, Elbert? It'll be the first time in forty years." With that said, she turned and walked out of the diner, head up, shoulders back, and looking at no one.

Though conversation picked back up around them, the table of the now threesome remained quiet. Eva couldn't help but wonder how many of Eden's residents felt the same as Maxine. Admittedly, when Eva first heard the official word on how Catherine died, she thought it sounded strange, but she'd accepted that was what happened.

No longer hungry, she left soon after.

THE DAY BEFORE, Eva had received a call from Stefan to see if she'd like to have lunch together. She agreed, telling herself it was not a date but just two people getting together to talk about history.

There was a little deli named Ray's near his office she'd never been to. When Stefan found out, he told her she couldn't live on the Outer Banks if she hadn't had at least one of Ray's sandwiches, adding the owner's grandparents were the ones who'd owned Sam's Sandwiches. Before her breakfast in the diner, she'd been looking forward to trying Ray's even if it was with Stefan. But after hearing Maxine talk about William the way she did, and the possibility that Catherine's death might not have been an accident, she didn't really feel like going out for lunch or looking at maps.

She ended up not calling Stefan to reschedule because it was too close to when they'd agreed to meet, and she hated it when people canceled on her at the last minute.

If Ray's had been closer, she'd have walked. Or maybe not, she decided once she stepped outside and the humidity surrounded her like a hot wet blanket.

Stefan, on the other hand, didn't look grimy at all, she noted, spotting him near the front of the deli. It amazed her how he managed to look perfect, standing there, waiting. All while wearing a light gray suit that looked tailor-made for him. He smiled at her approach.

"Good afternoon, Eva," he said. "This time and place still work for you? You look a bit stressed."

"Yes, the time and place are perfect," she replied, thinking *a bit stressed* was an understatement. "Thank you," she said when he opened the deli's door for her. "And yes, I'm a bit stressed. Just a lot going on."

"Not a good day for history?" Stefan asked.

"Just too much going on," she repeated, not wanting to discuss Catherine's death or its possible connection to Gabby's with a man who was little more than a stranger to her.

After placing her order at a window, Eva picked a booth not far from the entrance. Once Stefan joined her, she asked about his job, not in a mood to discuss anything about herself.

If he noticed the subtle switch she pulled on him, he didn't say anything. He launched into a story about the last conference he went to, keeping her entertained with the antics of his peers. He turned out to be quite the conversationalist, though that shouldn't have been a surprise, she supposed, seeing as how he seemed to be good at anything.

She glanced around at the crowd gathered inside the small restaurant. There was an odd combination of people. Almost half of the crowd was obviously tourists, as expected on a summer day, but a small percentage wore business attire and the remaining looked to be year-round residents. It wasn't usual for an establishment to appeal to that many people. Most of the places catered to one or the other.

What was even more surprising was how quickly their food was brought to the table considering the number of people eating at the same time.

"Wow," Eva said, looking her turkey, cranberry, and cheese. "That was fast."

"Years of practice, I expect," Stefan said.

Eva took a bite and quickly lost interest in anything else. The deli made their own bread daily, and the slices used for her sandwich were still warm from the oven. Heaven. She couldn't swallow the groan at how delicious the sandwich tasted.

"I can't believe I've never been here," she said, once she was able to put her sandwich down for a second.

"I can't either," Stefan said, with a smile. "Obviously, someone failed in their duties to show you how to be a proper year-round resident of the Outer Banks."

"Right?" Eva played along. "I hate to think what else I wasn't told."

They both laughed and spent the next few minutes talking about their favorite restaurants, which led to other favorites. It wasn't long until Stefan mentioned sports, and she shocked him by saying she didn't follow college basketball.

"You know they can kick you out of the state of North Carolina for that?" Stefan teased.

"I'll have to take my chances," Eva said. "I've never been a fan of basketball. Now baseball, on the other hand..."

They'd finished eating and had just made it outside.

"Would you like to walk instead of driving?" Stefan asked. "We can leave your car here, and I'll walk you back after our meeting. Or if you prefer, I can drive you back here."

"I'd like to walk," Eva said. "And since there's a bit of a breeze, it's much more bearable to be outside."

Stefan was right, the walk wasn't long or too far. Of course, it helped that he was also a baseball fan. They compared favorite teams and players as they walked.

"Just ahead on your left," he said, pointing.

Stefan's office looked like a small house. Made entirely of brick, it was tucked in the corner of the lot, just on the line separating the business and residential areas of the island. Eva wasn't sure what she'd expected, but somehow the house suited him.

He opened the door and let her enter first. She was met with a warm and inviting interior of muted yellow, green, and blue. His admin, Naomi, who Eva had called to set up the appointment, sat behind what looked like an antique desk. After an introduction from Stefan, Naomi offered to get water for them.

While she retrieved the water, Eva walked around looking at the various pictures Stefan had scattered throughout the room. She found several of him with a woman she took to be his mother but none with his father. An older-looking picture with muted colors sitting on a table near an armchair caught her eye, and she looked closer.

It couldn't be.

She picked the picture up.

No way.

"Eva?" Stefan asked.

"Where did you get this?" She showed him the picture she didn't remember taking. A group photo of all the members of the Six Pack, the first friends she'd made on the Outer Banks, all those years ago. Two rows of three. She was on the back row, and her grin was so big, it nearly broke her heart because she knew all the grief the girl in the photo would soon go through.

On her right side was Lady, and everyone considered her the leader. PC was on her left; the girls had called him Prince Charming until he convinced them to shorten it to PC. In the front row stood Noodles, named after what he ate for almost every meal. Mimi, the youngest of the bunch, was directly in front of Eva. The last member was Casper, a young boy who had a habit of disappearing.

"My mother took it." Stefan walked toward her.

From the corner of her eye, she saw Naomi appear and Stefan waved her away. Then he was by her side, a comforting hand on her shoulder. "Are you okay? You look like you've seen a ghost."

His mother. She looked at each of the boys in the photo. It had been so long, she'd forgotten the subtle details that made them all unique. But the boy standing to her side in the photo...

She looked up at Stefan. "You're PC."

His forehead wrinkled. "How do you know that name?"

She tapped the image of her younger self but didn't say anything.

"Jersey?" he asked, and at her nod, he exclaimed, "I can't believe it!"

After that realization, Stefan ended up having Naomi cancel the meeting he had scheduled next. Then he sat down with Eva in the small sitting area just inside the front door so they could catch up. The first thing he did was print off a copy of the photo for her. Then he told her to remain seated because he had more news for her.

Intrigued, Eva sat forward. Stefan told her to look closely at the girl standing in front of her in the picture. She smiled, remembering. "Mimi," she told Stefan. No one forgot Mimi. The youngest and shortest member had also been the funniest and one of the boldest.

"Yes," he said, grinning. "Look closer."

Eva relooked at the image of the eleven-year-old with two pigtails and tried to picture her aged. She gasped. "Amelia?"

Stefan nodded. "She'll flip when she finds out. Matter of fact..." He pulled his phone from his pocket. "I want to see her face when you call her Mimi. I'm going to send her a text to come see me right now. I'll tell her Jersey's here."

Eva giggled. How crazy was it that Jersey and Mimi were friends and that over twenty years later they'd meet as Amelia and Eva and unknowingly became friends again? "How about the other guys?" she asked. "Are they still around here?"

"Noodles and his family moved to Georgia—Atlanta, I believe—the summer before he started high school. We lost touch soon after. Casper worked for that movie they filmed around here several years ago."

"*The Marshlands*?" Eva asked.

"Yes, did you watch it?"

Eva laughed. "Only about a thousand times."

The movie had released a year or so after she finished graduate school, and she'd lost track of how many times she'd watched it. She remembered scanning the extras to see if she recognized anyone, which she did not, and the scenery to see if they'd filmed at any location she'd visited as a child. While there were several places she had, most of them had been unknown to her because a large part of the story involved Corolla and its wild ponies. Corolla wasn't an area she had explored with the Six Pack.

"What did Casper do on the film?" she asked.

"He was the vet they had onsite to watch after the ponies."

"Casper became a veterinarian?" Eva tried to picture the freckled-faced boy she remembered as a vet and failed.

"Yes," Stefan confirmed. "And that's not the best part."

"It gets better?"

Stefan gave her a knowing wink. "He fell in love with the supporting actress and moved to California. They've been married for ages now."

"No way." The only supporting actress it could be was Tensely Taylor, but Eva couldn't imagine that being possible.

"I can't make this up."

"Do you ever hear from him?" she couldn't help but ask.

"Not since his wife won her first Oscar a few years ago. Tensely Taylor?"

"The gorgeous redhead, who, besides being a beautiful,

accomplished actress, can also sing and make the angels cry?" At his nod, she narrowed her eyes. "Now you're just pulling my leg."

Stefan held up his hand. "Scout's honor."

"I don't believe you were ever a Boy Scout, either."

They both laughed. Eva pointed to Lady in the photo. "Do you know anything about where Lady ended up?"

All traces of levity left his expression, replaced by a somber look. He brushed a finger across the image. "Yes," he said, his voice sounding oddly pained.

She looked up from the photo to him, but his focus was on the picture.

"Lady was Catherine Harper."

EVA WAITED OFF to the side of Stefan's lobby, in order not to be seen from the door. She heard a car door slam, and several seconds later, Amelia.

"In four hours, I'm leaving for an out-of-town project. Are you out of your mind?" her friend asked Stefan, closing the door behind her as she stepped inside. "I haven't thought about that summer in ages." Amelia's gaze fell on Eva. "Hi, Eva," she said, then turned back to Stefan. "What's this about Jersey?"

Stefan tilted his head toward Eva. Amelia looked her way again, and Eva watched the understanding dawn across her face. "No way."

"I said the same thing," Eva confessed.

Amelia looked intently at her. "I can see it now that I know," she grinned. "This is the second-best day ever."

"Only the second, Mimi?" Stefan asked. "I'm crushed."

"You're a big boy." Amelia patted his chest. "You'll get over it."

"At least tell me what's at number one."

"Beaufort."

Eva had forgotten for a moment that Amelia had seen Emerson on Saturday. "You didn't call to tell me how it went."

"I was going to call you this afternoon before I left," Amelia said.

"Beaufort?" Stefan asked. "The only interesting thing about Beaufort is when one of those big houses has an estate sale."

Amelia and Eva both started laughing, exactly the way they had all those summers ago.

Stefan rolled his eyes. "Good to know some things never change."

I needed extra yarn today and went into Mary's room to check her supply while she was out with Alexander Edward. Her mending basket was unexpectedly heavy and I dug to the bottom to discover why. I cannot believe what I found and I hesitate to write it here.

Coins. A multitude of them. Gold ones with strange words. Could it be pirate treasure? I had observed Edward's men on occasion digging around the island, but assumed he bid them to do so in order to confuse any onlookers. Was there an actual treasure? And Mary had part of it?

— JOURNAL OF AN UNKNOWN WOMAN, EARLY 1700s

Chapter Twenty-one

After returning to her office much later than she'd expected, Eva found she couldn't concentrate on anything. Now that the excitement of learning Stefan and Amelia were Six Pack members had abated a bit, the ache of Catherine's death intensified. She kept hearing Stefan say, "Lady was Catherine Harper," over and over in her head. The ache wasn't the sharp pain of the day she learned Catherine was gone. She doubted she'd be able to describe it adequately. The closest she could come was to say the ache was for the girl Catherine had been that summer. The one she only knew as Lady.

Realizing she wasn't going to be productive for the rest of the day, she decided to head home early. William would be at her house in a few hours, and leaving early would ensure she had time to get everything ready.

When they'd made the plan for work, dinner, and baseball, she'd been looking forward to spending time with William. With the afternoon she'd had, however, she was looking forward to it even more. She said goodbye to Julia, told the front desk she was leaving for the day, and headed home.

She didn't notice anything strange until she'd parked her car in the driveway and walked toward her front door. Normally, she entered through the side door, but she assumed William would be entering through the front. There had been a thunderstorm the night before, and she wanted to make sure the stoop was somewhat clean since the wind had a habit of covering it in a fine sand.

Was it her imagination or did the curtain in her front window look askew? Probably her imagination, she rarely saw the window from this viewpoint. She made it to her front door when her phone beeped with an incoming text. It was William.

Decided to leave work early. Stopped by the Historical Society and saw you had the same idea. I'm on my way over, if that's okay with you? I'm almost there.

She rolled her eyes at his formality.

She replied, Works for me. See you soon. And added a smiley face just for fun. Unlocking her door, she stepped inside and froze. Papers, glass, and what looked like foam from cushions littered her floor.

Someone had wrecked her house.

Something moved out of the corner of her eye.

Someone was still in her house.

No, she decided, she'd only thought she'd seen something move. She remained still as if to prove she was right and it wouldn't happen again. Later, when she looked back and tried to remember what exactly happened in those next few seconds, she'd realize she'd been in shock.

As it happened, it was as if each sound, each sight, each everything played out in front of her in slow motion, with every sense she had operating on overdrive.

The silence of the neighborhood sounded strange compared to the near deafening noise she eventually recognized as the beating of her heart. She shoved her hand into the tote, desperate to pull her phone back out, but her fingers fumbled around it, unable to grab hold.

Have to get out.

She turned her head and saw it was much too late. Whoever it was had reached her and swung at her head. Pain exploded from the impact in a flash of bright yellow lights, engulfing her, and making her fall.

Fall.

Nothing.

AFTER A TIME, she began to hear the world around her, not as one loud combination of sound but each individual part. The steady beat she assumed was her heart. The whoosh of air through her lungs. Pain. Everywhere. She tried to sit up but couldn't get her muscles to agree.

Where was she?

There was a presence nearby. She felt it, but couldn't tell who it was. She couldn't see. Why couldn't she see?

Panic set in. *Oh, God.*

"Eva! Eva!"

Someone called her name, and she opened her eyes. William.

He was talking, but Eva couldn't hear anything he said, she only saw his lips move.

No matter. She was safe. She wanted to tell him something, but her body hurt too much, and she was so tired.

She'd close her eyes.

Just for a minute.

Mary insisted I write down her recollection of the day she met Edward. She told me I was to give it to Alexander Edward if anything happened to her. I told her she was being foolish. What could possibly happen to her? But she would not stop until I agreed. This is what she told me of that day.

Her head was down in thought as she approached the tide pools, which was why she didn't see him at first. It wasn't until she was almost right on top of him that she felt as if someone was watching her. She looked up and into the clearest green eyes she'd ever seen.

A second later, she took a step back, saw the rest of him, and knew immediately who he was. Everyone in the area had heard stories of Blackbeard. Her mind told her she should be frightened; she was in the presence of a man the world thought was a dangerous criminal. Yet she didn't feel frightened at all. She looked in those deep green eyes and only felt safe.

Actually, if she read him correctly, he looked more shocked than anything. She found that to be rather odd. Why would he be shocked? Had she come upon his hiding place and caught him off guard? If he knew the area the way she thought he did, surely he knew this was a popular spot for crabbing.

More than likely it was that he didn't spend much time around women. Or perhaps those that he typically came upon, or as in her case, those that came upon him, usually dissolved into a fit of vapors once they realized who he was.

She smiled. The one thing she was not going to do was have a fit. He blinked, and laughably, looked even more shocked. The smile, she guessed. He probably hadn't expected that.

Of course, she hadn't either.

"You might want to watch where you're going in the future," he said.

"Why?" she asked. "Is there somebody or something I should be on the lookout for?"

He chuckled. "You do know who I am, right?"

She put her hands on her hips and tilted her head. "Right now you look like a man in need of soap and a shave."

"I don't shave," he said.

"I can tell." Heaven help her. She was flirting with Blackbeard. She must be completely mad. But she didn't stop. "In fact, that was why I suggested it in the first place."

This time he was the one who smiled. She rather liked his smile. It made him even more handsome.

Gracious. Blackbeard handsome? Everyone would think her out of her mind.

Everyone would be correct. She had to be out of her mind because not only did she think him handsome, but she also liked his accent. It was different from anything she had heard before and sounded almost musical. If she listened hard enough, she could hear whispers of faraway beaches and castles she'd read about in some of the books the governor had.

"I see," he said and scratched his beard. "Unfortunately, I don't have time for either at the moment. I applied for a land grant and I have to finish gathering the details I need to correct what they have down as the property boundaries."

She was so caught up in listing to his accent, she almost failed to comprehend what he'd just said. "You bought this land?"

It was hard to imagine why anyone would want it, other than for the crabs. Most of it was boggy marsh as far as the eye could see, and there was very little land on which anyone could build a house. She told him as much, and he just smiled.

"Oh," she said. "I understand. You aren't planning to build a house, are you?"

"No," he said, a hint of amusement in his voice. "I'm not."

"Are you going to bury treasure?" She didn't understand how it was she could be so bold with him.

"Are you always so full of questions?" He raised an eyebrow, and in doing so emphasized a scar right above his left eyebrow. It had to have been a painful wound, right above the eye like that. His hat hitting it every so often.

"How did you get that scar? Was it a knife?" Seeing the scar should have driven home the fact that she was both alone and talking to a dangerous man, but it didn't. She didn't feel unsafe or fearful at all.

"I suppose that would be a yes to my previous question." He still sounded amused, and she detected no note of anger or irritability.

"If I don't ask questions, how will I learn anything?" she asked.

"Indeed," was all he said, leveling his glance and not looking away, even as she found herself once more captivated by his green eyes.

She blinked, trying to break whatever spell it was his eyes put her in. It was rather odd, she thought, for a pirate to apply for a land grant. Insofar as she'd never heard of a pirate owning land before. But of course they would, would they not? She doubted anyone could stay on a ship forever, and a pirate needed a place to bury his treasure.

She gasped as the truth hit her. "This is your land."

"Yes," he answered simply. "It is."

"And I'm trespassing."

"Yes. You are."

She narrowed her eyes. "Are you going to take me back to your ship and make me walk the plank?"

Mary couldn't stop the smile from covering her face as the infamous pirate roared with laughter.

— JOURNAL OF AN UNKNOWN WOMAN, EARLY 1700s

Chapter Twenty-two

"Sir." A gentle but insistent hand moved William away from where he'd been kneeling beside Eva. In his mind he kept replaying the moment he caught sight of Eva right as the dark figure hit her and darted out of her house. She fell, and William's heart stopped, even as he yelled for whoever it was to put their hands up.

They took off instead, and William wasn't able to chase after them, not when he saw Eva. Not that it would have made a difference if he had. The back of Eva's house sat adjacent to several acres of woodland; it'd be near to impossible to chase the man down.

Instead, William jogged up to her front door stoop where he found Eva unconscious. She didn't appear to be bleeding from what he could see, though a faint red hue started to bloom on her chin. But her breathing was steady, and when he took her pulse, it was strong under his fingers. He wasn't sure if she could hear him or not, as she zoned in and out in the handful of moments it took for the first responders to get to where they were.

"She opened her eyes once," he told the team assessing her. "I'm fairly certain she recognized me, but she didn't speak."

The two men did nothing to indicate they'd heard him. They placed a support around her neck and lifted her onto a gurney. "We're going to take her to the hospital in Nags Heads for assessment. If we need to, we'll carry her to Pitt County."

William hoped her injury wasn't severe enough to warrant taking her to Pitt County, which was a good two hours away. One of the downsides to living where they did was the location of the nearest level one trauma center. "I'll follow."

Two hours later, William couldn't stop his body from shaking. He stood with his back against the hospital waiting room wall, afraid his knees would give out if he stepped away. He still couldn't get over how fragile she looked when she fell. Since it'd been so long, he assumed they weren't going to transfer her anywhere, but no one had told him anything. He'd tried contacting Amelia but hadn't been able to reach her. After calling her office, he learned she was on her way to the southernmost point of the Outer Banks, with no cell reception. He left an urgent message to have her call him, but he hadn't heard from her yet.

"Chief Templeton?"

William looked up to find the emergency department physician on call, frowning at him. "Yes?" He took a step away from the wall.

The doctor appeared to be in his mid-fifties. His hair held more salt than pepper, and the wrinkles around his eyes suggested he did know how to smile. "We've stabilized Ms. Knightly and expect a full recovery, but we're going to keep her overnight because she took a significant blow to her head. Doesn't look like a concussion." His frown deepened. "We've transferred her to a room and have her as comfortable as possible, but I recommend you leave her for tonight and question her tomorrow."

No wonder the man was frowning. He was under the assumption William stayed at the hospital only for a chance to question Eva.

"At the moment, I'm not here on a professional level," William said. "Eva is a friend of mine, and I'm concerned about her. She's awake? Can I see her?"

The doctor didn't look convinced and continued to stare at him, assessing the truth of his words, perhaps. William refused to back down. Damn it all. He wasn't going to take a step outside of the hospital until he saw her with his own eyes.

The doctor nodded once. "Come with me."

William followed him down the hall and up a flight of stairs. They came to a stop outside of a door near the small nurse's station.

"This is Ms. Knightly's room," the doctor said. "I'll let the charge nurse know you're here. I suggest no more than fifteen minutes."

There was no doubt in William's mind that in fifteen minutes exactly, the charge nurse would be in Eva's room to ensure William left. It didn't make him angry or upset. It pleased him the hospital was so adamant about patient safety. He told the doctor he understood and would not overstay his welcome.

Once the doctor made it to the nurse's station, William knocked softly on Eva's door and eased it open. He stepped inside, surprised to see her awake and sitting slightly reclined in the hospital bed.

"I'm so glad you're awake," he said. He'd wondered why she hadn't said anything when he knocked if she was awake, but it only took a quick glance at the growing bruise on her chin to see why she hadn't.

She started to open her mouth, but he held up a hand to stop her. "You probably shouldn't be talking."

The look she replied with gave her opinion on that, but for whatever reason, maybe the doctor had advised her the same, she remained quiet.

"I only have a few minutes," he told her. "I promised not to stay over fifteen minutes and to hold my questions for tomorrow, but I had to come see you with my own eyes. I called Amelia and left a message because she's traveling this afternoon. I'm not sure when she'll be back in town. Is there someone else I can call for you?"

She shook her head and pointed to the door. He took that to mean the hospital staff had already taken care of that.

"Is someone coming?" he asked because he couldn't stand the thought of her being alone.

She nodded.

"Good." He took a deep breath. Finding her the way he did, the wait to find out how she was, and even now, seeing her in the bed with the bruising of her chin, it reminded him of how helpless he'd felt when they found Catherine's body.

By the time they allowed him to see his late wife for official identification, she was in the morgue, and though he never saw her on the beach, it was a scene his mind recreated for him. How broken she must have looked. He didn't sleep for months after, knowing that the images waiting to meet him in his dreams were worse.

"I'll be back bright and early in the morning." He squeezed her shoulder gently. "And get some rest because my top priority is to find out who did this."

He wouldn't stop until he found that person and made sure they were held accountable. A glance at the clock told him his time was up. Before he could say anything, the door swung open and a woman he recognized from the Historical Society, but didn't know personally, rushed in.

"Eva," she cried. "What in the world? I came as fast as I could. What happened? No, don't talk. Not yet."

Eva's eyes smiled as the woman approached her.

"Dear God," the woman said, taking in the sight of her chin. "The hospital called me and said you'd been attacked. Do they know who did it yet?"

Eva pointed to William.

The woman turned and leveled her green eyes on him, taking in his stance and badge. "Are you law enforcement?"

"Yes, ma'am," he said, holding out his hand. "Eden Police Department, William Templeton."

She shook his hand. "Julia Baxter. Why are you in here and not out there finding who did this?"

He liked that Julia was so protective. "I plan to join my men as soon as I know Eva's well and in good hands." He tilted his head. "How do you know her, out of curiosity?"

"Eva, hm?" She hummed, and he wondered if he should have called her Ms. Knightly. "I work with her at the Historical Society, but Eva saved my life once, and no one will hurt her on my watch."

Satisfied Eva was in good hands, William slipped out of the room a few minutes later.

Next on his list was to follow up with Mitch to see if he found anything.

It has always shocked me how often people misquote the Bible. I have heard the phrase, "Money is the root of evil," incorrectly stated as 1 Timothy 6:10 numerous times. However, the verse actually reads, "Love of money is the root of all kinds of evil." Someone, somewhere thought it sounded better with the "Love of," and "kinds of" left out and others agreed. But no matter how you say it, evil and money always seem to be together.

— **JOURNAL OF AN UNKNOWN WOMAN, EARLY 1700s**

Chapter Twenty-three

"How is she?"

Mitch waited for his return from the hospital, sitting behind the desk William saw as his.

"They're keeping her overnight but expect a full recovery. She was alert, and I was able to see her before I left. Has a friend staying with her." William nodded toward the computer Mitch was working on. "Find anything?"

"I followed his tracks down to the inlet, but lost him in the water. There were no boats."

"His? Him?" William asked. "Did you confirm the subject was male?"

"No, but it's unlikely they're a woman."

"Unlikely, yes. Impossible, no." It was a lesson he drilled into his force as many times as he could. "If we ignore the unlikely, we may be blinding ourselves to the actual. Don't assume we're looking for a man."

Mitch exhaled deeply. William didn't care if he was talking like he was the chief. He was and he would be again.

"Did you find any evidence at the scene?" William asked.

"Nothing was found in the area where Ms. Knightly was. They're still processing the house," Mitch replied. "But, like I said, there was no boat, and the dog lost the trail in the water. No abandoned cars were found anywhere in the nearby vicinity. Most likely means whoever it was probably arrived on foot."

"Without a car or boat at hand, it doesn't sound like they planned on kidnapping her." Not that William thought it likely, but one had to look at all the possibilities. Not to mention, it never hurt to be able to mark something off the list.

"We also have ears to the ground to see if this was a contract job," Mitch said.

"Is there a reason to think it might be?"

"One of the techs processing the house said it looked like a professional job to her based on how and what was damaged, and what was left alone."

"I thought they hadn't finished processing it yet?" William asked.

"They haven't. This was off the record."

William didn't like off the record. Off the record meant there was no responsibility. No accountability if the person off the record ended up being wrong. "Let's wait and see if that's the overall thought once they finish and are able to give us their thoughts on the record."

Mitch nodded.

"Anything else?" William asked.

"Were you able to talk to Ms. Knightly?"

"Not about what happened." William ran his hand through his hair. "The physician on call told me to wait and question her tomorrow. I'm on board with that decision, especially after seeing her. Her jaw's really bruised. But fortunately, she doesn't have a concussion."

Damn, he had to find out who did that to her. Out of the corner of his eye, he saw something flash across Mitch's computer screen. Mitch pulled something up and cursed under his breath, all while typing furiously.

"What's going on?" William asked.

"Ms. Knightly's next-door neighbor on the side you saw the subject flee?" At William's nod, Mitch continued, "They have a few security cameras around their house, and I was hoping one of them caught the guy. One of our men just went by there to ask. Apparently, the cameras are battery operated, and they stopped working last month. Batteries haven't been replaced. Damn it."

Damn it was right. It would have been nice to have video footage. But William had confidence in the men and women who worked for him. They'd find the person responsible.

"What's your plan for the evening?" Mitch asked.

"I have a few more things to work on before I head home."

Mitch nodded. "I'm going to call it a day. I've worked late every night for the last week, and I promised the family I'd try to get home at a decent hour today."

Listening to Mitch talk reminded Willian of all the times he'd worked late in the past. How often had he promised Catherine the same thing? But that wasn't the right question to ask. No, the right question to get to the heart of the issue would be, *how often had he promised to be home on time, and actually followed through?* Not very often, he feared.

"I do have one more thing I'd like to discuss," Mitch said. "Close the door, please."

Curious, William stood up, closed the door, and sat back down.

"This doesn't leave the office," Mitch said, and William nodded. "I know, officially, you're off Gabby Clark's case, and you were never on Catherine's. Unofficially, however, I wanted to let you know that if you were to do some investigational work on your own and happen to find something, I'm not going to tell anyone."

William's mouth dropped open, and for several seconds he couldn't speak. "Why would you do that? It could get you fired."

"Because Catherine was my friend, and I have a feeling there's more to her death than we originally thought. And I find it harder and harder to convince myself Gabby drowned. I'd feel better going up against whatever's going on with my chief at my side."

William remained dumbfounded. "Thank you," he finally said.

"Nothing to thank me for. Officially, I haven't done anything." Mitch stood up and punched his shoulder on his way out. "Don't stay here all night."

HOURS LATER, William wasn't sure what time it was, Peggy walked in and stood next to the cubicle desk he'd taken over. He'd stayed late in an attempt to get through at least some of the endless paperwork he never seemed to get caught up on.

"What are you still doing here, and what time is it?" He moved to sit up and his back told him in excruciating detail why it wasn't a good idea to sit in the same position for a long time.

"I'm not sill here. I left and came back." She lifted a paper bag. "I brought you dinner."

Fried pork chops, probably with green beans and mashed potatoes based on the heavenly scent floating from the bag. His stomach growled an angry reminder at how long it'd been since he'd had something to eat. "You did?"

"Yes." Peggy moved so she stood directly in his line of sight. "I was at the diner buying a pie for my Sunday School girls. We have a luncheon tomorrow and I didn't feel like making one. As soon as I got out of my car, I saw your truck still sitting here. I knew you had been here almost all day and probably hadn't stopped to have dinner. It's nearly nine." She eyed the mess of papers on his desk. "Are you going to eat here or should I take it out front?"

"You can take it out front," he said. "I need to get out of this chair."

Peggy gave him a look he translated into, *that's for certain.* But when she spoke it was to ask, "How's Eva doing?"

"I saw her a few hours ago, and she was awake," he told her. "She should be able to go home tomorrow according to the doctor. I'm going to go by the hospital in the morning around eight and ask her a few questions. I'll have Mitch take her statement later." He realized he sounded like he was rambling, so he stopped talking and stood up. "Thanks for picking up dinner. I'm starving."

"Do you know where she's going tomorrow?"

William stopped and turned to look back. "Who?"

"Eva," Peggy said. "I can't imagine she's ready to face that house just yet."

Damn. He blamed the hours of paperwork on his head not quite working right because normally he'd have been on top of the housing situation.

EVA WAS ALONE in her room when William stopped by the next morning. The bruising on her chin was more colorful, but otherwise, she looked better than the last time he saw her. She was sitting up in bed as opposed to reclining, and the color had returned to her face.

"Good morning," William said. "I won't ask how you slept because you're in the hospital, so it's a given you slept like crap." That at least, got half a smile from her.

"You don't look like you slept all that well, either," she said.

He shrugged. "Part of the job. Crime never sleeps and rarely takes a day off. Has your friend left?"

"Julia? Yes, she left early this morning. She had to go into the office because she has half a dozen volunteers starting today. I told her she didn't have to stay last night and that I'm fine, but she wouldn't listen. She said to let her know when they released me and she'd come pick me up."

"What time are they going to do that?"

"I'm not sure, but I hope it's before noon."

"Once you've recovered a bit more, I want you to come by the station, and Mitch is going to get your statement from yesterday."

She went a bit pale at the mention of the day before, and a hint of fear touched her eyes. "Did you find them?" she asked in a whisper.

What he wouldn't give at that moment to tell her yes, that they had captured the person who had attacked her, put her in here, and destroyed her home. That she shouldn't worry because justice would be served.

He sighed. He couldn't.

"Unfortunately, no, we didn't, but we will. You can count on it."

She nodded and looked away, but not before he saw the tears pool in her eyes. "I figured that's what you'd say."

"It's only a matter of time before we find the person responsible." William had stopped by the station before heading to the hospital so he'd have an update to give her. "It appears as if the subject was looking for something, and you interrupted them."

"Two questions," Eva said. "One, why do you call him the subject? It makes him sound like something you're studying as opposed to someone who wrecked my home before knocking me unconscious. You don't think I did this to myself, do you?"

"Of course not. It's the way the American justice system works. Innocent until proven guilty. The word *suspect* implies guilt."

"I get that," she said. "But you need different words to use in cases like this."

"I'll tell the higher-ups at the Department of Justice you think so."

She rolled her eyes. "Question two, why do you think he was looking for something?"

"That's the assumption based on how and what was damaged," he said. "In addition, there were several valuable items left untouched. Typically, if someone had broken into your house for a simple robbery, those items would be gone. When you feel up to doing so, you need to go through everything to see if anything's missing that we might have overlooked." William was thankful all the coins were in a safe deposit box at the bank.

"Speaking of," Eva said. "I see my purse, but do you know where my tote bag is, or at least who has it?"

"Your tote bag?" he asked, trying to remember if anyone had mentioned one. He thought back to the scene yesterday. Was there a tote bag on the porch with Eva? He didn't think so, but then again, he didn't remember seeing the purse either and it had obviously been nearby.

His hesitation and expression must have been all Eva needed for an answer because her face paled. "Oh my God," she said. "He has my tote bag."

William was already reaching for his phone. "What was in it?"

"My laptop."

"Damn it," William muttered under his breath.

"Okay, Ms. Knightly," a chipper nurse nearly sang, opening the door and stepping inside the room. "I have your discharge papers."

Recognizing she'd stepped into something, she looked from Eva to William and then back to Eva. "Everything okay here?"

"Yes," Eva said and plastered a fake smile on her face. "We're fine."

"Will he be the one taking you home?"

Eva and William answered at the same time.

"No."

"Yes."

"Actually," the nurse said, in an obvious attempt to leave. "I need another signature. I'll be right back."

Eva turned to William after she left. "I told you, Julia's coming by to pick me up."

William narrowed his gaze at her. "Julia with half a dozen volunteers starting today?"

"Yes."

"Tell me what kind of sense it makes to call and have her come all the way back here to pick you up, when I'm standing here now and can take you?"

"When you put it like that, it doesn't make any sense at all," Eva said. "But I'm sure you have better things to do than to drive me around."

"Not at the moment. Where will you be staying?"

She winced. "Julia said I can have her couch. Justin's mom is in town and staying in their spare bedroom. When Amelia gets back into town, I'll see if I can stay with her."

"Or you can stay with me at Nana's," William said. "I'd offer you the house in town, but I think you'll be safer at Nana's. There's probably nothing to worry about, but it'd make me feel better for you to be there, at least until whoever's responsible for your attack is caught. There's an extra bedroom with a bed, and you'll have your own bathroom. But the big benefit is you won't have to share your space with a woman you don't know."

He thought he had her with the mention of her own bathroom. Nana had a second bath put in when he moved in with her permanently after his parents died his freshman year of high school. But Eva didn't appear to be that easily swayed.

"If I'm completely honest," she said. "I haven't been looking forward to calling Julia to pick me up for those very reasons. And Amelia will be gone for a few days. Or at least that was the impression I got when I talked with her yesterday. But you know how people in Eden think. If I stay with you, whether it's in town or at your Nana's, within five minutes of us leaving the hospital in the same car and not stopping at either the police station or my house, people will start talking. And I don't have to tell you what they'll say."

He knew exactly what they'd say. At best, they'd think the two of them had recently hooked up. At the worst, they'd think the hook up happened months ago, and that one or both were instrumental in Catherine's death as a result.

Why did he suddenly find he didn't care?

"Frankly," he said, "It doesn't matter to me what they say. I'm tired of trying to conform to everyone's idea on how I should act. I've come to the conclusion people are going to talk no matter what. Your home was invaded, and you were attacked in broad daylight. The best option for you is to move in with me, at least until we find out who attacked you, or with Amelia when she's back and we can ensure the security of her place. If the town of Eden can't understand that, we can't make them."

"Don't hold back," she said. "Tell me how you really feel."

He shrugged. It'd felt good to say it all. "I'm tired of living under the microscope."

"You're right," Eva told him with a determined lift of her chin. "I'll call Julia and tell her thanks, but no thanks."

EVA FELL ASLEEP on the way to his Nana's house, and when they arrived, he half carried her to his Nana's room. He'd been serious when he told her he knew she hadn't slept much the night before, but he hadn't realized just how little she must have got. While she slept, he called and left a message for Mitch to call him back with an update.

He called less than ten minutes later.

"What have you learned?" William asked.

"Our suspicion last night was correct," Mitch said. "It appears as if someone was looking for something. Slashed pillows and curtains, but many valuable items left untouched. All of which suggest something other than a robbery. Also, there was no sign of the violence we commonly see in personal disputes." He hesitated before adding, "No one's been able locate the tote. We're going to assume the subject took it with them."

William thanked him, and they agreed to touch base later. He didn't expect to get any new or additional information from the scene. Just knowing the most likely reason was enough knowledge for him.

Eva slept for three hours and seemed to be more rested and calmer once she woke up. The house wasn't unknown to her, she'd been by a few times with Catherine before the separation.

"Thank you, for basically insisting I stay here," she said. "Because at the moment, just thinking about being in my house, knowing he's still out there, is enough to send me into a panic attack."

She seemed more annoyed over the loss of her tote than worried. The laptop didn't bother her too much, she told him. She synced it with her online storage account daily, so in that regard, she hadn't lost any data.

The question they couldn't answer was, what was the person who took it looking for?

"I'm not sure what they thought you had," William said. "I think you surprised whoever it was when you came home early. Probably, they took the tote for the laptop. Maybe they thought there was some information they could use on it?"

Her phone buzzed.

"Hello?" Eva said, a smile overtaking her expression while listening to whoever was the other line. "No, it's fine. Don't even think about it."

William took a step away to give her privacy, but she lifted a finger and mouthed for him to wait a minute.

"That sounds interesting…As long as you aren't asking out of guilt…Okay, see you then."

Eva was still smiling when she disconnected.

"Must have been a pretty good phone call," William said.

"It was Stefan," Eva said, her smile not as bright as it'd been seconds before.

"How's Mr. Stefan-with-an-f doing?" He wasn't sure why the thought of Stefan calling to check on her bothered him.

"You can't hold the way he spells his name against him," Eva said, echoing what he'd told himself before. "That's on his parents."

"Maybe, but it still looks pretentious. What did he want?"

"To apologize for not calling sooner. He's been in Charleston, and just got back home today. He also asked me to dinner, said he had something he wanted to show me."

William almost told her that was the world's worst pickup line, but judging by the look in her eyes, she wouldn't appreciate it.

"It's nothing really," she said. "I only like him as a friend, and he's fun to be around."

He remembered seeing them sitting together in the diner. There had been nothing friendly about the way Stefan looked at her.

"Why do you care?" she asked.

He opened his mouth to say he didn't but couldn't form the words. He did care, he realized. Very much so.

I believe talking with Mary would be much easier if I carried paper and quill on my person at all times in order to write down all the questions coming to mind every time she speaks. She has not been herself recently.

— JOURNAL OF AN UNKNOWN WOMAN, EARLY 1700s

Chapter Twenty-four

Two days later, just after one in the afternoon, William was finishing up the paperwork on a minor car accident he'd worked earlier in the day, when Mitch stopped by his cubicle.

"Come with me for a moment," the acting chief said, giving no hint as to what he wanted.

William stood without speaking and followed Mitch to his cruiser. Once inside the car, Mitch passed him a handful of papers.

"This just came in," he told William. "I'm going to question him, and I want you to go with me."

William looked over the papers, his anger rising. Disgusted, he slapped them down on the dash. "Are you kidding me?"

"I wish I were."

HAMILTON'S EYES GREW wide as he took in the sight of William and Mitch on the doorstep of the modest home he'd inherited from his parents. "What are…uh, I mean…I didn't…"

Based on the man's reaction and the way he couldn't talk,

William assumed Hamilton recognized the pissed expression he wore while waiting on his doorstep. Since William *was* pissed, he didn't care.

"Perhaps we should go inside to avoid becoming your neighbor's entertainment for the evening?" Mitch asked, in a tone that conveyed his feelings matched William's.

They had driven by the hardware store first and not seeing Hamilton's truck parked anywhere, took a chance they'd find the young man at home.

William looked over at Hamilton's next-door neighbor's house and saw the curtains move.

"Right," Hamilton said, opening the door wide enough to let the two men pass and then closing it behind him.

William hadn't paid attention to the home's decor the last time he'd been inside, soon after Gabby's death. He looked around now, and from what he could gather, Hamilton hadn't moved much of his parent's furniture out. Instead, it appeared as if he did little more than shove tables and chairs aside if he needed more room for a particular gadget. From the way it looked, Hamilton's intent was to own every piece of technology possible.

Hamilton led them to the living room, and the two officers took seats on opposite ends of the couch. Hamilton sat in a nearby chair, fidgeting until he realized neither William nor Mitch were talking but watching him.

Since Mitch was the acting police chief, William let him lead.

"Where were you the night Gabby died?" Mitch asked.

Raleigh was where everyone thought Hamilton had been, at the business conference he'd mentioned after Gabby's body was found. William had checked it out, and yes, Hamilton was listed as being registered and having attended. William also confirmed the conference ended with a breakfast meeting on Friday morning, and, according to the conference records, Hamilton was scheduled to stay for that last meeting.

Now, Hamilton's lack of reply confirmed those plans had changed.

"Here's the thing," Mitch said. "When we checked Gabby's incoming calls, we also pulled where those calls came from. It's in your best interest for your answer to match what the report says. Where were you the Thursday night Gabby died?"

Hamilton sank into the couch, and mumbled, "Elizabeth City."

"How long is the drive from Elizabeth City to Eden?" William asked at the nod Mitch gave him.

"About two hours."

"Much shorter than the drive from Raleigh to Eden."

William hadn't asked it as a question, but Hamilton answered it, anyway. "Yes, sir."

William nodded for Mitch to continue.

"I don't know why you left Raleigh early or why you spent the night in Elizabeth City," Mitch said. "Frankly, I don't care as long as the reason wasn't illegal and didn't involve Gabby. What I do care about is why you allowed everyone to think you were in Raleigh. In fact, according to the statement you gave Officer Templeton, when you called Gabby that Thursday night, you told *her* you were still in Raleigh. Do you see what I'm getting at?"

Hamilton scowled. "I didn't do anything to Gabby."

"Is there anyone who can confirm your whereabouts Thursday night?" Mitch asked.

"I don't know."

"You don't know?" Mitch asked, obviously trying to keep his anger in check. "I suggest you figure it out relatively soon. What time did you arrive in Elizabeth City?"

"I don't know, I didn't check to see. I know it was dark."

William thought that might have been the most unhelpful answer he'd ever received. He supposed he should be happy that it at least narrowed the timeframe down to about nine hours, but he wasn't. "What were you doing in Elizabeth City?"

William got the impression Hamilton wasn't going to talk, but just before William could open his mouth to tell him it didn't matter if he kept quiet, because they had more than they needed for a warrant, Hamilton surprised him.

"Gabby and I had been having problems," Hamilton said. "She'd be fine one minute, and then the next, she'd be yelling at me for something. Usually, it was for going by a place when she was working. I knew I wasn't supposed to be with her while she was cleaning, but she'd keep sending me texts asking where I was and wanting to know if I was with another woman. I'd tell her no, but she wouldn't believe me. Then, when I'd show up to prove it, she'd get mad."

William raised a quick eyebrow in Mitch's direction and was answered with a curt nod. Good. That meant Mitch had read William's note from when he interviewed Doris and was aware that Gabby had said the exact opposite.

"Are you certain it wasn't you sending Gabby texts asking her if she'd invited men to visit her while she cleaned?" Mitch asked. "And you weren't the one stopping by where she was working to make sure she wasn't lying?"

As if realizing they knew the truth, Hamilton nodded. "Sometimes I'd show up unannounced at places while she worked so she'd know how it felt not to be trusted."

William didn't believe him at all, and based on Mitch's expression, he didn't either.

"Out of curiosity," William said. "How many times when you showed up to a place where she was cleaning did you find a man with her?"

"None."

"And how many women were you dating along with Gabby?" William asked.

Hamilton sighed deeply. "I got tired of always being accused of stuff I had no intention of doing. Then, about five months or so ago, I was at this bar in Elizabeth City, and met this woman. And I thought to myself if Gabby's going to be mad as a wet hen and act like I cheated, I might as well go ahead and do whatever it is she's accusing me of."

"You were with this woman the Thursday night Gabby died?" Mitch asked.

"Yes."

Mitch leaned back in the couch and crossed his arms. "Then why did you say you weren't sure if anyone could confirm where you were Thursday night. Why can't she?"

"I'm not sure she'll do it." Hamilton scrubbed his face with both hands. "She found out about Gabby that night. She got pissed off and broke up with me."

Good for her, William wanted to say. What was it with people thinking cheating was acceptable behavior? "We'll still need her contact details," William told him. "What time was it when this happened?"

"I don't know." Hamilton fisted his hand and hit his knee. "I didn't know I should keep track. Jesus. Are most people actually able to answer that crap?"

William didn't reply but instead asked, "Where did you go after leaving her?"

"I drove to a bar there in Elizabeth City and got plastered. When they kicked me out, I slept in my car right there in the parking lot. I know better than to drive when I'm in that condition."

Thank goodness for that at least, William thought. "And you don't think the bar employees would confirm your actions?"

Hamilton shrugged. "I don't know. But it was after seven Friday morning before I left that parking lot."

It was obvious Hamilton didn't understand how grave the situation was. "My problem with what you've told us so far," William said, "Is that we can't rule out you arriving earlier to Eden than you claim."

"And if I arrived earlier, there's a possibility I killed Gabby?"

Both William and Mitch remained silent, allowing Hamilton to arrive at his own conclusion. As a result, Hamilton's next statement didn't come as a surprise.

"I want a lawyer."

Real beauty comes from deep inside a person's soul. Before, I might have stated that the pirates such as Edward didn't have one. However, I can no longer say such a thing.

— **JOURNAL OF AN UNKNOWN WOMAN, EARLY 1700s**

Chapter Twenty-five

Three days later, Eva stopped herself before she threw her phone across her office. One of the food vendors she'd been trying to work out a deal with for the Festival had just sent an email letting her know he'd signed up to work somewhere else that weekend.

Unable to sleep, she'd finally given in at four-thirty and got up. She was in her office by five-thirty. It was now ten, and she'd already gone through a pot of coffee. What she really needed to do was hit something.

Preferably the owner of the food truck.

She had been assured by the board that they had not yet released any information about the possibility of the Festival's cancellation. Nor, she was told, did they plan to do so until they knew with certainty one way or the other. The reassurance should have made her feel better about the one vendor, at least she shouldn't have to worry about a barrage of other vendors calling to withdraw, but it didn't.

Before she could find a way to track him down, her phone rang. It was Amelia. She smiled. Amelia would help her. With the two of them, surely, they'd be able to find a food truck.

"Hi, what's up?" Eva asked in greeting. "Are you back in town?"

"Yes, finally," Amelia said. "Hey, if I send you a picture, are you in a position to look at it?"

"Sure. It's just me and the Blackbeard Festival, and to be honest, I'm ready for a break."

Amelia's silence made a chill run up her spine, even as Eva told herself she was being ridiculous over a picture. She held off on asking if anything was wrong.

"Okay," Amelia said. "Sent."

"Do you want to stay on or for me to call you back?"

"I'll stay on."

It took less than thirty seconds for the picture to show up in her notifications. As soon as it did, she switched on the speakerphone. "Got it." She went to the message to check out the picture and almost dropped the phone. The photo had been taken in a storage room of sorts, judging from the boxes and shelves occupying the background. But her eyes were drawn to an upper shelf. Completely bare except for what looked like her stolen tote bag. Eva had mentioned her missing bag a few days ago when Amelia had found an area with good reception and called to see how she was doing the day she was released from the hospital.

"Where are you?" Eva asked. "Where is it?"

"Eden Methodist. I took the day off to help Mom because she's running their Vacation Bible School this year; the woman who was supposed to be helping her broke her hip and is in the hospital. Anyway, we're pulling out all kinds of crap from this storage room in the church. I swear they used this stuff back when *I* went to Vacation Bible School. There are all these shelves and boxes everywhere. We're pulling out what we need when I look up, and I see that on one of the top shelves. Is it yours?"

"It looks like it." Eva couldn't say with any certainty without a better look. "I'm not one hundred percent sure, though." What was it doing in Eden Methodist?

"Mom and I will be here for another hour or so, if you wanted to come by and see if it's yours."

Eva glanced down at the phone and decided tracking down a food truck vendor could wait.

EVA MET AMELIA at Eden Methodist's back door because she didn't want to chance running into Reverend Neighbors.

"I know this isn't your favorite place," Amelia said. "But I didn't know what else to do."

"It's okay." Eva remembered how uncomfortable and angry she'd felt that day being berated by Reverend Neighbors when all she'd done was be a good friend to Julia.

"I don't know why Mom continues to come here," Amelia said. "Other than it's what she's always done."

Julia's mother, Elizabeth, greeted Eva warmly. The older woman gave her a hug and started talking, not once asking why she appeared at the church out of the blue. Eva was relieved she didn't mention the last time they'd been in the church together. Maybe she didn't remember.

"Hey, Mom," Amelia said. "Why don't you go get some lunch? You need a break, and Eva and I can finish this box. I have some cash in my purse if you want to grab it."

"Are you sure?" her mom asked. "I actually am feeling a bit hungry."

Amelia convinced her mom the two of them would be fine, and they both breathed a sigh of relief when she left.

"Odds are she'll run into someone she knows, they'll start talking, and she'll lose track of time." Amelia motioned for Eva to follow her, and they walked down the hall to the storage room. "I went ahead and pulled it down so you could see it better."

It only took a few seconds for Eva to confirm the tote was hers. She had tied a red ribbon to the shoulder strap when she first bought it, and it was still there. Even though it was light and she knew what that likely meant, she unzipped it and looked inside.

Nothing.

"I should go tell William," Eva said, realizing she probably should have called him before heading to the church.

"Help me get these boxes put away, and I'll go with you," Amelia said.

They worked quickly, putting the boxes they didn't need back into the storage room, and moving the ones they did into an empty Sunday School room. Amelia called her mom and told her they'd finished and where she could find the boxes she needed.

"And I'm catching a ride home with Eva," Amelia added. "I'll call you later tonight."

Mary told me today that she had no need to worry about a thing because I always did the worrying for her.

— JOURNAL OF AN UNKNOWN WOMAN, EARLY 1700s

Chapter Twenty-six

William had been in law enforcement since he'd graduated from college. In that time, he'd seen foul and depraved behavior of a kind he wouldn't have thought possible before viewing with his own eyes. Likewise, he'd seen unfathomable self-sacrifice and generosity so sweet, thinking of them years later nearly brought tears. As a result, William thought very little, if anything, could surprise him.

Eva walking into the police station with her missing tote proved how wrong he was.

He'd been in the front office, on the phone with the police chief of Mateo discussing several acts of vandalism occurring in both towns when the door opened. He glanced up and saw Eva walking in with Amelia at her side. The smile he gave them froze on his face when he saw what Eva carried.

"Keith," William said to the man on the other end. "I'm going to have to call you back on this. I have a situation that just popped up."

"I've been upgraded to a situation now?" Eva's words were teasing, but neither her voice nor her expression matched them.

"I thought it sounded better than saying someone had just shocked the life out of me." He pointed to the bag on her shoulder. "Is that your tote?"

"Yes," she said. "Minus my laptop. Amelia found it at Eden Methodist."

He looked over to Amelia in question.

"It was on a top shelf in a storage closet," Amelia said.

"Looks like you need to go have another chat with your friend, Reverend Neighbors," Eva said.

He wanted to tell her she should have called him instead of going to the church and getting the tote herself. Let her know that he needed to know and see exactly where the tote had been found. But at the moment he couldn't get his brain to form words.

"Should I leave this here?" Eva held up the tote. Obviously, she wasn't having difficulties forming words.

He nodded. His plan for the day had been to work on the department's budget for the coming year. The mayor had *suggested* Mitch allow William to handle it, but William had a feeling he only did so because William knew his preferences concerning the report. Mitch didn't mind at all and had been more than happy to pass it along. As much as William dreaded working on the budget, he'd rather spend the entire next week working only on those numbers as opposed to having the conversation he now had to have with Robert.

"You don't really think this means Reverend Neighbors is behind the attack at my house, do you?" Eva asked as she turned to leave. "I mean, he's not my favorite person. Hell, I avoid him at all costs, but I can't reconcile him being involved in anything of the sort."

William couldn't either, but with two of the rare gold coins being from the church and now with Eva's tote being found there? "I think it's possible he knows more than he's letting on." He ran his hand through his hair. "I'll talk with him this afternoon and let you know if I learn anything pertinent to your attack."

"Thank you," she said. "I hope it goes well and you get some answers."

"I hope I'm ready to hear them."

ARE YOU feeling okay?" Robert asked William two hours later.

William had stopped by the church after lunch, or at least after most people had lunch, since he hadn't felt like eating when noon came.

"Not really," William answered.

"Does this have to do with Ms. Knightly, Ms. Clark, or Catherine?" Robert asked, sounding exactly like his normal jovial self and not at all like someone capable of keeping dark secrets.

William snorted. "Yes, all three of them." Robert looked as if he was going to say something, but William didn't wait to hear what it was. "You heard about the attack on Eva Knightly?"

"At her house, right?" He shook his head. "Shocking someone could be that bold. Ms. Knightly is okay, though? That's what I heard, anyway."

"Yes, she's fine," William said, watching the reverend closely. "And we didn't announce it in the press, but a tote she had and the laptop inside were taken from the scene by the attacker."

"If you didn't announce it to the press, why are you telling me?"

"Because the tote was found this morning, minus the laptop, in one of the church's storage closets."

"*This* church?" Robert asked as if it was impossible.

"Yes, this church. The very same church where two odd gold coins were found in the offering plate after Gabby Clark died. The coins that ended up in Eva's hands."

"Are you saying someone at the church had something to do with the attack on Ms. Knightly?"

"I'm saying it's strange how Eden Methodist keeps getting brought up. How else can you explain it?"

Robert sat completely still. The only part of his body that moved was his mouth. "Someone put it there."

The way he remained nearly frozen in his seat made William think that not only did he know more than he was telling, but he was also scared for some reason.

"But you don't know who?" William asked.

"No." Something flashed briefly across his face. "I don't know."

Fear, William decided. Definitely fear. If he continued down his current path, Robert might shut down completely. A change of topic was needed, but Robert beat him to it.

"Gabby Clark had a strange coin found on her body," Robert said. "Then two coins show up in my offering. Don't you find that odd?"

"No," William said, which was obviously not the answer expected. "If someone wanted to get rid of them, it makes complete sense. Did you ever see the coin Gabby had or did she mention it to you?"

Robert's cheeks flushed. William only noticed because he'd never seen them do so before. "Not that I remember. When she was here, she was working. Just like I was working. We didn't chit-chat, no matter what you may have heard. Is it the same type of coin they found on Catherine?"

"You know I'm not involved in her case. Even so, since we were separated, and I didn't see her very often, let me ask you, did Catherine seem different to you in the months before her death?" William asked. "Like she was afraid or worried?"

It seemed to take longer than necessary for Robert to answer the question.

"Catherine wasn't like everyone else," he finally said, not answering the question, but his shoulders appeared to relax a touch. "Maybe it was the artist in her, but she seemed to feel emotions more intensely than most people. It's what made her a great painter, but carrying around that level of intensity, all day, every day was incredibly draining."

William frowned. "I'm not sure I understand what it is you're trying to say to me."

"Being who I am, I can't, and don't, condone such things, but I'm also human, and prone to sin myself, and God does say all sin is equal before Him. With Catherine being as intense as she was, the guilt she felt—"

"What are you talking about?" William knew there had been gossip when he and Catherine separated. But even with all the speculation, he was unaware anyone knew one hundred percent the reason why.

"I thought you were talking about her infidelity."

"No," William said, trying to calm himself and come to terms with the fact that Catherine's affair wasn't as secret as he'd always thought. It shouldn't bother him, really, but it did. "I was wanting to know if she ever spoke to you about someone threatening her. But before we get to that, I want to know what you know about her infidelity. Who was he?"

Robert's reply came so smoothly, it sounded rehearsed. "I may have been Catherine's friend, but I was also her pastor."

"Yeah?" William asked. "Well, I was her husband, and I want to know who he was."

"I'm a member of the clergy first," he said. "And that supersedes any friendship I have."

"Including mine?"

Robert held perfectly still. "I'm sorry," he said, telling William all he needed to know. The office suddenly felt too warm and too small. William stood up.

Robert held out his hand. "Please don't leave yet."

"Why?"

"Because you need to know how she felt."

William wasn't sure he wanted to know how she felt. Hell, he wasn't sure how *he* felt. Was there an emotion that encompassed guilt, rage, and despair all at the same time? He didn't want to ask

Robert to tell him how Catherine felt, but on the other hand, he didn't want to leave the office without knowing, either.

Robert cleared his throat. "The last time I saw her, she told me she'd loved you since high school, and though she did many things wrong, the one thing she did right was to marry you."

The breath left William's body and he dropped back into his chair. Robert might as well have punched him in the gut. He took a deep breath and closed his eyes for a second. When he was composed, he gave a sad chuckle. "That certainly explains why it was so easy for her to toss aside our vows like yesterday's garbage."

"She took full responsibility for that and was looking for a way to redeem herself." Robert spoke with a conviction that told William every word of it was true.

William nodded and silently stood. He didn't trust himself to know what might come flying out of his mouth if he opened it. Instead, he left Robert's office and went out a side door so he could avoid running into Evelyn and being forced to make small talk.

THOUGH WILLIAM wanted nothing more than to go home, or to the marsh house, or anywhere except back to his cubicle, he had too much to take care of to leave early. He planned to sit at his desk and not interact with anyone. He'd never missed an office door so much before, but fortunately, his scowl was enough to keep people away.

His plan lasted until Peggy buzzed the phone on his desk, not even an hour after his return.

"No," he said before she could get a word out.

But Peggy had worked for too many of Eden's police chiefs to be deterred that easily. "Evelyn Davis is here to see you."

There was probably nothing else she could have said that would have made him react faster. "I'll be right there."

He hurried to the front where he found Evelyn clutching her

purse and looking at the door every so often as if she were expecting someone to barge in any second.

"Evelyn?" he said to get her attention.

"William, I'm sorry to bother you." She glanced at the door again. "And I only have a second. I told Reverend Neighbors I was stopping by the diner for a minute."

"You're no bother," he said to try to calm her down. "What can I help you with?"

She bit her lip, obviously wanting to say something, but hesitating for whatever reason.

"Should we go sit down?" he asked.

"No." She looked at the door again. "I really do only have a second."

But she didn't continue.

"You've already made it here," William tried again. "You might as well go ahead and get it out."

She took a deep breath. "I'm sorry, but it's a small office and I couldn't help but overhear. Especially with the door wide open. But Reverend Neighbors *did* talk with Gabby about coins."

William placed his hand on the wall to steady himself. That was not what he'd expected her to say. Hell, he didn't even know why he'd asked Robert that question. It wasn't one he'd planned to. Evelyn's glances to the door made sense now.

"What did you hear about the coins?" he asked.

"To start with, I knew he had two gold ones, or he did, in his desk." Evelyn tilted her head. "I knew this because he was out of the office one day, and I had to get into his desk for something, and I saw them."

"Yes, I know about the coins he had."

Evelyn leaned closer to William and dropped her voice. "The Wednesday before Gabby died, she was cleaning the church, and he must have had them out. He'd do that sometimes, take them out, hold them, that sort of thing. But only when he didn't think anyone was watching. Anyway, Gabby stepped into his office, and because the door was open, I could hear everything."

William was getting the impression Evelyn saw and heard a lot more than people gave her credit for. He wondered how many secrets Evelyn had heard over the years because of open doors.

"She told him she'd recently found a coin exactly like the one he had. She was so excited, said she'd bring it back with her when she came Friday to clean." Evelyn gave a snort. "The odd thing was the reverend didn't act excited at all. He told her it wasn't necessary, and she'd be better off putting it back where she found it. Told her she shouldn't mess with old coins because they might be cursed."

It took a few seconds for the entirety of what Evelyn said to sink in, and when it did, he froze in place. Robert had lied to him. Hell, he'd lied to everyone. If Robert had talked to Gabby about the coins on Wednesday and Evelyn saw them prior to that, they hadn't been put in the collection plate the Sunday after Gabby's death.

"When did you first see the coins?" he asked.

"About two months ago."

"Why would Gabby go to Reverend Neighbors if she thought she'd found something of historical importance?" he asked. "Why him instead of someone from the Historical Society?"

"She said she was going to set up a time to meet with Eva Knightly." Evelyn shook her head slightly. "But she was showing him because she'd see him first due to her work schedule and because he and a few of his friends consider themselves to be history experts."

The hair on the back of William's neck stood up with her words, but he managed to keep his expression neutral when he replied. "They do?" He even managed a little laugh. "Which friends?"

"Umm…" She squinted her eyes. "I'm not sure I know their names. I've never been formally introduced to them. I just over-hear things."

"Have you told anyone else? Either about the coins or the friends?" He didn't think she had based on how hard it'd been for him to get the information out of her.

"No." Her grip on her purse tightened so much her knuckles turned white. "I almost didn't tell you."

"Why?"

Evelyn glanced at the door again. "I've worked with Reverend Neighbors since he arrived in Eden, and I think I know him fairly well. I don't believe for a second he hurt either Catherine or Gabby. But I do think something's going on." She hesitated before continuing. "I didn't say anything earlier because I didn't want to get him in trouble, but when you asked him directly and he lied, I knew I had to tell someone."

William could appreciate how difficult it had been for her to come by the station and feel as though she were ratting out her boss. He placed a hand on her shoulder. "Thank you for coming by and telling me. We'll keep your involvement confidential. He doesn't ever need to know you even came by."

Tears shined in her eyes. "Thank you, William."

"No thanks necessary. Just doing my job."

In a totally unexpected move, she stood on her toes and gave him a quick hug. "I'm so glad you decided to come back here to work. Eden wouldn't be the same without you. Harvey and I are going to have you over for dinner soon, okay?"

He smiled. "Just let me know when."

She agreed and hurried out the door with a wave. Even if she never followed through with the dinner invitation, for the first time in a long time, he felt normal for a moment. He'd forgotten how nice that felt.

Today at the market, I overheard the governor's wife talking with a strange man. She told him he needed to inform his master that it was time. The one they'd been waiting for was due to arrive soon. Her words chilled me for some reason.

— JOURNAL OF AN UNKNOWN WOMAN, EARLY 1700s

Later that day, a few minutes before six, Eva parked in one of the few spaces in front of Stefan's office. From the corner of her eye, she thought she saw the blinds flutter in one of the front windows. Even walking up the short walkway to the front door, she couldn't ignore the feeling she was being watched. Before she could contemplate who it might be, however, the front door opened.

"Eva," Stefan said, stepping aside to let her pass. "Come inside. Forgive me for watching from the window. I sent Naomi home and I feared I'd miss your knock if I went back to my desk."

"Your work must be engrossing in that case." Relief swept over her. It had been Stefan watching, not some stranger hiding in the shadows.

He chuckled and moved to stand beside her. "You do remember I practice real estate law?"

"Of course." She smiled. "Don't tell me it's *that* boring. I'm sure you could tell a story or two."

"Come on back to my office, I thought I'd show you a few things before dinner, if that's okay? We can walk to the restaurant, but I called and they can't seat us until seven." He waited for her to nod before leading her toward the back of the building, into what she assumed was his personal office. "And you're right, I do have a story or two I could tell, but doing so would probably get me disbarred."

"We can't have that now, can we?"

"No, we can't." Stefan pointed to an open door. "Right this way. How are you doing?" He tilted his head, studying her. "That's a nasty-looking bruise."

Eva thought she'd done a good job covering it up with makeup, but she guessed not. "It'd look even worse if something had been broken."

"Thank goodness nothing was." He narrowed his eyes. "Have they found the person who did this?"

"Not yet."

He didn't look pleased. "I'm sure they're doing the best they can."

The room they entered was larger than she expected; matching every preconceived idea she had of an attorney's office and looking exactly like a stereotype made real, it held a massive wooden desk. Framed diplomas adorned the walls, and a high-back leather chair, probably worth more than her car, completed the picture. "This is gorgeous, Stefan."

"Thank you," he said, full of pride. "I combined the two bedrooms back here into one so I could have more space. Never regretted doing so."

"I would think not, especially if the end result was an office like this." There were several maps of various sizes adorning the walls, and she walked along the wall closest to her to look over a few. "These are amazing."

They were multicolored, which had shocked her the first time she saw an authentic antique map. She'd always assumed that they would be plain black and white. While many were, there were also numerous ones that had been hand-colored with natural pigments at the time of creation.

"Are they real?" She looked over her shoulder to see him watching her with an amused expression.

"I had them authenticated when I was living in Charleston."

"Charleston? I'd assumed you lived here your entire life."

He motioned her to a sitting area off to the side of his desk, and they each took a seat in two of the plush leather chairs he had there.

"No, I moved to Charleston shortly after high school, and that's where I went to undergrad. I kept a residence there even while I was in law school. I'd always sworn once I graduated from high school, I'd leave the Outer Banks and never come back. Dad died when I was fifteen. After mom passed, seven years ago, I found I missed this place after all."

"I'm sorry to hear about your parents," Eva said. "I don't remember your dad from that summer, but your mom was the sweetest lady."

"She was," he agreed. "I know you weren't able to come back that next year because your mom died. Is your dad still around?"

"Yes, he's around, all right." Eva rolled her eyes. "Recently married wife number four. She's younger than I am."

"Ouch," he said.

"Yes," she agreed. "Needless to say, we aren't very close. I see him around Christmastime, and that's enough for me."

"I'm sorry to hear you aren't closer with your dad," Stefan said.

Eva shrugged. "It is what it is, you know?"

"True, but that doesn't make it hurt any less."

She nodded. It was nice to talk with someone who understood, but they'd spent enough time talking about the many ways their parents disappointed them. "So, tell me what you have that you want me to see, and then I can beg you to let me display it at the museum. Assuming it's historical."

"It is, but you might be unimpressed, and not want it any-where near your museum," he said, standing and picking up a large wooden box from the floor and putting it on the coffee table in front of them.

Stefan lifted the lid off the box, flipping it so the inner lining was exposed. Eva felt just like a child on Christmas morning as she thought of all the things that could be in a box that large. But she wasn't expecting what he pulled out.

"Wow," she said, gaping at the cutlass Stefan had withdrawn and itching to get a better look. "That's an amazing weapon."

Stefan placed it on the soft liner of the box top and motioned for her to get closer. "Go on and look at it. Pick it up if you want."

Based on what she could tell from the handle and the blade, she estimated the cutlass to be about three hundred years old. "Late 1600s to early 1700s?" she asked. "And no way would I even think about touching anything that old without gloves on."

"You can't hurt this old thing," Stefan said. "It's been in my family forever. If we haven't managed to mess it up, I doubt you can."

"How long is forever?" she asked, wanting to hear the history behind the sword. Surely a weapon that old had a story.

"Family gossip says it's the sword that killed Blackbeard."

Eva frowned. "Spotswood's?"

"No," Stefan said. "I thought Mimi showed you?"

She loved how he still called her Mimi, even though everyone called her Amelia. "Showed me what?"

"My family tree."

"She showed me…" Eva gasped, remembering what Amelia had said. "You're Mr. X!"

"I'm who?"

"Mr. X." Eva laughed at his frown. "That's what she called you to keep your identity secret. She said you were related to Gover-nor Eden. But I don't understand the connection to Blackbeard and the cutlass. Eden wouldn't have killed Blackbeard."

"Why not?"

"Blackbeard was working for him. Giving him a cut of his treasure," Eva said. "Why would he slaughter his golden goose?"

"Blackbeard was recently married when he died, right?" Stefan asked. "What if Blackbeard wanted out?"

"So Eden decided to kill him?"

"Easiest way to get rid of the problem, wouldn't you say?"

"If you don't mind a little murder, I guess."

"I doubt Blackbeard's hands were all that clean, either."

"True." Eva studied the cutlass. She hadn't heard of any accounts mentioning Eden being on the boat with Spotswood when Blackbeard died. Eden was well known in the colony, and she didn't see how he could have been anywhere near Blackbeard at the time of his death and for no one to have recorded anything. More likely than not, it was just a family myth passed from generation to generation, along with a really cool cutlass. But even if it wasn't real, it was an impressive replication.

"Any way I can convince you to let me display it at the Blackbeard Festival?" she asked.

"Of course," he said. "But I want to be listed as anonymous."

"I'm sure I can arrange that." She wasn't sure why he wouldn't want to be listed, but she wouldn't argue with him about anything so trivial.

"You think it's an odd request?" he asked.

She didn't like that he could read her so easily and gave a half snort, half laugh to cover her discomfort. "Yes. I don't know why you wouldn't want people to know."

"My father was a history nut. Self-taught, though. He learned everything by reading and thought of himself as an expert. Drove people crazy around here. I'd rather be anonymous than to remind people of him." He gave her a smile. "Ready for dinner?"

"**REVEREND NEIGHBORS** is an ass," Eva told William later that evening when they had both returned to the marsh house. "I didn't want to say as much before because I knew you were friends with the guy, but he truly is. And another thing, if he's such an expert in history, why has he never talked to me about Blackbeard? It's not a secret I did my thesis on him. I would say he should have recognized the coins, but I won't since I didn't know what they were either."

They sat on the screened-in porch, drinking glasses of iced tea and enjoying the slight drop in temperature that followed the sun setting. She was trying to both enjoy the moment as well as make sure her heart understood such moments were temporary.

"Maybe he did know exactly what they were, but he decided to use them as a way to get close to you."

She made a face at him and changed the subject. "Why does Evelyn think he's a history expert? Obviously, he's saying or doing something to make people think he knows more than he does. I mean, Gabby went to him instead of me or someone else from the Historical Society when she found that coin."

"My biggest problem with him is that I can't believe he knows who Catherine was with, or at least pretended like he does, and he won't tell me."

"I agree," Eva said. "That's worse than claiming to be a history expert."

"The thing is, his behavior doesn't match the man I know him to be. There has to be another reason he acted the way he did today. I can't believe he would refuse to tell me just to be an ass."

"I'm sticking with him being an ass." Before he could reply, she asked, "Do you think there's a connection between Catherine's death and Gabby's?"

"What makes you think that?" he asked. "Other than the coins, their deaths had nothing to do with one another."

"Nothing in particular," she said. "It's just a feeling I have."

"Wish I knew these so-called history experts who Robert is friends with," William said.

"The difficulty is it could be any number of people," Eva said. "Anyone who's read more than two books on Blackbeard probably calls themself an expert."

"This whole thing is crazy." William sighed and ran his hand through his hair. "The more things we turn up, the more we find we don't know. It's like the Bermuda Triangle of mysteries."

"We should go research that when we finish Blackbeard."

"That would be something, wouldn't it?" He seemed to get her sense of humor, or maybe he was only relieved that in the aftermath following the assault, she still managed to crack a few jokes. Either way, it hit her in that second how comfortable she felt around him even when they disagreed.

"I know," she said. "Next we solve the mystery of the Lost Colony."

"If we can figure out this tangled mess, we probably could."

Alas, pirates! We are not known for our gentle ways.

— LETTER FROM BLACKBEARD TO HIS WIFE, MARY, 1718

Chapter Twenty-eight

Since Robert had to work on Sunday, he typically took Mondays off. Which was why William pulled up to the small house he resided in just before noon on Monday. William had thought all weekend about the best way to approach Robert and considered everything from officially bringing him in for questioning to doing nothing. It was only in the dark, early hours before dawn on Monday he decided.

As expected, Robert didn't look any happier to see William than William was to be there.

"William," his friend said.

"Can I come in for a minute?"

Robert didn't answer but opened the door wider and stood to the side to let him pass.

With his police hat in his hands, William stepped into the tidy home he'd been in uncountable times before. Robert followed several steps behind until the two men made their way into the living room.

"Would you like to sit?" Robert asked.

"I think it's best if I stand."

Robert didn't question his reply, only nodded, and waited.

"I've asked you this once before, and I promise you, I won't ask again," William said. "The only thing I want in return is the truth. If you can't give me that, tell me now, and I'll leave and never darken the doorstep of your church or home again."

Robert looked at him with wide eyes, his face pale, and nodded.

"Where did you get the two coins you gave Eva?"

Robert closed his eyes, mumbled something under his breath, and said, "From her." Then he whispered, "Catherine."

William thought he'd prepared himself for her name to be the answer given, but the sudden ache in his chest told him otherwise. He tried to school his expression, but he knew he failed horribly.

"Why did you change your answer?" William asked. "Before, you said they were placed in the collection plate the Sunday after Gabby died."

"I placed them there," he said, hesitating.

William couldn't tell if Robert was trying to decide what to tell him, or which parts, but neither was acceptable. "Go on."

"Catherine was conflicted the last year of her life. I don't know the details other than it involved another man and infidelity. There was more, but she said she didn't want to burden me with the information. I accepted that. I was afraid whatever it was would turn out to be illegal and I would have to turn her in."

William wondered what he thought now that she was dead, but didn't ask because he didn't want to interrupt.

"About a week before she died, we met outside of the church. It was late one afternoon. She planned the entire thing. Said it had to look like we'd accidentally ran into each other. I thought it was the craziest thing I'd ever heard, but went along with it because it was so hard to tell her no." Robert took a deep breath and continued. "That's when she gave me the coins. She said she was afraid you wouldn't be safe if she gave them to you."

"Did she tell you why?" William asked.

"No," he replied, and William saw no evidence of deceit in his body language.

"What were you supposed to do with the coins?" If Catherine gave them to him, she had to have a reason.

"She said she'd let me know. That we couldn't talk in the street, and that she'd call me the next week," Robert said. "But she didn't have a chance because a few days later, she was dead. I didn't know what else to do, so I kept them. Then, when I heard a coin was found on Gabby, I was afraid someone would see or know that I had two similar ones, and they might think I had something to do with her death. I thought by saying they were given to the church, I'd be removing any suspicion from me."

"It never occurred to you to bring them to me and tell me the truth?"

"Of course it did."

"Then why didn't you?"

"Because Catherine thought you wouldn't be safe with them, and I had no way to find out why." Robert dropped his head. "I didn't want to lose another friend."

"You still should have told me."

"I know," Robert said, and William had never seen him look so dejected. "There was something else Catherine told me."

"What?"

"I asked her where she got the coins. She said she'd put the key to the map in the Carolina Coastal Museum." Robert shrugged. "After she died, I went there to see if I could find what she was talking about. The children's section has a mural she painted, and I went a few times to look at it, but I've never seen anything that looked like a key."

William had been putting off going to see the mural, but based on what he'd just learned from Robert, he couldn't wait any longer. "I'll go look."

Robert looked pained. "I'm sorry I didn't tell you sooner. I thought I was doing the right thing."

"I know you did." William wanted to be angry with him but found he couldn't. "But you've told me now, and I'm going to get to the bottom of this."

Robert drew him to a stop as William walked past him on his way to the door. "I don't think either Catherine or Gabby died accidentally."

William didn't say it, but he was starting to think the same thing.

WILLIAM TOOK A deep breath to prepare himself and stepped out of his car at the sight of Julia exiting the Historical Society and crossing the parking lot. He met her at the front door of the Carolina Coastal Museum.

"Thank you for letting me in, Mrs. Baxter," he told her as she unlocked the doors.

He'd called Eva after leaving Robert's to ask her if he could come over to see the mural. Since it was Monday the museum was closed, which was fine with him. He'd prefer to be alone. But Eva had surprised him by saying she'd decided to stay at the marsh house today to research the cutlass Stefan was letting her display for the Festival, adding the quiet of the place allowed her to work faster. It wasn't an issue, though, she said, she'd call Julia and ask her to let him into the museum.

"No problem." Julia stepped inside to turn the lights on. "Just make sure to close the door behind you when you leave. The lock will engage automatically. And I feel the need to warn you, though I don't think it'll be an issue, but I'll be back over here in two hours to give an orientation to new volunteers."

He waited until she left to close his eyes and make sure he was ready before attempting to locate the children's section. It took only a handful of seconds and a look to his right for it to become obvious he was nowhere near ready. For a brief second, the world tilted at a crazy angle.

He took a deep breath and told himself to pull it together. He was not going to lose it because of a mural. Another deep breath, and he felt better. "You're fine," he whispered. "It's only paint."

He walked closer. As he'd assumed from the photos Eva had given him, it was large, taking up almost the entire wall. Catherine had been most known for her landscapes, which was what she normally painted. The piece before him looked nothing like those, and it was very much more than paint.

The mural had an air of whimsy to it, even while appearing to be an educational piece. Off to one side, a timeline of important Outer Banks dates had been painted, including the arrival of European settlers and the first flight. The main portion was a depiction of the local area but an odd combination of past and present. She'd even added playfully drawn landmarks and historical figures. Altogether, it was a fantastical eye-catching piece.

And she'd never felt the need to share it with him.

As if he could somehow connect with her, he ran a hand over the mural. With one finger he traced the path she painted leading to one of the many lighthouses found along the Carolina coast. Too many to include on the mural, but she'd picked the Currituck Beach Lighthouse to highlight. The sight of it had his heart in his throat. Anyone else painting such a mural would have certainly painted the more well-known Cape Hatteras Lighthouse. Or even the oldest lighthouse in North Carolina on Ocracoke Island. Even the sketch Eva had given him, which he assumed was Catherine's rough draft, was of a different lighthouse. But for her final selection, Catherine had picked Currituck Beach.

The place he'd proposed to her.

He would never have the chance to ask her why she painted that particular lighthouse, and he wasn't going to spend a lot of time thinking about it. With no one able to contradict him, he chose to see it as a positive sign. A sign that, had she still been alive, pointed toward a possible renewal of their marriage. Just like Robert had said.

Maybe their relationship hadn't been as hopeless as he'd thought. It was possible he'd given up too easily.

Had he?

Maybe.

The real question was, could he have forgiven her?

That, he wasn't sure of.

"What happened to us, Cat?" he asked the mural in a whisper, using an old nickname for her. He wasn't sure what made him stop using it, but he didn't think he'd called her Cat for many months after they'd married.

But as beautiful as the mural was, and as much as it reminded him of Catherine, it was only a painting and held no words of wisdom for him. Yet he still felt, somehow, Catherine heard him when he whispered, "I won't stop looking into your death until I'm completely satisfied and any needed justice has been served." He almost added that was his vow to her, but there had been enough vows between him and Catherine, some broken and some not. Either way, there was no need for another.

He took a step back. Robert said she'd told him she'd put a key to the map in the Carolina Coastal Museum. She'd had to mean she painted the key into the mural. It was the only thing that made sense.

But he didn't see a painted key anywhere, leading him to believe she meant a figurative key, not a literal one. Which meant it could be almost anything. Could be, but it wouldn't be. Whatever it turned out to be would have to be obvious to the person it was meant for while not drawing attention to itself from the people it wasn't.

He looked over her depiction of the lighthouse first because that was what had originally caught his attention. However, after several long minutes, he found nothing about the historical land-mark that stood out to him.

Damn.

His eyes drifted over the entire piece. Maybe the overall shape alluded to something.

But there was nothing that he could see.

The timeline held nothing out of the ordinary, either.

With each passing minute, the sinking feeling in his stom-ach intensified at the realization that maybe the key wasn't in the mural at all. A glance at his watch told him he'd been in the museum longer than he'd anticipated.

"Show me what I'm missing, Cat," he whispered into the silent room while looking over the mural again. "My gut tells me it's here."

His gaze fell on a pole painted above the words, WHERE ARE WE? In answer, she'd painted numerous signs on the pole, each containing a place such as New York City or Raleigh, with both a directional arrow and mileage. He looked at the sign on the bottom and a chill ran down his spine.

Nana's: Hop, Skip, and Jump

I would soon discover for myself things are not always what we think. This is especially true of people.

— JOURNAL OF AN UNKNOWN WOMAN, EARLY 1700s

William knew he should get to Nana's sooner rather than later, but in order to get there he had to go back past Robert's house, and he wanted to make a quick stop before he continued. He'd never seen the man look as down and defeated as he had earlier. William wanted to let him know he'd figured out the clue, to assure his friend it was nothing that he'd have noted. Maybe that would cheer him up.

For the second time that day, he parked next to the late model sedan Robert drove. Feeling lighter than he had earlier, he sprinted up the front stairs and rang the doorbell, stepping back to wait, wearing a big grin. But Robert didn't answer.

William rang it again.

Still nothing.

"Robert?" he called.

The grin left his face when he tried the knob and it opened. He reasoned with himself the door would likely be unlocked if Robert hadn't taken the time to lock it after William left earlier. But something seemed off. William pulled his gun out of its holster.

He pushed the door further open with a tap of his foot. The resulting creak was the only sound before his stern, "Hello?"

No reply.

"Police. Robert? Anyone home?" He spoke louder. "Robert?" Still nothing. He could call for backup, but wouldn't he feel stupid when it turned out Robert had fallen asleep watching a game or something? No, he wouldn't call right this minute, he'd wait until he knew what was going on. It wasn't likely Robert would have left, not with the house unlocked and his car outside.

William stepped into the foyer with a sense of dread, prepared to find destruction everywhere. But as he looked around, nothing appeared to be out of place, much less destroyed.

He peeked into the small living room where they had stood only hours before and made a note that the large flat screen TV remained in place. Moving deeper into the house, he stopped momentarily at the doorway to Robert's good-sized, recently updated kitchen, and let his eyes skim over everything. It was all as he remembered, right down to the laptop on a table tucked into the far corner and the framed, autographed New York baseball jersey of his favorite player on the back wall.

"Robert," he called again, just in case he'd fallen asleep after William left.

No reply.

Damn. Where was he?

William's sense of dread grew as he walked toward the one bedroom in the house. The door was partially open. He pushed it wider, and his breath caught. Robert rested on his back beside the bed, unmoving. Eyes open, but not seeing.

He rushed to the man's side, pulling his radio of his pocket, calling for urgent back up and medical help. "This is Templeton ten eighteen, ten fifty-two," he said, giving the reverend's address.

Seconds later, he heard multiple confirmations of message received.

"Robert," William said, kneeling beside the man. "What's wrong? Can you tell me what happened?"

William couldn't find a pulse and Robert didn't move, but his body held a bit of warmth. If he was dead, it hadn't been for long. Just in case there was a chance, William began CPR.

Time ceased to exist as he cycled through the repetitive motions in a vain effort to revive Robert. He may have chanted, he wasn't sure. For those long moments between when he called for help and when the paramedics pulled him away, he didn't remember anything other than willing the man under his hands to breathe.

It was clear from the look on the paramedics' faces when they took over that it was a futile battle, but they left with Robert in the ambulance, anyway. William waved them on and said he'd follow up later.

It was no coincidence, in his opinion, that this happened the day Robert spoke the truth about Catherine and the coins. Was someone afraid of what he might say later? It couldn't be anything he'd said to William today. The only people who knew what had been said were him and Robert.

He stood to leave, noticing as he did, a beer can. It was probably nothing, but he called into the station to give an update on what had happened and to request that someone be sent over to collect evidence including the beer can in the bedroom. Not wanting to disturb anything more than he and the paramedics already had, he walked outside to wait.

Once JJ and Darrius arrived, William spoke to them briefly before heading toward the marsh house. He was about halfway there when Mitch called.

"Yes, sir?" William answered.

Mitch didn't bother with any pleasantries. "I just received a call from the lab with the results on Gabby *and* Catherine."

Mary's voice was calm as she told me what she'd heard from the governor's housekeeper. "Edward wants out of pirating, but Eden won't let him because he knows too much. His wife found out about the baby and said she'd kill him herself and that'll bring Edward to his knees. I'll stand with Edward, but I need for you to take our child to safety."

— JOURNAL OF AN UNKNOWN WOMAN, EARLY 1700s

Chapter Thirty

I t hadn't taken Eva long to fall in love with the house William inherited from his Nana Ruth. Not that she hadn't been in it before, she had, but it had always been with both William and Catherine with her and only for short periods of time. Now that she'd been at the house for a few days, her outlook on it had changed.

She didn't have to stretch her mind too much to see a young William running around the yard, playing under the watchful eye of his grandmother. Growing up in the city like she had, this place looked like a child's dreamworld.

Frankly, it looked a lot like an adult's dreamworld as well. Or at least her vision of one. The quiet and peaceful location boasted a jaw-dropping view of the marshlands. And as spectacular as that view was during the day, it was even more so at both sunrise and sunset. She wasn't sure she ever wanted to leave.

It boggled her mind Catherine thought differently. Eva remembered how she'd complain following a stay. There were too many bugs. The birds were too loud. The air smelled funny.

And that was just the outside. Inside, she found the bed too small and uncomfortable, the closets weren't large enough to hold her clothes, and the bathrooms were ancient.

Eva thought all those things only added to the charm of the place, with the notable exception of the bugs. Bugs would never be charming, but that problem was easily solved by staying in the screened-in porch.

When she mentioned in passing to William the day before how beautiful she found the area and how she couldn't believe there weren't more houses around, he'd replied that the government owned a good deal of the land and that much of it wasn't buildable. To Eva, that simply meant he was able to keep the area to himself. She bet he wouldn't mind. The thought of a resort hotel or golf course taking over the area made her sick to her stomach.

Though she'd planned to drive into the office on Monday morning, at the last minute, she decided to stay where she was. No need to drag the heavy cutlass all the way into town when she could do everything she needed to right where she was. She put on a pot of coffee and had just sat down to see if she could find a reliable source connecting Governor Eden and the ship Blackbeard had been killed on, when William called.

She felt a little bad about not being with him the first time he saw the mural. But after giving it more thought, the more sense it made that William would want to be alone. She made a note to call him in a few hours to see how he was doing.

Time normally ceased to exist when she submerged herself into research, and this time was no different. The sound of tires making their way across gravel announced a vehicle pulling up to the house. She looked up from the notes she was making. According to her watch, it was too early for William to be home.

She wasn't expecting anyone, and William had mentioned before he never had people drop by unannounced. Curious, she walked to the front window and looked outside.

A car had parked behind hers, making it impossible to see it or who the driver was until they stepped out from behind her car. Stefan Benson.

Now, she was even more curious. Why would Stefan drive all the way out here? Hell, how had he known she was here? They hadn't spoken since their discussion about his relation to Governor Eden the week before.

His face was flushed and his eyes lit with excitement when she opened the door to his knock.

"Stefan," she said, not knowing what else to say.

"Eva." A smile covered his face. "Julia Baxter told me you were here. I hope you don't mind."

"No. Not at all." She stepped aside to open the door wider. "Would you like to come inside?"

"I actually found something, and I want to show you, but I have to take you there." She hadn't imagined his excitement; it was even evident in his voice. And it was obviously contagious because she found herself smiling.

"What is it?"

"It's a surprise."

"I hate surprises," she told him, which was definitely not a lie.

"You'll like this one. I promise." He held out his hand. "Come on."

She almost said no, but then told herself she was being ridiculous. This was Stefan. She'd met him when she was twelve for crying out loud. And he looked like a child on Christmas morning. "Let me get my purse."

Once they got in his car, a sporty little silver thing that probably cost more than a lot of houses, but would no doubt leave you squashed like a bug if you were in an accident, Stefan still wouldn't tell her where they were going. Eva tried guessing, but he laughed at every suggestion she threw out saying, no, it was someplace even better.

"I'm going to start naming islands in Hawaii just to hear you say, 'well, maybe not that good,'" she teased.

He flashed her a smile. "What makes you think Hawaii is better than where we're going?"

"Seriously?" She rolled her eyes even though she knew he couldn't see. "Because it's Hawaii, and no matter where we're going, it'll be in North Carolina. And the last time I checked, North Carolina is not Hawaii."

"Oh, you of little faith," he said. "Trust me, why don't you?"

She did trust him. Otherwise, she wouldn't have gotten in his car to begin with. Especially since she had no idea where they currently were, other than it wasn't toward any town she knew about.

Her phone buzzed, and she looked at it, surprised she had service. Maybe they weren't as far away from civilization as she'd thought. The display flashed with William's name.

She answered with a cheerful, "Hey there. What's up?" and hoped he could hear her over the static on the line.

"Eva," he said. "Can you hear me?" He sounded worried.

"Yes, mostly. What's going on?"

"We got the labs back. They relooked…and I thought you should know…" Static interrupted and drowned his words.

"I didn't get that last part," she said, heart racing. "What do you think I should know?"

"There were skin cells found under Catherine's fingernails. The DNA is a match to Stefan Benson. You need to be careful until we're able to bring him in."

Don't look at Stefan.

Don't look at Stefan.

Don't look at Stefan.

Doing everything she could to keep her voice steady, she replied, "Too late," seconds before her phone lost all signal and disconnected.

"**EVA!**" William all but yelled. Damn it, what had she meant by *too late*? He debated calling her back but didn't. He'd be at the marsh house soon; he'd talk to her there.

Less than three minutes later, he pulled up to the house and parked beside Eva's car. He made his way inside, calling her name, but didn't get a reply. Where was she? Her car was outside, so she hadn't gone far. Walking into the kitchen, he saw the note she left taped to the refrigerator, and his heart sank.

Out with Stefan. Be back soon!

He jerked the note down with a curse. That was what she'd meant by too late. She was already in his hands. And William had no idea where they could be headed.

The key to the map...

It was a long shot, but at the moment, it was all he had.

He walked the short distance to his Nana's room, the room Eva was currently residing in. Apart from Eva's suitcase in a corner, the room looked the same as it had when Nana had been alive. The decor and furniture hadn't been changed since her death. A handmade quilt Nana's mother made for her when she'd married his grandfather covered a full-sized mattress, a worn-looking black leather Bible sat on a nightstand, waiting to be picked up and read, and the numerous crayon and marker pictures taped to one wall, showing the whole of his artistic career.

There was only one picture on the next wall. A drawing like the others, but created with a bit more finesse, done in charcoals, and definitely not by his hand. A rabbit, a dog, and a cat were the focus. The trio was walking in the woods, and appeared to be talking.

The simple drawing never failed to make him smile. Catherine had drawn it as a birthday gift for Nana before they'd even been engaged. The animals were all characters out of William's favorite book as a child. Every night he spent here, Nana would read the story to him. Even though he knew every word by heart, he still delighted listening as Nana created her own voices for the three characters.

Named Hop, Skip, and Jump.

As soon as he'd seen the small sign on the mural, he'd known it couldn't be a coincidence. She'd painted all three words as if they were proper nouns, she had to be referencing the book. Unfortunately, he had no idea where the book was, nor could he remember the last time he saw it. Catherine didn't reference the book title, however, only the names of the characters in it.

And the picture…

He took a step forward and gently lifted the picture off the wall, expecting to find a hidden safe or a map taped to the wall, something, but when he moved the picture, all he saw was the wall.

"Damn."

He'd expected anything other than that. Nothing.

A sheet of paper fell from the back of the picture. He turned the frame over and took the paper from the floor. Taking care to hold the frame as gently as possible, he walked to the bed in the middle of the room. There, he put the picture face down on the bed.

The back of the drawing's frame had a handmade pocket of sorts. Based on its haphazard appearance, namely the uneven cut lines and misaligned corners, whoever made it had done so in a hurry. A hole had formed along the bottom edge, or had never been secured in the first place, he couldn't tell which. It was probably what had allowed the paper to slip through.

Why would Nana have an envelope hidden on the back of a drawing?

He carefully lifted the envelope from the back of the frame, cursing as it ripped and the contents fell to the bed. He looked down and froze.

Four gold coins.

He picked one up and dropped it immediately, scanning the

other three. Emerson would have to be called back to verify, but to William's untrained eye, they looked like the first four that had been identified.

He collected the paper that had been stored with the coins, and unfolded it, expecting it to tell him something about what he'd just discovered, maybe certifying the coins were indeed part of Blackbeard's treasure. Instead, what he found took his breath, and he sat on the floor.

A hand-drawn map. A map hand-drawn by Catherine. If he hadn't known by recognizing the strokes she used when drawing, the title written in her neat script would have told him.

Where I Found the Coins

All at once, he remembered her trying to show him a map. It had been after work a few months before the separation, and he was on the deck, attempting to forget the day with a beer. Catherine had walked out and sat next to him. He expected her to ask about his day. Surely after years of being married to him, she knew when he'd had a bad day. But no, she started talking about a real treasure map. He'd snapped and told her he had no interest in the map, treasure or not. Undeterred, she tried again, and that had been when he'd looked at her and said, "Really, Catherine? You, too? Do me a favor and throw that garbage away."

He had so many questions, they swirled around in his brain, until they all slowly morphed into one: Had his actions, or more to the point, his inaction, inadvertently contributed to Catherine's death?

The room tilted oddly, and he broke into a cold sweat. Thankful he was already sitting down, he dropped his head between his knees and forced himself to take several long, deep breaths. Eventually, the dizzy feeling passed and the shaking stopped. He stood up.

He couldn't help Catherine anymore, but he could help Eva.

"I'm not going to walk away from the only friend and sister I've ever had and leave you to face what could be..." I told her, but couldn't make myself finish.

"Edward and I will find you once we take care of the Edens," Mary said so calmly, I almost believed her.

— JOURNAL OF AN UNKNOWN WOMAN, EARLY 1700s

Chapter Thirty-one

"Stop the car, and let me out right now," Eva told Stefan.

"We're in the middle of nowhere," he said, glancing her way, but not stopping. "Are you being serious?"

"I know," was all she said in reply. She was too busy trying to plan the best way to open the door of the moving car and jump out.

"You know what?"

Maybe if she told him, he'd stop the car. Even if he planned to hurt her, as soon he slowed down, she'd open the door and hop out. She inched her finger toward the seatbelt latch and hoped he didn't notice.

"I know you had something to do with Catherine's death," she said. "The lab found your DNA under her fingernails."

He didn't get mad or attempt to slow down. Instead, he laughed. "Let me get this straight. My DNA was found under Catherine's fingernails and that means I had something to do with her death?"

Of course it did, but she wasn't going to tell him that.

"I think you've been watching too many police dramas on TV," he said. "The presence of my DNA under her fingernails doesn't mean I had anything to do with her death. All it means is that she scratched me."

She must have looked confused, because he continued, "Have you ever clawed a lover's back in a moment of passion, Eva? I don't think Catherine ever left my bed without marking me. She was a wildcat. In fact, we'd had a couple of intense rounds the night before her disappearance. I distinctly remember her drawing blood at one point."

Her blood ran cold. "You were who she was having an affair with." This was the man who had ruined William and Catherine's marriage. The man whose name Reverend Neighbors wouldn't give William. Even though she'd already told herself she wouldn't date Stefan, she'd never felt so disgusted and dirty.

"Affair sounds so dowdy. Catherine and I were lovers. It's not a big deal." He spoke so matter-of-factly, he probably believed what he was saying. "Man wasn't made for monogamy. In fact, I was hopeful things would eventually progress between the two of us."

Surely, she was hearing incorrectly. "You and me? I don't think so."

"Don't dismiss the idea so quickly. Give it some thought."

"No," she said. "And if that's the only reason you brought me out here today, you can turn around and take me back."

"Relax, Eva. I'm not a child who throws a fit when things don't go my way."

She sighed and crossed her arms, looking to her side and out the window to avoid him as much as possible.

Stefan pulled off whatever road they'd been on and kept going on an unpaved one. Wherever it was they were going, Stefan seemed determined to get there quickly. Apparently, he cared little about his car's shocks. Every time the vehicle ran over a rut in the road, she bounced around the front seat.

"Sorry," Stefan said. "We're almost there."

She didn't think her patience would last much longer, but

fortunately, Stefan had been correct, and within a few minutes, he pulled the car to a stop.

"This is it," Stefan announced brightly.

Eva's heart caught in her throat as she looked around. She had no idea where they were, other than it was in the middle of nowhere. Coming with Stefan had been a bad idea. The note she'd left for William was useless because he'd have no way to find her.

"Come on," Stefan said. "You're going to love it here."

"I'm not sure I can walk at this point," she said, trying to stretch out her legs in the sports car.

"Don't move," he said. "I'll come around and get your door for you."

Stefan opened the car door for her and helped her out. They walked away from the car, and when he told her to turn around, she did, and gasped.

Before her was an abandoned house, near collapse. There were several broken windows and weeds fought with long sea grass for space between the wooden slats of the porch. But even in its disrepair, it had obviously been lived in at some point in the not-too-distant past.

"What is this place?"

"My father found it after studying some of his maps."

"The ones in your office?" Eva asked. She had the strangest feeling she should know where they were, but nothing looked familiar.

"No," he said. "The maps showing this place aren't in my office. Too risky someone would see and recognize what it was they were looking at, and that would be a problem."

"It'd be a problem if people saw a map of land an old house is on?" she asked, unable to stop her sarcasm.

Stefan's expression didn't change at all. "At the time, the land belonged to William Templeton's grandmother, Ruth. I'm not sure if she even knew this old place exists. Hell, I doubt William knows it's here. But while my father was searching around the property, he found an old gold coin."

She gasped.

"Like the ones found on Catherine and Gabby?" Eva asked.

"I would assume so," he replied. "That would make the most sense."

The coins had to be part of Blackbeard's stash. It was real, and it was somewhere nearby. She didn't know how she knew, but she was certain. And on William's land.

She couldn't imagine William knowing about this place. Not with the way it looked and the way he kept up his grandmother's house. If he knew this house existed, it would look much different.

"My father died of a heart attack when I was fifteen. Mom kept all his maps and such packed away. I didn't find them until after her death." Stefan laughed. "You would have loved to have seen all the things he had. Most of it was junk, but he had those maps and the cutlass. I think deep down, he wanted me to find it."

"Find what?" she asked.

"Blackbeard's buried treasure," he said as if she asked something silly. "In his notes, my father claimed this was the house Blackbeard built his new bride, but I don't know how he came to that conclusion."

Eva looked at the house with renewed interest. It seemed impossible the dilapidated home before her had been built by Blackbeard. *But it makes sense*, something inside her whispered. And it was William's land. Knowing that, it was plausible Catherine found this place and the gold coins. Though that didn't explain how Gabby found hers or how the other two made their way to Eden Methodist.

"Wait," she said, processing something he'd said. "Why would your father want you to find the treasure? It's not your land."

Something akin to anger flashed so quickly in his eyes, she thought she imagined it. "Do you remember who I'm a descendant of?"

"Governor Eden." Eva's mind spun trying to work everything out. Adding the first governor of Eden into the story wasn't helping.

"Right, and by burying the treasure, Blackbeard cheated Eden out of his rightful share," Stefan said. "They had an agreement. Eden would turn a blind eye to any laws Blackbeard broke, and in return he would turn over a certain percentage to Eden. He couldn't turn it over if he buried it, now could he?"

She supposed he couldn't, but for some reason she felt as if she'd be agreeing to something greater if she said so.

"Therefore," he continued. "Any treasure found would rightfully belong to Eden if it had been found while he was alive. Since he's not, it belongs to me—as his heir and descendant."

It took her a second to realize she'd actually heard what she thought she had. "I don't think that's how the law works," she said, trying to cover her shock. "In fact, I know it's not."

"Eva," he said calmly. "We aren't talking about the law. We're talking about history and what's right and wrong. Surely you can see that?"

"Are you sure it's not just you trying to get your hands on the treasure?" Because that was what it sounded like to her.

"If you help me find it, I'll give you part of it."

She opened her mouth to reply, but nothing came out, which was probably for the best because she wasn't sure what the words would have been. He looked completely serious.

"Do you know where it is?" she finally asked.

"Not exactly, but it's got to be around this property somewhere." Stefan sighed and shook his head. "I should have gone about it differently. I thought you were just as much into finding the treasure as I was. I apologize if that's not the case."

"It's not that I don't want to find the treasure, but that I…."
But that she what?

It wasn't right to be on William's land, looking for treasure for which she held no claim. She didn't think Stefan would agree, however, so she needed to word her objection carefully.

"I think a lot of us have these grand ideas about finding Blackbeard's treasure and what we'd do with it and all." Eva looked straight ahead, still trying to wrap her head around everything. "But that's all they are, ideas and plans we know deep down we'll never have a chance to put into place. Now, though, you've made it seem a lot more real. I find I have to ask myself questions I've always thought I knew the answer to, and what I'm discovering is I'm not sure I do know my answer." She glanced his way. "Does any of that make sense?"

"Yes," he said, and his smile comforted her because she saw he did understand. "You were right, you know, when you said a few days ago about how it didn't make sense that Governor Eden would want to kill Blackbeard."

"Oh?" she asked, because that was the only reply she could come up with in response to the statement he appeared to have pulled out of the air.

"He *did* kill him," Stefan continued. "But he didn't want to."

Eva stared at him, not understanding where he was going with the conversation or where it came from in the first place.

"What are you talking about?" she finally asked.

"Have you heard the tale about the Devil's Coins?"

"The one where Blackbeard cursed anyone who found his treasure and wasn't an heir?"

"Yes." His eyes lit up, as if surprised she knew it. "Remember what happened to Mary?"

Something about the conversation put her on high alert, but she couldn't put a finger on what. Was it the land and its home, and the fact she stood on it? Or Stefan and his talk of a long-ago tragedy?

He looked as if he was waiting, so she told him what she remembered. "According to the story, she ran into the devil and he killed her, but she was able to tell Blackbeard about their son before she died."

"That is what the tale says, but of course, it wasn't *actually* the devil who killed her."

Eva forced a small smile. "I didn't *actually* think it was. Was it Governor Eden?"

"Not quite, but close. His wife, Penelope. Or if not by her hands, at least at her request."

Was the legend of the Devil's Coins based more on historical fact than anyone had ever realized? "How do you know?"

"I found letters from Governor Eden that my father had. He doesn't come out and say it explicitly, but if you read between the lines, it's obvious."

He spoke of it as if it were nothing, not just a huge historical deal. At least in her mind it was a huge historical deal. "Do you still have them?"

"No," he said. "If I did, I would have shown them to you. I don't know where they are now." He leveled his gaze at her. "Do you think this could really be Blackbeard's house?"

"I can't say with any certainty that it is, but on the other hand, I don't have any proof that it's not."

It may have been her mind playing tricks on her, but something about Stefan looked different. She couldn't put her finger on exactly what. His eyes were bright and shining with an excitement she couldn't understand. And maybe it was nothing more than the way the light of the setting sun fell across his face, but he looked wild and a bit unhinged. Suddenly, she just wanted to get back to Eden.

Giving what she hoped seemed a nonchalant shrug, she replied, "We should come back and look when we have more daylight. It's going to be too dark in about an hour or so to see much of anything."

He laughed and she froze, fear paralyzing her. It was not the sound of a sane man. It didn't even match the laugh he'd had no more than a few minutes ago when she'd brought up the DNA.

"Come back when we have more daylight?" he asked. "Oh, yes, and let's bring William with us."

"Since you mentioned it, that's probably a good idea." She tried to stay calm. "It is his land, after all."

He stopped laughing immediately. "No."

The anger in his voice surprised her so much, she took a step away from him.

"I gave you a choice. A chance to work with me, but you declined to even help me look." He took a step toward her in return. "Which means there won't be another time for you to come visit here, Eva, because you won't be leaving." He lifted a gun she hadn't noticed and pointed it at her. "Not alive, anyway."

Mary placed a hand on my arm and asked if I remembered her words the night she married Edward.

I nodded knowing they would echo in my heart for eternity. "If I were to die tomorrow, I would fly to heaven as free as a bird for having known this happiness."

— JOURNAL OF AN UNKNOWN WOMAN, EARLY 1700s

Chapter Thirty-two

Eva made herself remain upright and willed her body to stop trembling. "You're going to kill me because I won't help you search land you don't own for something you have no right to claim?"

"I never thought you'd agree to help me, but it didn't seem right not to at least pretend that you had a choice." He gave a sick chuckle. "Besides, if I merely wanted you dead, I'd have killed you long before now. However, I need you alive at the moment."

She clenched her teeth. "You won't get away with this."

"Oh, but I will. I assure you." He reached in his pocket with his free hand and tossed her a pair of handcuffs. "Put these on."

There was no way. To do so would be to sign her death certificate.

"Now, or I shoot out your kneecap and then have you do it, anyway." His voice left no doubt he would do as he threatened. "It won't do you any good to scream, if you're thinking about it. There's no one around for miles."

From what she gathered of the journey here, as well as what she saw of her current surroundings, she believed him.

He watched her with a studious expression. She also believed he'd shoot out her kneecap.

She cuffed her wrists together.

"Good," he said. "Now we're going inside to have a chat. Walk up the stairs."

He followed behind her, acting for all the world as if he owned the place. Maybe in his mind he did. Though she wanted nothing more than to stand in the midst of her surroundings and breathe it in before studying every nail that held the house together, she had to focus on getting away from the madman at her side.

The very fact they had been able to walk up to the porch and open the door told her someone had prepared for her arrival. Every step he took screamed of confidence. He was so certain of his plan's outcome, it kept her off-balance. *Because his plan's outcome is your death.* She had to do something to get away. She swallowed hard, telling herself to calm down and not to panic, that she would somehow get away from Stefan. Some opportunity would present itself.

She hoped.

He pushed her into a chair he clearly had waiting for that purpose, then proceeded to tie her legs together and then to the chair, leaving her hands cuffed in her lap. "Wait right here," he said and then laughed before moving out of her field of vision.

It sounded like he was rolling something over the floor. Whatever it was gave him a hard time, due to the uneven floorboards she guessed, and he cursed under his breath several times. She almost smiled when he came into sight struggling with a table on wheels, but as he neared, she saw what was on the table. A laptop. A phone. An unlabeled liquid-filled bottle.

But not just any laptop or phone. Looking closer, she realized she recognized the phone case and the laptop. "Is that Catherine's phone? And why do you have my laptop?"

But she knew. Deep inside she knew, even if she didn't want to admit it.

"Yes," Stefan said, sounding pleased she'd noticed. "It is. Do you know why I have it?"

"Because you killed her."

"I'm shocked you think so little of me. Catherine wasn't supposed to die," he said, like that somehow made it all better. "That wasn't my plan. I needed her to tell me where in this godforsaken property or shack she found the coins. The sand hole she fell into filled up quicker than I thought it would, and she was gone before I could do anything."

"You dug a hole for her to fall in?"

His eyes narrowed. "Of course not. It was some idiot tourist who did it, more than likely."

"I guess they made it easier for you," Eva said before she thought about her words.

He glared at her. "Do you think I wanted Catherine to die?"

"I'm not sure." She wasn't sure why she became mouthy suddenly, but it kept Stefan talking which meant he wasn't trying to shoot her. It wasn't much in her favor, but every little bit helped. "You don't seem all that upset that she's gone."

His eyes grew wild, and she feared she'd gone too far. "You don't know anything about me," he said. "Nothing."

"Where did you get her phone?"

"She left it on the sink in the bathroom at the bar that night. A woman brought it right after Catherine had walked out and left it behind. I saw and told her I'd give it to her because she was with me."

"How did Catherine get from the bar to a sand hole?"

"I'm not going to talk about Catherine anymore other than to say she knew where the coins were, she refused to tell me, and now she's dead."

Stefan hadn't killed Eva yet, and he'd had plenty of opportunities, which meant he still needed her alive. At least for the moment. No matter what, she needed to show how useful she was until she could find a way to get away from him.

"I can help you find it."

He gave her a self-satisfied smile. "That's a lovely offer, and I truly appreciate it, but I already asked you once, and you turned me down. The offer is no longer an option."

If she couldn't find a way to help him, she needed to keep him talking. Anything to keep him talking.

"Did you finally find this place by looking at your father's maps?"

"Of course, and I've known about this place for ages. You see, what most people, including William, don't know is that Catherine and I dated off and on in college. Not anything serious. When the high school reunion came up, she wanted to go alone in case William was there. She'd always had a thing for him." He chuckled. "Of course, William was there and hooked up with Catherine. I didn't care, I knew she'd come back to me. And she did. It didn't bother me that she was married when she did."

What?

She didn't realize she'd said it out loud until he laughed.

"Oh, yes," he said. "I can be a patient man when I need to be. All I had to do was bide my time."

"Why would you think she'd come back to you when she was married to William?"

"I knew William couldn't keep her satisfied," Stefan said, as if they were discussing nothing but the weather. "Not with as much time as he put into his job."

She hoped she was able to keep her face as neutral as possible and that her expression wasn't showing the disgust she felt. If Stefan knew how she really felt about him right now, he'd no doubt put a bullet through her head.

He looked even more unlike the Stefan she thought she knew. The air around him pulsed with a dangerous undertone. So tightly wound, he trembled, he was a man on the edge and ready to detonate. She didn't want to be anywhere nearby when it happened.

"But enough talking," Stefan said. "I did bring you here for a purpose."

"And what is that?"

"You're going to confess to Catherine's murder," he said, his voice deadpan. "Then because you're so guilt ridden, you're going to kill yourself."

Her chest felt tight, and the tiny cabin grew warmer with each passing second. She wanted to tell him that he was out of his mind, but feared he'd take it as a compliment. "Did you kill Gabby, too?"

"Gabby drowned. I may have helped her along, but unless the ME is specifically looking for what I gave her, the tox screen will come back negative. You must realize, I didn't want to have to kill Gabby," he said. "But she showed up in my office flashing that gold coin for anyone to see." He shook his head. "It wasn't a risk I wanted to take."

Her stomach clenched hearing about Gabby. "No one's going to believe I killed Catherine."

"Don't play ignorant, the part doesn't become you. You and I both know you're much smarter than that." The gun was still leveled at her. "They'll believe anything you tell them because your confession will be just what they're looking for."

"What does that mean?"

"Everyone's going to eat up the story you'll tell about being in love with your friend's husband, how she confronted you, and in a moment of passion you killed her."

"That's the stupidest idea I've ever heard," she said, hoping he had no clue how she really felt about William. "You'll never be able to convince anyone of that."

"It won't be as hard as you might think." Stefan seemed pleased to share his plan with her. "It's certainly been to my advantage you've decided to shack up with William at that tiny little place in the marsh. Not only because everyone knows you're there, but also because there's been no one staying in the house in town. The house I have a key for because I took Catherine's and had a copy made. Thanks to a few items that were taken from your house—underwear, an old hairbrush, those sorts of things—it'll look like you had a well-thought-out plan."

"We haven't been shacking up."

"What a child you are, Eva. What you actually do doesn't matter, it's what people *think* you do that counts." He bent down to look at her eye level, and when he did, something moved nearby. "Don't you worry the details, I have it all under control. Now, I have to go get a few more things. We'll start when I get back."

She watched as he turned and walked away, noting he shoved the gun in the back waistband of his pants. Maybe he'd shoot himself in the backside.

She glanced to where she thought she saw movement seconds before, but nothing was there. Her mind probably made it up or she was seeing things. Or maybe it was a bird or a rat. At this point, it could be anything. Anything other than someone coming to recuse her. No one other than Stefan knew this place even existed.

Being alone, or at least without Stefan pointing a gun in her direction, gave her time to think and to plan. She would find a way out of here.

The first thing she had to do was untie her legs from the chair. How to accomplish that with her wrists cuffed together, however, was another problem altogether. She thought wistfully about the case of lock picks she had in her purse. The purse that was still in Stefan's car.

Damn it.

Why hadn't she thought of putting the picks in her pocket? That way she might have more than a snowball's chance in hell of living through the day.

As it stood, there would be no knight on a white horse coming to rescue her. If she couldn't find a way to get out of this stupid chair, she would more than likely die here, and since no one knew about the house, her body would never be found.

"The Lord allowed me to have Alexander Edward to have as a representation of our love and through him we will continue," Mary told me while tears rolled down her cheeks. "There is no one else other than you, dear sister, that I would trust to care for my heart. Take him and keep him safe."

— JOURNAL OF AN UNKNOWN WOMAN, EARLY 1700s

From what Catherine drew, there was an abandoned house on his property. William could only assume it was where Stefan was taking Eva. If that assumption was correct, that would be the most likely place to find both Stefan and Eva. If he was wrong...he couldn't think about that.

As he drove, William didn't allow himself to dwell on the numerous unanswered questions left in the wake of those assumptions. Why Stefan would take Eva there. What his plans were. If Eva went voluntarily or if he'd forced her. And how were parts of his land and property he'd never seen before involved?

There wasn't time for questions, only planning. Using the map Catherine drew, he parked far enough away from the abandoned house, the location he thought Stefan and Eva most likely were, so as not to be seen or heard. He tried to see everything as an uninvolved third party, but the truth was, he didn't know what he'd do if he lost Eva.

The sun had started its descent by the time he made it to the house. He let out a sigh of relief at the sight of Stefan's car parked outside. A quick peek through a window, and he saw Eva's purse on the front passenger floorboard.

Someone inside the old home was talking. Fortunately, the marsh was filled with noise, the wind whistled through the tall grass and birds chirped everywhere. William silently made his way to the house, walking as quickly as possible toward the window on the side of the house closest to where he thought the sound came from. Peeking inside, he caught a glimpse of Eva tied to a chair. Stefan stood in front of her, talking.

He didn't let himself feel thankful he'd found her and she was alive, because he knew if he didn't do something soon she wouldn't be for long. Based on how Eva's chair and Stefan were positioned, if William entered through the door, there was a chance Stefan would see him. The best chance he had of getting in without notice would be the very window he was at.

There was no glass in the windows, only a set of wooden shutters to keep the elements out. Thankfully, they were currently open. Not that he'd have a problem getting them open if that hadn't been the case, but it wasn't a very quiet activity.

He listened to Stefan, trying to gauge the best time to enter.

William's blood ran cold listening to Stefan's plan. From the way the man spoke, it had not been a hastily made decision to kidnap Eva, but rather a small part of a much larger agenda. From the way it sounded, Stefan hadn't been getting together with Eva so much as he'd been grooming her. For the last several weeks, she'd been unconsciously slowly molded into the perfect scapegoat.

William forced himself not to dwell on the fact that he was looking at the man responsible for his marriage falling apart. To think Stefan had more than likely used Catherine in the same way he'd been using Eva, but on a much larger scale and for a much longer time, threatened to send his rage in an upward spiral. However, rage was a luxury he couldn't afford at the moment. Not if he had any hope of getting Eva out of this situation alive.

Stefan turned to leave, and William prepared to spring into action, replaying in his mind the moves he planned to make. As soon as Stefan made it out the door, William lifted himself up and over the windowpane, landing lightly on his feet.

Eva's eyes grew wide at his entrance, and a large smile covered her face. She lifted her hands. They weren't tied but handcuffed together. Retrieving the key he kept on his keychain, he glanced toward the front door.

A car door slammed.

"Quickly," Eva said in a hurried whisper.

William unlocked the cuffs and Eva worked to get them off while he took his pocketknife and started cutting through the ropes on her leg. William wanted to catch Stefan off guard and glanced again toward the front door. Things were less likely to grow violent if he could apprehend Stefan while the man's hands were full.

The last of the rope fell to the ground, but William knew they'd made noise in the process. The question was, how much, if anything, had Stefan heard? No matter the answer, William needed to get Eva out of the way and somewhere safe.

"Go out the window I used," he told her in a whisper.

"Are you coming?" she asked.

He shook his head. "Not yet. As soon as I arrest Stefan." He narrowed his eyes, hoping to convey how serious he was. "Go."

"I'll wait."

"No," he said. The car outside beeped. William could only guess Stefan had locked it and was heading back inside. Eva needed to go. "Now."

She took one step in the direction of the window, but then stopped at the sound of footsteps.

"What are you doing here?"

William turned to see Stefan standing in the middle of the doorway. He had removed his suit coat and tie. The first few buttons at his throat had been undone, and his shirt sleeves were rolled up. A fine sheen of sweat covered his face. Stefan carefully placed the box he'd carried inside on the floor. William felt a sense of relief when he stood back up, without a weapon in hands. That relief fled when he looked in Stefan's eyes because all William saw was evil.

William kept his hands where they could be easily seen. Stefan wasn't holding a weapon, so William didn't draw his. Maybe they could end this without violence. "I'm taking Eva back home, and then you and I are going to go to the station."

Stefan didn't say anything, but William saw his intent the second his decision was made. Moving faster than William would have thought possible, Stefan let out a yell and took off toward him with his hands out in front of him.

"Eva, go!" William had a chance to shout while pulling out his gun. Before he could take aim, Stefan made it to him and grabbed his wrist. They both fought for control of the weapon.

Out of the corner of his eye, William saw Eva hadn't moved. Nothing he could do about it now. The more desperate Stefan became, the stronger he grew. It took all of William's strength to keep a grip on the gun.

They struggled for long seconds. Stefan's face contorted into rage, and he let out a scream. William's grip slipped. Stefan jerked hard to the right, and William's gun flew across the room.

Stefan's lips lifted in a slow grin. "I'm going to kill you."

"Stop now, Stefan."

William looked over Stefan's shoulder and saw Eva holding his service weapon. He hadn't seen her pick it up.

"You won't shoot me," Stefan taunted. "You don't have it in you."

"I swear to God, Stefan." Her voice was steady with no trace of fear or nerves. "Stop now, or I shoot your knee."

Stefan laughed and reached behind his back, pulling out a gun. "When I finish him off, I'm coming for you."

A gunshot rang out, and William braced himself for pain, but it was Stefan who dropped to the floor with blood curdling howl, clutching his knee.

Shaken, but knowing he still had work to do, William picked up the weapon Stefan dropped, ensured the safety was on, then took the one Eva held out to him.

"You shot me!" Stefan yelled at her.

"Returning the favor," she said.

"I didn't shoot your kneecap."

Eva waved her hand in dismissal, though she looked a bit pale. "You threatened me with it. Same thing."

As William Mirandized and handcuffed him, Stefan continued his verbal assault. Not even stopping his tirade when William did the best he could first-aid wise for the gunshot wound.

Since it would take at least twenty minutes for anyone to make it to where they were, after radioing for paramedics and backup, William attempted to get Stefan as comfortable as possible. Eva sat on the floor across the room, likely going through a bit of shock. Hell, after seeing the way she shot, *he* was in a bit of shock. He wished he could clone himself and help her through it, but at the moment, he needed to stay close to Stefan.

"Tell me why?" William finally asked Stefan. If he insisted on rambling, William would rather hear something useful instead how of he planned to sue the Eden Police Department if he wasn't allowed to press charges against Eva. Which didn't make any sense at all, but William chalked it up to how painful that knee had to be.

"Why should I tell you anything?" Stefan asked.

"Because one day my words might be the deciding factor between whether or not you end up in a cell or on death row."

The look in Stefan's eyes left no doubt in William's mind that Stefan wanted nothing more than to tell him to go straight to hell. But after a long moment of silence, Stefan shifted his position, grimacing as he moved.

"I'll start at the beginning," he said. "When I was fifteen, my father decided he wanted to leave his high-paying job as an attorney to become a priest. I thought he was joking at first and laughed, but then he backhanded me and said God didn't make jokes."

William kept silent. He hoped Stefan wasn't going to blame everything he did on the way his father treated him.

"Of course," Stefan continued, anger burning in his eyes, and his voice laced with hate. "He couldn't be a priest with a wife and a son, so he planned to have his marriage to my mother annulled. Going through that would have ruined her. For days, she did nothing but cry and beg him to reconsider. He refused, and I could never forgive him for that. Fortunately, he had a massive heart attack before he could go through with his plan. Mom sold most of his things or gave them away. The only things of his she kept were his maps and a few other historical items. I didn't even find those until she passed."

William kept his expression neutral, not sure if he was ready to hear the next part or not. One thing keeping him calm was he didn't want Stefan to think he'd gotten the best of him.

Stefan was kept from continuing by the sound of sirens approaching. He simply looked at William and said, "Guess you're going to have to wait for the rest of the story."

By the time the first responders and the various law enforcement officers left, it was dark. William and Eva were the only two people remaining. He watched her as the car carrying Stefan pulled away and wondered why she hadn't left before now. She'd refused to go to the hospital because she said she was fine and Stefan hadn't touched her.

"Shit," he said as it hit him. "You don't have a car here."

"I was hoping I could get a ride back to town with you," she said.

William looked around the run-down house. "Well, I'm not about to leave you out here by yourself."

"I have been camping, you know," she said. "I would be fine staying here until someone could pick me up or bring my car."

"It wasn't your survival skills I was questioning," he said dryly. "I'm afraid if I leave you here, you'll somehow get yourself into another pile of trouble."

She looked as if she wanted to argue, and surprised him when she said, "Yes, you're probably right about that. Do you mind if I stay at the marsh house one more night? I think I'll stay there tonight and move back home tomorrow."

"Are you ready to go back to your place?" he asked, thinking about the mess she would have to deal with. "Have you been inside?"

"Yes, I think I'm ready, and no, I haven't been inside," she answered. "But Doris sent in her crew to clean it up for me when your team had finished with everything they needed."

"Doris is good people."

Eva nodded. She looked exhausted, but he had a few more questions before they left.

"Where did you learn to shoot like that?" he asked.

"I once dated a Marine who was a designated marksman." She shrugged. "He liked to teach, and I was a quick learner. I now know how right he was when he said it's much different when you're shooting people."

"It didn't cross your mind at any point to tell me you could shoot?"

She gave him a teasing smile and a wink. "A girl likes to keep some secrets. Besides, I did tell you I could come in handy riding shotgun."

"Next time tell me when you mean for me to take something literal," he said with a laugh.

He kept a close eye on her as he drove them back to the homestead because she was right. It *was* different when you were shooting people. She still trembled every now and then. He supposed she would for a time. But she was a smart woman, and she'd let someone know if she needed help. No doubt she was still trying to come to terms with the fact that the boy she met when she was twelve and the man who almost killed her today were one and the same.

Mitch called when they were a few miles away. Once they were off the phone, he updated Eva.

"We lost Robert," he said, blinking back tears. "The medical examiner will be getting involved since it's a suspicious death. They're also going to test the beer can for toxins."

Eva nodded, and he saw a tear roll down her cheek. "I can't believe he's gone. He was never my favorite person, but I never wanted him to die, and he was a good friend to you and Catherine."

"Yes, he was, and of course you didn't want him to die. No one wanted that," William said, thinking how unfair it was that Stefan was alive and three other people weren't.

Silence filled the car for a minute.

"Thank you," she said, after a long silence.

"What for?"

"For coming to get me. For saving my life. For finding me."

"Just doing my job," he said. "No thanks are necessary. Besides, you're the one who really saved the day."

He felt the weight of her stare but didn't turn toward her or acknowledge her in any way. "You're a good man, William Templeton. The world needs more men like you."

He wasn't so sure about that, but before he had a chance to reply, Eva was snoring.

IT ENDED UP being four days before William was able to speak with Stefan. After finding it so difficult to get the attorney to speak following the shooting, William had anticipated him being obstinate and uncooperative, but prison life did not suit Stefan, and bail had been denied. Apparently, he thought answering William's questions again might benefit him in the future, though William had never even hinted anything of the sort. Either that or Stefan knew it'd be painful for William to hear, and he wanted to be part of that pain.

They spoke of Gabby first. Stefan recalled how she burst into his office that Thursday morning. Excited, she told him, because she had found more coins, *just like his.*

"I had the gold coin my father found in my top desk drawer," Stefan said. "She confessed she'd opened the drawer one of the first few times she cleaned my office, looking for paper to leave a note, and saw the coin. What she wanted to show me that Thursday was a coin she found earlier in the week."

"Did she find it at Nana's while cleaning?"

"I assume so, I didn't ask her because I didn't want her to think I was interested. She might have gotten suspicious before I could take care of her." He didn't look remorseful as he continued. "Understand, I had no hard feelings toward her. I didn't want her to die. But she knew just enough about the coin to be dangerous if she started talking. So, she had to go."

"Why did you leave the coin on her?" William asked.

"I thought about taking it, but I knew she'd mentioned the coin to Robert. I knew I could keep the reverend quiet, but I didn't know who else she might have spoken to or if she'd used my name. I thought the best course of action, all things considered, was to leave the coin."

Stefan drove to her place that night, knowing she'd be alone because he'd overheard her telling Naomi that her boyfriend was in Raleigh. Poisoning her water had been easy. The hardest part was ensuring she was still unconscious when he dumped her in the ocean.

William's stomach turned at how easily Stefan talked about taking someone's life. "The attack on Eva?" he asked.

Stefan waved his hand in dismissal. "A man hired to get evidence to plant in your house in town."

"Contact details?" William asked, and Stefan told him where to find them in his office files.

"And, yes," Stefan added. "Before you ask, I planted the tote bag at the church as a distraction." He snorted.

They were down to one topic. William wasn't sure he wanted to know, but he knew he needed to hear. "Tell me about Catherine."

A smile flickered at the corners of Stefan's lips, but didn't make it to his face. "I trusted her too much. Trusted that her feelings for me were stronger than the ones she had for you." He shook his head. "You were so wrapped up with your job and keeping up your grandmother's place, you didn't see how lonely Catherine was. About two or three years ago, I saw her at The Tattered Flag and invited her to lunch. It had been a while since we last saw each other, but it didn't take long for us to catch up."

William's stomach twisted. Had he really been so busy he neglected his wife? How had he been so blind? Anger and disgust fought for dominance, but he swallowed them both down to deal with later.

"When I first mentioned the possibility of treasure on your land, at a property you didn't know about, she was excited," Stefan continued, seemingly aware of William's turmoil based on the smirk he wore. "We'd make plans for what we'd do when we found it. She'd go exploring on your property when you were at work. But in the end, she was too weak. She tried to tell me she wasn't able to find anything, but I could see behind her lies."

Stefan's hands were clenched in tight fists, betraying the utter calm of his voice. If someone wasn't paying attention, it was possible to overlook the rage suggested by those fists. William had a feeling it would be unwise to do so.

Stefan eyed William, and obviously realized what he was doing, because he relaxed his fists before continuing. "I was watching her. I saw her talk with Robert. When I confronted her, she told me she'd made a mistake with me and that our relationship was wrong. She claimed she was going to work on her marriage and wanted out. I told her there was only one way out."

The hair on the back of William's neck stood up. At the moment, Stefan hadn't been charged with anything pertaining to Catherine, but if premeditation could be proven, that could change. Was Stefan's "one way out" statement a confession?

"We'd had an argument that day, before she died," Stefan said, oblivious to what he might have let slip. "I knew she had more information than what she was telling me. I wanted to know what she'd talked to Robert about. She cried and claimed she hadn't found anything. But she was lying. I followed her into the bar that night, making sure she didn't see me, and waited outside once I overheard her telling the bartender she was leaving."

Stefan flashed a sadistic smile. "I was glad she was too drunk to drive because that meant I could follow her on foot. From past experience, I knew she could be more...*forthcoming* after a drink or two. I'm sure you know what I mean."

William made himself sit very still and not show any emotion.

"Unfortunately, when she realized she was being followed, I sensed her panic. She took off running." Stefan shrugged. "I followed."

The scene played out vividly in William's head, and an overwhelming sense of grief swept over him. He vowed not to let Stefan know how much it affected him to hear of Catherine's last moments.

"I thought when she hit the beach, she'd stop. But no. She took off for the dunes. Bad decision. I can only assume it was an alcohol-based one. I doubt she'd have taken the same path if she'd been sober. Of course, maybe she thought she knew them well enough to hide."

William couldn't help but think back to what he'd been doing that very night, probably around the same time the monster sitting before him now was stalking his wife. At the time, the most important thing to him was trying to limit the potential damage of the upcoming storm. And while his job was important, how often had he placed its importance above that of his wife's?

Stefan seemed to sense William's discomfort and an unholy glee covered his expression. "I could tell when she hit the sand because she slowed down considerably. I matched her speed because I thought doing so would show that I wasn't dangerous, I only wanted information."

But to what lengths was he willing to go to get that information?

"She hadn't gotten far when she looked over her shoulder. She never stopped running, though, and before I could say anything, she disappeared." He snapped his fingers. "Just like that. I kept walking toward the place I last saw her, and it didn't take long before I found her. The top of the hole was above her head, and she was panicking. Clawing the sand. Trying to climb out. Only thing that did was to make more sand fall on top of her. By the time I made it to her, the sand was up to her thighs. She stood completely still, which was good, because that stopped the sand from falling."

William fisted his hands under the table, telling himself he couldn't give in to the urge to strangle the man, no matter how tempted he was.

"When she saw me," Stefan said, but William could tell he was still on that beach with Catherine, using a monotone voice showing neither regret nor remorse. "She flailed her arms. A mistake because the action made the sand fall again. At that point, there was nothing I could do. Every time I moved, it only made the situation worse. I couldn't save her."

"You didn't try," William said, purposely keeping his voice low, knowing if he yelled now, he might not stop. "You didn't even call for help or tell anyone. You left her there."

Stefan said nothing.

William knew he wasn't getting the entire story from Stefan. He wasn't even sure how much of what he'd just been told was the truth. All he knew was it was in his best interest for him to get away from Stefan Benson as quickly as possible.

Every afternoon before I prepare the household for dinner, I sit in the parlor and talk with my mother. Some days I might have as many as fifteen minutes, and other days as few as two. The amount of time never matters. Not to me, I am happy to have a free moment. Nor does it matter to my mother, who is dead.

No one knows, of course. Kind as our neighbors are, I doubt their kindness large enough to encompass a woman conversing with dead people. Not that they could overhear. I remain silent, speaking to my mother with the words I write as I remember the past.

— JOURNAL FROM AN UNKNOWN WOMAN, MID 1700s

Chapter Thirty-four

Yesterday, the State Medical Examiner's Office released autopsy results on Eden resident, Gabby Clark. Clark's body was found weeks ago at a local fishing hole in Eden. According to the report, her death was a homicide.

There were also questions brought up about the death of Catherine Harper, local emerging artist and estranged wife of Eden Police Chief, William Templeton. However, her death is still considered accidental according to authorities.

Though Templeton was not a person of interest in either death, he agreed to step down as Chief of Police during the recent investigations. Mitch Montague, who was appointed as Acting Police Chief, turned the job back over to Templeton yesterday. In a brief message to the press, Templeton thanked Montague for his service to the town of Eden and praised him for his handling of a "dark time in our community's history." He also reminded residents and visitors to the Outer Banks that holes dug in the sand should never be deeper than knee level, and any holes dug should be refilled with sand before leaving.

Related, Nag's Head real estate attorney, Stefan Benson, has been *charged with the first-degree murders of Gabby Clark and Reverend Robert Neighbors, both of Eden, as well as multiple charges including kidnapping and assault of Eva Knightly, a local historian. Benson is currently in custody. His request for bail has been denied.*

"ALL OF THIS heartache and death over a bunch of stupid coins," Eva said the following weekend, placing the newspaper she'd been reading down on the table beside her.

William had stopped by to check on her after leaving work. They hadn't had a chance to talk much since Eva moved back to her home the morning after everything went down with Stefan. William was certain she was fine, but he wanted to see with his own eyes. Currently, they were sitting on her back porch.

"I hate humans sometimes," she added.

"I do, too," he said. "I have to keep reminding myself that for every Stefan, there are ten other men who are nothing like him."

"Does that work?" she asked.

He had to be honest with her. "Only about thirty-five percent of the time."

"Stupid coins," she mumbled under her breath.

"Does this mean you aren't interested in Blackbeard's treasure?" he asked.

"I still want it found for historical purposes, but now I'm more concerned about who finds it and how they come to find it." She sighed. "I don't know, maybe it's for the best it's never found."

"You don't really still believe that, do you?"

"I don't know. Sometimes." She turned her head to look at him, holding her hand up to shield her eyes from the sun. "Seriously, look at everyone who's died as a result of those coins—Catherine, Gabby, Robert."

"You're still alive," he said, his breath hitching at the thought of how close they came to that not being the case. Though, he had to admit she did have a point. Death and destruction did seem to follow the coins around.

"Only because I was lucky that you figured out where I was." She dropped her hand. "I'm pretty sure Blackbeard hid his treasure somewhere nearby. Probably in more than one place. But a lot of people have walked this area since Blackbeard and his peers. Maybe the best possible outcome is someone found it ages ago and kept quiet about what they discovered."

"So, if I were to tell you that the day after Stefan was arrested, I was looking around that old house and came across an old wooden chest under some floorboards, you wouldn't want to know what was inside?"

Her eyes grew wide. "Did you? You aren't joking, are you? Please tell me you wouldn't joke about something like that."

"I'm not joking," he said, and swallowed a laugh at the way her eyes grew round with surprise. She looked lovely.

"What was in it?"

"I haven't opened it yet." He'd thought she looked surprised before, but that was until he saw the look she gave at that statement.

"Why not?"

"I decided to wait and open it with someone a little more knowledgeable about its possible contents." She wrinkled her brow, so he added, "I've been waiting to open it with you. Between both of our schedules, this is the first time we've been in the same space long enough for me to mention it."

"Oh my God."

"Do you want me to get it?" William asked. "It's sitting in my truck right now. I'll bring it into your living room. We'll be able to see better in there. Unless you think it's been cursed."

She reached out and punched him on the shoulder. "You've been sitting here for ten minutes and the entire time, you've had a wooden chest in your truck?"

He laughed. "Is that a *yes*?"

"Yes." She stood up and shooed him away with her hands. "Go get it. Now."

He wasn't surprised to see her not-so-patiently waiting, standing in the living room when he returned. "It's much lighter than what I think treasure should weigh," he said.

"I don't care if it's empty. Look at that woodwork." She ran her finger along the delicately carved lines of the chest.

"I agree, it's beautiful craftsmanship," he said. "But don't you want to look inside?"

She took a step back. "Put it down and let's open it."

William put the box down. "It has a lock, but no worries." He flashed her a smile and withdrew his set of picklocks from his back pocket. "It's no match for me."

He'd expected her to laugh or at least smile, but her eyes were wide with shock. Did she find picking locks to be distasteful? Too bad if she did, he had no other way to get past the lock. He went to work, and within seconds the lock was off the box.

William caught Eva's eye and pointed to the wooden chest. "I think you should be the one to open it since you were the one who had their life on the line that day."

"Are you sure?" she asked.

"I wouldn't have said it otherwise." William didn't care what was in the box, just seeing Eva's reaction was enough.

Eva knelt in front of the chest and slowly lifted the lid. Sitting at her side, William watched as she pulled out a handmade baby quilt. Next were two outfits that looked too tiny for a human to ever fit into.

But it was the next garment that took his breath. It was so long, Eva had to stand up in order to see it all. He stood up as well.

"I know exactly what this is," she whispered. "It's a wedding gown."

"It's blue," William said.

"Wedding gowns usually weren't white until the Victorian

era." She showed him the bodice of the gown. "See how pearls and crystals have been hand-sewed? You wouldn't find anything like that on just any dress." Reverently, she brushed the material. "Satin. I wonder if this was what Blackbeard's bride wore when they got married?"

"No matter what it turns out to be, it's an exquisite gown, that's for sure." Not that William knew one fabric or color from another, but even he knew outstanding artistry when he saw it. "And so well preserved. Hard to believe it's been inside that chest for over three hundred years."

"Maybe it's a magical chest," Eva mused.

"Was that the last thing in there?" William asked.

"I don't even know." She handed the gown to William. "Hold this."

"Wow." He shifted his arms at the unexpected weight. "That's a lot heavier than I thought it would be."

Eva threw him a knowing smile. "That's because it's real satin and real pearls. Can you imagine wearing that all day? With a corset?"

He winced. "I'll never complain about having to wear a necktie again."

But Eva's mind was obviously back inside the chest. "Looks like there are letters or something. And what looks like a journal." She looked like she'd just been handed millions of dollars. "This is unreal. Here, put the gown back inside for a minute, and let's see what this says."

She picked up the delicate piece of paper on the top and held it so they both could read.

November 1758
Dearest Cousin Mary,
It's so hard to believe it's been forty years since I said goodbye to you that fateful day in 1718.

I remember walking away from the house first because you said you wanted Alexander Edward's last vision of you to be of you waving him on and not walking away. He was so tiny then, but I like to think he remembers.

I was so scared. Me. Alone except for a child that wasn't mine. I later sometimes pretended he was mine, but only for a second because I always knew he was yours. I changed my first name to Mary so your son and I would always remember you. I changed our last name, I didn't think it wise to use Teach, it was and still is too closely associated with the pirate Blackbeard. I went with Templeton, which at least starts with the same letter.

We left North Carolina on foot. Fortunately with the money you gave me, we were able to get a coach and we made our way to Boston. It's very different here. It's much colder, and the sea doesn't look the same.

All these years, I've never stepped a foot back into North Carolina, though Alexander Edward has promised to take me one last time. We leave tomorrow.

Speaking of your boy, I know you would be proud. He is a merchant and has done very well for himself. He married a lovely Boston girl from a good family and they have made you a grandmother six times over. They have five boys, but the youngest is a girl and, unlike her brothers, her hair is blond. I think she looks like you.

I don't know what to expect going back to North Carolina. I've been in Boston for so long, I wonder if I'll even remember it? Or if it will feel like home? If it wasn't for your son, I would think my early years all a dream.

Alexander Edward's youngest son will travel with us. He's a doctor and they need them badly in the South. We hope the deed I have will be all that is required to prove ownership of the land and homestead. I still have much of the gold you gave me and I recall several of the places you told me Edward had buried more. I think I shall pretend I'm a pirate and bury it on your land where it *belongs. Maybe someday two hundred years from now a Templeton heir will come looking.*

I hope he (or she!) finds it.

There is unrest everywhere and talk of war and independence from England. Is it bad that I don't care one way or the other? I find myself growing weary and tired. I only want to sit in the dunes one more time, to feel the breeze through my hair, and taste the salt in the air.

I can almost see you in Heaven smiling at the wishes of a silly old woman. I know Edward is right by your side. I shall see you both soon.

Ever yours,
Millie

William tried to read the letter but gave up. He recognized his surname, Templeton, in the text, but that was about all he could make out.

"Templeton," Eva lifted her head. "Does this mean…"

"Hell," he said. "Don't ask me what it means, I can't make heads or tails out of that. I know those words are written in English, but that doesn't mean it's easy to read the script."

Eva was silent as she read the letter again. "I want to say it implies that the descendants of Blackbeard changed their last name from Teach to Templeton."

He was a descendant of Blackbeard? The only remaining descendant of Blackbeard?

It sounded preposterous in his head; he couldn't imagine how much more it would be to say it out loud. No wonder Eva hadn't been able to finish her question.

"It can't mean anything," he said. "It can't. It's too crazy to even think about, much less consider as fact for even a second."

But Eva wasn't listening to him. No, she had that faraway look in her eyes again. "If you do consider it as fact, though, for a little bit longer than a second, you'll have to agree it does make sense."

He shouldn't ask her. He knew he shouldn't. But he did anyway. "How does it make sense?"

"Whose property was all this found on? Whose family has owned this land for years? Whose last name is Templeton?"

Hearing her talk almost made it seem possible. Almost. In reality, it was nothing more than Eva's overactive imagination, and her wanting there to be a connection with Blackbeard. "I hear what you're saying. I promise," he told her. "But there's no proof there. Everything you have is circumstantial. Seriously, I think I would have heard that we were somehow related by now."

"I wasn't aware that we were in court or that you were an attorney." All at once, her smile grew wide and her eyes danced.

Heaven help him. Eva had a plan.

"You want proof?" she asked him. "I'll get it for you."

He narrowed his eyes, but he had to admit, he was curious to see how she planned to prove his heritage. Or more to the point, his *supposed* heritage. "How?"

"Amelia's into genealogy, and I've seen her work. Pretty impressive."

"Amelia, Elbert's granddaughter, the engineer who is also running for mayor, Amelia?" Surely, there had to be another one he didn't know.

"Yes."

"Does she ever sleep?"

"Probably not much." Her head titled. "I think we just discovered why she always hit a dead end when looking to possible descendants of Blackbeard."

"We did?" he asked, certain he was missing something. "When did we do that?"

"Just now with the letter. She's never been able to locate a descendant of Blackbeard's because she never knew he was raised by a woman with the last name of Templeton. This letter makes it sound like there's numerous places Blackbeard's loot is buried, and I just said that same thing less than thirty minutes ago. Now I'm willing to bet a good portion of it is on your land."

"Maybe," he said, not convinced yet. "I drove back to that house yesterday. I'm trying to decide what to do with the property. I don't want to tear down something that could be historically important."

"You didn't see any other chests, did you?"

He shook his head. "No, but I came across a shack someone must have used for storage."

"Storage?" she asked, like the shed was filled with untapped treasure waiting to be discovered.

"Yes, but just stuff," he said. "You know, things people don't want to get rid of, but can't keep in their house for fear of being labeled a hoarder kind of stuff. Not the good stuff you're thinking about."

"William Templeton," she said in a dry voice. "There are two things you should know about me. One, I never joke about history. And two, everything in storage can turn out to be the good stuff. Even hoarder stuff. Maybe especially hoarder stuff."

"In that case, I give you permission to go through the storage shack all you want."

She smiled, her entire face beaming with excitement, and she rubbed her hands together. "I can't wait to start. Let's go tomorrow."

The next day was Sunday. "I could probably be persuaded."

"We'll make it a date then. First though, I want to look through the rest of this." She bent down and picked up the remaining letters and the journal. "By the way," she said, offhandedly. "Have you ever gone by the name Billy?"

Teach is not a name that will be forgotten quickly. If you ever wondered why I changed your last name, now you know.

— LETTER TO ALEXANDER EDWARD FROM MILLICENT, 1758

Chapter Thirty-five

Two Months Later

Sunrise had been her most favorite time of day. It seemed
only right for William to get up early enough to share
one with her on the first day of the Blackbeard Festival.
The only thing he carried with him was one yellow rose. He
arrived while it was still dark and placed the rose on top of her
tombstone.

Her final resting place was simple, as was the stone marking it.
Her name and dates, his name, and a quote from Ferreira Gullar,
"Art exists because life is not enough," were the only things it held.

He didn't stop by very often. Before now, he'd always told
himself it was because he was too busy and never had the time.
Looking back, he saw that for the lie it was. The truth was, he
always found time to do the things he wanted. He'd rarely stopped
by because he'd been angry with her and didn't want to make the
time. Standing in the near darkness, he watched as day slowly

traded places with night—the light too intense to leave anything hidden.

He placed his hand next to the rose, the chill of the night still clinging to the stone's surface. "We certainly knew how to make a mess out of things, didn't we?" he asked. "I've been trying to think of a marriage messier than ours, and I can't. And in looking into our mess, I've realized it wasn't all you, and it wasn't all me. I thought about saying it was fifty-fifty, but since you can't argue, let's call it an even seventy, thirty."

He took a deep breath. "Seriously though, I wish you'd felt safe enough to tell me about Stefan, but I can understand why you didn't. And I'd like to think that if you had, my response would have worked toward bringing us closer together, but I'm pretty sure it wouldn't have."

Somewhere close by, two birds began to chirp as the land stirred to life for the day.

"I hope you can forgive me for the ways I failed you. For not looking into your death more. For not stopping Stefan before he could kill again. For not realizing how desperately wrong everything was at the end. For pushing you aside when you tried to show me the map. For everything."

He traced her name with his finger. "There's a chance I might be related to Blackbeard. Can you believe it?" He chuckled. "Yeah, you probably can. I'm still friends with Eva, she…she helps ground me in a way no one else has. I think that's what Robert did for you. Hell, maybe he's still doing it. If he is, thank him for me. For being there for you when I wasn't." He took a deep breath, filling his lungs with air and slowly letting it out. "I have to leave for work, but I promise it won't be so long between visits next time." He rapped his knuckles on the stone. "Part of me will always belong to you."

As he turned to leave, a warm breeze caressed his cheek and he swore it felt like a paint brush.

THE BREAKFAST foursome had been a threesome ever since Maxine's unexpected confession months earlier. Elbert, Herb, and Francis still sat at the same place nearly every morning, but it wasn't the same. Their conversations weren't as lively, and they all three seemed a bit depressed. Eva had almost given up on any reconciliation between the four friends, when Maxine walked into the diner the morning of the last day of the Blackbeard Festival and marched over to stand by their table.

"I was wrong," she said. "It doesn't happen often, but I'm big enough to own up to it when it does. Though you have to admit I was partially right, it was someone they knew."

"That's the worst apology I've ever heard," Francis said.

Eva felt the entire room held its breath, waiting to see how things would turn out for the old friends.

"Sit down and stop your yammering," Elbert said, to the relief of all present. "You came just in time. I have news."

And just like that, the world seemed right again.

"Cut the suspense and tell us," Herb said. "I'm only getting older by the second."

Elbert leaned in toward the middle of the table to whisper, but Eva could still hear. "Someone in this town is a direct descendant of Blackbeard."

"Who?" they all three asked at the same time.

"I don't know, Amelia's been doing this genealogy, family history stuff, but she won't tell me who it is. Only calls him Mr. Y."

"What kind of name is that?" Herb asked.

"A fake one," Maxine answered. "Speaking of, Elbert isn't that Amelia who just walked in? And with a man."

Eva's head shot up. Sure enough, Amelia stood at the front of the diner with Emerson. According to what Amelia told her, they'd planned for him to spend the night after the Blackbeard Festival ended, and then they were going to go camping for a few days along the coast. Eva would have waved them over to her table, but she knew they were getting their breakfast to go.

"Who is that with her?" Francis asked.

"Emerson Jefferys," Elbert said. "I met him yesterday. Fine young man."

"Isn't he the coin expert that went to Duke?" Maxine asked.

"He graduated from Duke?" Herb asked in such a manner to insinuate doing such a thing was a grievous sin. "Are you seriously going to let your granddaughter date a Yankee?"

"Welcome to the twenty-first century, my friend," Elbert said. "Grandkids get to date whoever they want, and I can't use sweetener that comes in a blue packet."

WILLIAM WALKED along the beach while the sounds of the crowd enjoying the last few hours of the Blackbeard Festival faded away behind him. He kept his head down as he went, looking for sand holes. Part of him felt ridiculous, but part of him accepted it was something he'd always find himself doing from now on.

It was a habit he'd picked up shortly after being reinstated as chief and, he could now admit, started mostly as a means to avoid the press. They had all but moved into town following the arrest of Stefan. Peggy swore she'd used her *no comment* mantra more in the last two months than she had in the entire forty-five years preceding. Mitch adjusted by wearing earbuds whenever he went out and pretending not to hear anyone. And William had learned the press didn't want to interview him enough to follow him along the shore.

He always walked at approximately the same time of day. Sometime around seven in the evening while it was still light enough for him to see, but late enough for most people, visitors and residents alike, to either be out at dinner or, as was currently the case, in town enjoying something taking place there. As an added bonus, he found walking gave him time to think and reflect, even more so than jogging.

He'd thought about a lot of things while walking. His marriage. Catherine. Eva. He'd thought *a lot* about Eva. She'd spent the last month applying for grants that would allow her to work almost exclusively on the letters and journal they'd found in the chest. Her initial findings suggested they were authored by a cousin of Mary's, Millicent Reyes. He was hopeful at least one grant would come through.

And of course, he thought about Stefan. The anger he'd had toward the man was not completely unexpected. But the level of rage came as a shock. He was still working through that part.

Not that he blamed Stefan entirely. William knew there were two people in a marriage, and that both he and Catherine were to blame. But, it didn't seem fair to dump blame on a dead woman, so he bore his part of the blame, and threw the rest on Stefan.

After his visit with Stefan, it struck him that it probably wouldn't hurt to talk to a therapist. He'd decided when things calmed down a little, he'd see if he could find one. But he soon saw that right as he solved one issue, two more would pop up in its place. Now that he'd been walking daily, he wasn't sure he needed to see anyone.

The other surprising benefit of walking almost the same path each day was the ability to see in detail the ever-changing landscape. Though he'd lived in and along the Outer Banks his entire life and witnessed the wind and sand do some pretty crazy things, he'd never noticed the almost daily changes. He remembered a miniature golf course from his childhood that was now completely submerged by sand, and somewhere buried under the forever shifting sand of the dunes was a hotel. Strange to think about all the unknowns he could be walking over.

Of course, it worked the other way as well. Every so often when one went walking, a ship long since lost at sea could be seen reemerging from the sand, exposing secrets safely buried for a century or more.

He was glad the festival was over for another twelve months. As Eva had hoped would happen with both deaths accounted for, an unprecedented number of visitors had flooded the area over the last few days, making everything more anxiety-provoking than normal. The Historical Society had been more than willing to fund additional security staff. However, even with the additional manpower, William knew his staff was stretched thin.

The crowds were due in part because of Eva and the planning committee's vision and hard work. But the real draw was due to the national attention the town had received as a result of the deaths and Stefan's involvement in them, as well as the historical findings and never-before-seen artifacts.

Though he'd never admit as much in public, William thought it a bit creepy for the Festival's theme to be focused on the secret romance between Blackbeard and his young bride while the town itself was currently in the spotlight because of an altogether different man who was now known only as being a murderer.

He'd made a decision while walking a few days ago. He had no need for two homes, and it was foolish for one to be empty while he lived in the other. Selling his Nana's house wasn't an option he'd ever consider, but he'd found he had no desire to sell the house he'd shared with Catherine, either. Instead, he planned to rent out the house in town.

"I thought I'd find you out here."

He stopped, smiling at the sound of Eva's voice, and turned to watch her approach. She was dressed in a casual sundress, and a pair of sandals dangled from the fingers of one hand.

"I thought you'd be at the center of the Festival since today's the last day," he joked with her.

"I have been, but I needed a break, and when I looked at the time, I decided to come help you."

He'd never told anyone what he did, and Eva's directness took him aback for a minute. "Help me?"

"Look for holes. That is what you're doing, isn't it?" She raised an eyebrow.

"Yes," he confirmed. "Just felt like something I should do."

"I can understand."

They walked a bit in silence. William glanced out of the corner of his eye. Eva walked looking down at the sand, a smile still on her face.

"Rumor has it this year's festival attendance is a record breaker," he said, and her smile grew even bigger.

"The rumors are true," she said.

He knew she'd been worried about keeping the crowds entertained and spreading out the different venues, so people didn't feel as if they were right on top of each other. "How's the guest feedback look? Do you have a general idea?"

"From what I've heard so far, most of it is very positive, but it'll be a few days before we know enough to say for sure." She tucked a windblown strand of hair behind her ear. "Our initial numbers show Amelia's pirate logo contest and the Blackbeard exhibit in the museum drew the most interest. Thank you again for letting us display the chest contents."

He waved the thanks away. "It's the least I can do. How did Paul and Mac's silent auction go?"

"Pretty good, I think, but then again, we don't have actual numbers yet." She hesitated before adding. "They've petitioned the board. They want all proceeds from the silent auction to go toward building a public baseball park in Eden, named after Robert."

He hadn't heard about their plan, and tears prickled his eyes, even as he smiled. "Robert would have loved that."

Eva nodded. "Apparently, the three of them would try to get together to watch whenever New York and Boston played."

"I wasn't aware they knew each other that well."

"Surprising, what we don't know about people."

If that wasn't the honest-to-God truth, William didn't know what was.

They were silent for a moment, until William spoke. "I'm interested in how the Eden resident-only auction they did for a long weekend in Boston went over with the town." William had chuckled when he first heard what they were doing. Mac said it was a sneaky way to 'bring more culture into Eden.' William had wished him luck.

"Right? Have any of these people ever been outside the state of North Carolina?"

"Eva," he said in a serious voice. "A lot of them haven't been beyond sixty miles of this city."

"I expected as much. How far have you been?"

He leveled his gaze at her, trying to determine why she asked. "I took a bus to New York City during fall break my sophomore year at State. And I did a work study program in San Diego for a semester my junior year."

She nodded, as if expecting as much. "What did you think of San Diego?"

He ran a hand through his hair, remembering. "Wouldn't live there for all the money in the world, but I don't mind visiting. The food was pretty amazing."

"West Coast food is pretty great."

"True, but it's just not home, you know?"

"I do." She didn't speak for a few seconds. "I always knew I wanted to come back to the Outer Banks, but part of me worried it wouldn't be the same. That maybe in my head I'd remembered it better than it actually was. I mentioned that to Catherine one of the first times we met. And she told me something I'd never forgotten." She looked at him. "Have I ever told you this?"

"No." In fact, he couldn't remember Catherine ever mentioning anything similar, either.

"She said she always viewed the Outer Banks as a teenager—

unsettled and volatile. With the land, ocean, and weather always changing. How new islands could appear and disappear again in a matter of weeks. Or the wind could rearrange the sand dunes in such a way that they buried entire buildings. And yet, she said, no matter how or how much that teenager changed, they would always be recognized by those who loved them."

She wiped a tear away, and William found himself doing the same.

"That's why you'd never be at home in San Diego," Eva said. "And why Catherine never tried to leave. Both of you love this place too much to leave."

He thought about what she'd said, mulled it around in his head. "That's the burden of love, isn't it? Being tied to something and not being able to let go?"

"No," Eva said. "That's the best part of love. Being tied to something and knowing you're finally home."

He didn't know how to respond to that, so he said nothing.

"There is something I wanted to ask you," she said.

"Ask away."

"I was wanting to know if you'd go with me to the dance tonight?"

Each year, the Blackbeard Festival ended with a public dance at a local park near the ocean. The last time he'd attended was the year before Catherine died. So far this year, he'd been asked four times prior to Eva's invitation, and he'd turned them all down.

He didn't want to turn Eva down.

She'd obviously taken his silence to be hesitation on his part. "It was just a suggestion. I mean, you can say no. I just thought if you were free and I was free, then we could go together, but I know I'm really late in asking, so I totally get it if you don't want to go or if someone's already asked and you're going with them, or—"

"Eva, stop." William stopped walking, took hold of her shoulders, and turned her to face him.

He had tried to be careful where Eva was concerned. He'd tried to stay away since Catherine died, knowing they both needed time and space. It had been one of the hardest things he'd ever done, but he'd forced himself to do it because he thought it was the right thing to do. The sensible thing.

He was sick of being sensible. Where had it ever got him? To who and what he was today? A thirty-something widower still living in the town he grew up in, looking for buried treasure that may or may not exist, and holding onto land for a home no one wanted? Forget that. It was time for a change, and that change started now.

He moved closer to her, but in a movement that was one hundred percent Eva, she realized what he was doing and moved closer to him at the same time. Their lips met somewhere in the middle, crushing against each other. With uninhibited need they took their time tasting and teasing the other.

Her arms came around him and as he tightened his around her, she dropped her sandals. God, it had been too long since he'd kissed anyone. Hell, he couldn't remember the last time he'd held a woman. More than likely, both of those last times had been Catherine. But he didn't want to think about anything else other than Eva in this moment.

He clutched the back of Eva's dress and then forced himself to release the thin material and placed his hands on both her shoulders. It took all his willpower to pull away from her.

"I'm sorry," he said when he could breathe again. "I shouldn't have done that."

She placed her hand on her hip and cocked her head to the side. "You are such a man. You shouldn't have done that? I believe there were two of us involved, and I'm not sorry at all."

EVA SNATCHED HER sandals from the sand and shot William a pointed look, daring him to say he was sorry again. She stomped along the sand, vaguely aware of his following. Seriously, what was his problem, kissing her like that and then apologizing for it? There was no way he could have thought he'd taken advantage of her, not when she'd been just as into the kiss as he was.

Thankfully, he didn't apologize again. He grabbed her hand and tugged gently. "Come up here."

They'd reached a public dock, though there was no one on it at the moment. They walked to its end and stood.

"I need to tell you something," he said, dropping her hand. "Just give me a minute."

She waited.

The sounds of an evening at shore echoed around them. Waves slapped against the wooden stilts of the dock. Overhead, a seagull called out, and in the distance, another answered.

When he finally started to speak, his words were not what she expected.

"I've only been with one woman my entire life," he started. "For years after we got married, I did everything I could to make her happy. I know I wasn't perfect—far from it—but for whatever reason, I couldn't do it. We couldn't do it. I'm not sure if it was the artist in her or the cop in me, but we didn't do marriage very well."

He shoved his hands in his pockets, still not looking at her, but gazing over the water. "After she died, there was a feeling, almost like a relief, that I didn't have to live that way anymore. I never planned to date again. Couldn't imagine ever wanting another woman. I certainly wasn't expecting you."

She gasped.

He turned his head and gave her a weak smile. "I'm scared to death I'm going to mess up, and I don't think I could bear to have you one day look at me the way Catherine did that last year. I want nothing more than to go with you to the dance, but I'm not sure if I should. I don't want to hold you back from anything, simply because I'm going too slow."

She tilted her head and looked at the man whose heart was so broken he thought it beyond repair. The man who had completely captured her own.

He'd been throught a lot the last few months. Learning things he'd never known. Discovering connections never imagined. Coming face-to-face with the knowledge that things aren't always the way you thought they were.

He'd dealt with a large amount of emotional baggage, too. He was *still* dealing with a large amount of emotional baggage, having never confronted his feelings about Catherine before.

It was hard on a man.

Going slow.

She could live with that.

"If there's one thing I've learned from all of this," she said, "It's that you'll never regret taking a risk for what you want. You'll only regret what you were too afraid to do. I'm willing to go slow for you, if you're willing to take a risk on me."

He was so quiet, she feared he'd turn her down. But then, ever so slowly, he began to smile until only joy was visible in his expression. "In that case, Eva. I would love to be your date for the dance."

He held out his hand.

She took it.

Discussion Questions

1. Early in the novel William mentions to Robert his guilt over Catherine's death and how he wasn't able to love her the way she deserved. Should he feel guilty? Why or why not? Does his guilt color how he acts with others? If so, how?

2. What do you think would have happened between Catherine and William if she hadn't died? How would this impact Eva?

3. The summer spent in the Outer Banks as a child impacted Eva's life significantly. Have you ever experienced a similar event? How did it change the direction of your life?

4. Throughout the novel, we see glimpses about the pirate known as Blackbeard. While the journal entries were fictional, the discussion Eva had at the festival planning meeting was all based upon historical record. Do you think history painted him accurately? Has your impression of him changed? How does this change your perception of other historical figures?

5. Eva mentions that Blackbeard was a marketing savant. Can you think of ways that you market yourself or how the people around you market themselves differently depending on who they are with? Why do you think we do this and how can it help/hurt us?

6. Throughout the novel, we see many characters struggle with grief. What character did you feel most understanding of and why? How did you feel finding out Catherine was Lady?

7. Eva talks about her "love affair with history." What was your favorite historical aspect in the novel? Just as we see Blackbeard teach Eva, how has a historical moment shaped you?

8. How do you feel you chose people in your life? Are you a cautious person who takes time to consider someone a true friend? Do you feel drawn toward certain people like Eva and Amelia? How has a friend changed your life, or do you feel you would be the same person even if you never knew them?

9. Did Stefan and Eva's past as children affect how you felt toward the end of the novel? Why or why not?

10. William says at one point "It's like the Bermuda triangle of mysteries." What was the most shocking twist for you and why was it so impactful?

Acknowledgements

As I sat down to write this, I realized that this manuscript has seen three presidents and four title changes. By the time you hold it in your hands, it will have seen my youngest child through the entirety of her teenage years and my oldest through his high school, undergrad, and graduate graduations. I would say it's been a journey of love, but the truth is there were times I despised everything about it and wanted nothing more than to delete it forever.

But the story wouldn't leave, the characters wouldn't be quiet, and I could never convince myself to move it to the trash can.

While most of this story is fiction (the devil's coins myth and unknown woman's journal are both products of my imagination), there are plenty of historical facts embedded as well. Blackbeard was betrayed by an unknown person, and evidence does point toward him working with Governor Eden. There were even a few things I thought I made up that turned out to be true, like Blackbeard's marriage to a woman named Mary, and his interest in a shipwreck off the coast of Florida.

Needless to say, there have been many, many people who have read a version or two of a draft, and the vast majority of those gave their thoughts or advice. There is no way I can personally thank each of them (mainly because my memory's shot) but if you're one, know that this book would not be what it is without you. You have my eternal thanks for the steps you took alongside me.

Many thanks to Megan Trank and the entire team at Beaufort Books for believing in this story as much as I did and for taking a chance on it and me both.

Much love and thanks to my husband, who has read more drafts than anyone and didn't flinch when I asked, "One more time?" and our two kids, both of whom write better than me but still ask for advice.

Finally, my upmost thanks to you for the privilege of telling you a story.

About the Author

Writing allows **CAROL ANN COLLINS** to combine two of her favorite things, history and romance. Her work is a combination of historical fact, pure fiction, and a vivid imagination. An avid reader since childhood, she is also a *New York Times* bestselling author under a different pen name. Though she is an introvert who had no problem staying inside during quarantine, she enjoys traveling with her husband and two adult children. In her spare time, she is an avid book collector and bargain shopper who loves to combine the two. To date, her favorite find is an 1869 edition of *Innocents Abroad* by Mark Twain purchased for $10.